The Magwitch Story

The Magwitch Story

Tony Lester

Published in 2010 by New Generation Publishing

First Edition

Part one

Made A Gentleman

Magwitch's Story

Introduction

Many having read in "Great Expectations" how Magwitch returned from New South Wales to see "his" gentleman must have wondered how he could have financed the trip and indeed how he was able to send money to the lawyer, Jaggers, to pay for Pip to be made into a gentleman. When Magwitch returned he originally told Pip and Herbert Pocket a little about his early life, and he also touched on his life in New South Wales. But he never told it all.

But Pip was determined to hear the full story, so after walking Magwitch to a distant point near the river, where Pip knew they would be undisturbed, he pressed him to tell him everything. They went there, having spent the night in the Ship Inn, before the day when Pip hoped to get Magwitch away on a boat to France. As we know now, this never happened.

Faced with Pip's firm insistence, he told his complete story to him, having first made him swear that he would never tell a living soul, harbouring the delusion that having made Pip into a gentleman he would now remain one, always providing that no-one knew how this had been accomplished. Of course Pip swore to remain silent, and in fact he never did actually tell anyone person in his lifetime; a lifetime that Pip also wrote about and which appears in another place. So while they were waiting the best part of a day for the boat in which Pip and Herbert had planned they would get Magwitch onto the Hamburg steamer, Magwitch told Pip everything, overcoming his dislike of telling his story like a song or story book.

Pip kept his promise, holding Magwitch's history in his mind. Then while the details were still fresh he wrote them down. He was extremely miserable following the death of Magwitch and he wrote Magwitch's story as a way to pass the time and to assuage his sorrow.

Luckily the manuscript where he set down, not only what happened to Magwitch in Australia, but also an account of his early years, has survived, and I have tidied it up here and there in order to produce this account. One thing that had to be dealt with was Abel Magwitch's language; Pip made an attempt to reproduce Abel's actual words but obviously he used his own words when he came to write his account. I have amended them slightly so that the reader can more fully understand this interesting account.

At this time I cannot reveal how the manuscript came into my possession; that is quite another story!

Chapter 1

My early years

I was sold by my mother for five shillings. I have never blamed her for this. I was six years old, a sturdy child, well able to look after myself and handy with my fists if I needed to be. It was because of my fisticuffs that I was bought by Jed Plummer, a pugilist who ran a show in a tent where local youths were encouraged to go a few rounds with one of Jed's several "gentlemen of the ring". Jed always called them this, never boxers or pugilists, and it was partly this that made me determined to be a gentleman myself.

You can't imagine what it was like for me, a small boy, having it to make my way in the world of the boxing booths. My job was to do anything that anyone wanted. They wanted water? I would bring it; they wanted Porter? I would go to the Ale houses and buy a jug full. I would clean boots, horses, saddles; fetch and carry all day long; and then, when I was worn out, I was allowed to sleep with the horses.

Most days I got fed, broken meats usually with some bread. Now and then, if we had done well, I would get a treat, some bacon. Of course, I were no angel, and was always ready to lay hold of anything that did not seem to have an owner. And, if I had not helped myself occasionally to spare vittles I should have starved.

In time I moved up from the occasional thievery to a regular way of life. You have to remember that I was surrounded by rogues, all who had their own speciality.There were smatter-haulers, note-passers, roadsmen, dips and the like. Fairs were good places to get money. I remember one in a big town.

Blackwater was the name of the nearby town. I remember it was a large town with coaching inns and some ale houses. Every year it had a great two-day cattle fair. Up to the times of the beginning of the fair the countryside around would be alive with all sorts of cattle, pigs, sheep, and horses, all being brought to be sold. Some would come from as far as the west country. The folks who brought them from Devon were real rustics, chaw bacons whose speech was very slow and measured, but they were not as daft as they looked. The noise at times were overwhelming and so were the stink of sweat, manure and dog's turds.

During the days of Fair there would be enormous excitement with a tremendous amount of to-ing and fro-ing. There would be a farmers, drovers, gypsies, blacksmiths, cheapjacks and all manner of hucksters. All sorts of penny gaffs would be set up and during the evening they would set the lamps alight and the fair would go on in the glare of the lamps and flares. Somehow at night it were not only more exciting but almost beautiful.

It would be held in the open land around the town, and included lots of sideshows and, of course, boxing booths, and that was where I was employed.

Of course, I never knew my father, come to that I hardly knew my mother, poor soul. I don't blame her for what she'd done. She had no choice really. I was a bastard child got by my mother by being too trusting, according to what she told me. It was common tale, but she always gave me to understand that he, my father, was a real gentleman. At first, so she said, he supported her, then she was turned out, and after some wandering round the country she made up her mind to get me settled. She knew that boys of my age and strength (I was a big boy for my age) could work, so I was sold to Jed Plummer. Then, almost as soon as the money changed hands my mother was off.

"You be a good boy" she said, "and work hard", then she was gone.

I never saw her again.

Jed Plummer not only ran a boxing booth that went around the fairs but he also worked with the gypsies in all sorts of half-way legal ways. He was half gypsy some said. He certainly knew Romany ways and spoke some of their language; he also spoke thieves cant, which be something I picked up myself.

So by the time I was eight I could saddle a horse, box a little, and by a little bit of good chance I could even swim. We had moved to Blackwater for their fair, or at least we had moved to the outskirts on a piece of land that had a pond on it. And I fell into it, and I would have drowned if Romany Ted hadn't gone in and pulled me out.

Chapter 2

My work in the booths

He cursed me for making him get himself wet, particularly his new breeches. Then he stripped to his drawers, made me do the same, and got me back in the water, where he showed me how a body could float, and by moving his arms and legs, could move about in the water. Of course, I just splashed about at first, but eventually after several days I became quite good at it, though not as skilful as Roman Ted. I was to find out later why he took this trouble with me; this was after we had all attended the Blackwater Fair.

I had been there the previous year with Ted Plummer, and helped with the boxing booth. Jed told me that boxing would one day be the most popular of sports and would replace sword and cudgel fights. He often said this, saying there was a Academy in London where it were practised, and that Dan Mendoza had made the sport more scientific. Whenever he said this many of his listeners laughed, and truth to tell, having seen the knock-down smashing, face-pulping exhibitions in the booth I thought the sport were brutal.

But there were no doubts in my mind that anyone who stepped into the ring shown real pluck. And many a plucky young man, anxious to impress his mates, and some young woman, would take the challenge to knock down Jed Plummer. Mind you, I never did see anyone do it, but many went off bloody but pleased for themselves; and many a young lass seemed ready to staunch the blood of her country hero. To be fair to Jed he did seem to be skilful in avoiding the blows of these yokels, some of whom had mightily strengthened their arms with all manner of country pursuits.

Jed used to cry:

"Come on you truly English men and prove you're worth more than two or three Frenchies."

That used to get the young bloods going. The recruiting sergeant used to hang about the booths too, trying to enlist any likely looking lad. And on more than one occasion I also saw an officer who looked very dashing in his red coat with gold buttons, which I was to learn in due course were really only brass, strutting along like a cockerel in his white breeches and white gloves with his officers sash round his waist. Sometimes it seems to me the officer's face would glow as red as his red coat, having taken a few drinks to fortify himself for the recruiting.

Jed always went to Blackwater Fair as it were the largest cattle fair in the south of England. In 1800, when I suppose I must have been 10 years old, we were there again. I knew it were 1800 as everybody were talking about it. I also remember clearly as it was the last time I helped put up the booth and did the fetching and carrying. The talk was of how the next year was to be something special.

As I was now older I could wander round more and see all the horses, pigs and sheep being brought together. They intrigued me. They were all so different. Most people think that a pig is just a pig, but there are so many varieties, and some are brighter nor some men I have met.

For a long while before the actual fair began, all the animals, including cows would be brought to the common land that was around Blackwater. When the cows were milked the milk was sold to whoever had a ha'penny and something to put the warm milk into. I would watch the milking and beg the girls to let me try. From the very start I could do it; the girls would sometimes give some milk for nothing if I helped them.

Then musicians, blacksmiths and hucksters would arrive. The gypsies, with their painted wagons, would come trailing along, leading long strings of horses. You would hear all sorts of accents as some of the people came from as far away as Wales. I used to think that was a far off country. Of course, I never dreamed then that I would go half way round the world. There was endless noise and smell as hundreds of animals and people came together. Then in the evening, when lamps were lit up, the garish show went on with gypsies, hucksters, petty chapmen, tinkers and traders of all sorts, intent on separating people from their money setting out their wares. It was an exciting time for me and I forgot to go back to attend to Jed, so by the time I did get back he was waiting for me with the strap.

Chapter 3

I escape from the Booth, and go on the road with the gypsies.

But no sooner did he lay into me than Roman Ted stepped in and pulled the strap from his hand. I don't know what Roman Ted said for it were in Romany, but Jed just shrugged his shoulders and turned away. I do know that some money passed between them too before I were then led away to a caravan where I were fed and told to sit and wait. Later on I was dressed in a coat with big pockets. When it got dark I was taken around the fair with some of the other gypsies. Suddenly there was an increase in the noise and cries of "stop thief". A Romany lad pushed past me, and as he did so he pushed something into my pocket and then was gone. Some of the crowd chased after him, and my companions indicated by nods and winks that I was to go too. Totally bewildered by all this I went back to the caravan where the woman who had give me the coat took it off me again. I followed this procedure several times and I think that it was because I were so fair-headed that no-one gave me a second look; they were looking for gypsies.

After Blackwater fair we all went round the country wherever there was a sizeable gathering, and at each I was made to play my part. I also learned other things from the gypsies, including how to use herbs, such as willow what they boiled up to make a nostrum to relieve aches and pains; but, apart from counting, I never at that time learned to read nor to write. Meadowsweet was another herb to help with pain, but all country people knew about that one just as they did for Figwort. We collected Figwort for wounds, laying it on with cob's webs to heal cuts and such. Penny Royal was for women and so was poppy, but they were most often used for having young-uns so I were never privy to how these were used. All country gardens had Comfrey of course. Its other name was Knitbone so you can imagine what a poultice made out of pounded Comfrey was used for. I can't remember now all the names of all the country herbs that we used to gather. If I had been able to write well then I might have put them down, but I couldn't at that time so I didn't.

Inevitably I got caught. It was in Gloucestershire in a hiring fair on Candlemas day on the 2nd February where a goodly number of people had gathered together hoping to be hired. Some were hoping to leave a situation that was not to their liking, but unrealistically expecting that in their next employ they might be happier, poor souls. I had on the old coat as usual and into the pocket Jack Green had slipped some money what he'd lifted from a cully in the crowd. Unfortunately for him though, the cully's wife had seen this and screaming like a mad women ran after he, then seeing him slip the goods to me, she stopped chasing Jack and grabbed me instead, holding me tight to her so that no matter how hard I kicked and struggled I could not make her let me go. Her husband quickly caught up with her and saying:

"Caught you, you little devil", he delved into my pocket and found the cash.

My luck was really out, I thought, as within an hour they had me before the local beak. He had come to the fair, and was able to deal with me immediately.

"It's North Leach for you" everyone said as I stood there totally cast down. I had no idea of what North Leach was, but after being locked temporarily in a room in the local inn with two other criminals I soon learnt that was it a new prison built by the High Sheriff of Gloucestershire. It had been built to a design what the world and his wife thought to be brilliant but the inmates thought otherwise! However, my stay there was a short one, for on appearing at the magistrate's court, a Mr Jordan, who was friendly with the beak, took it upon himself to speak for me. Apparently it was his habit to try to save lads like me, saying that given a chance they would turn away from their previous bad habits. I can't be sure of his reasons. Perhaps he were a good Christian soul, or mebbe I was just cheap labour and unwilling to run away from a place where I got fed.

So that's how it was that I first came in contact with gentry. Of course they were simple country gentry, not your high ton London or Bath sort, who tended to look down on country Squires however long the Squires' pedigree might be. At first I was the lowest of the very low in a household of servants, most of whom the made it very plain that they resented my coming into the house. I slept in the attic, and ate for the first time in my life regular good food, often what was left over from the Squire's table, once the other servants had had their share. I also had an allowance of ale each day. I drank it as it were provided free, but I never really took to it.

Mr Jordan's wife did not like me, and made this a very plain, so it came as no surprise to me that when Mr Jordan had a stroke and died that I was immediately put out of the house. And here again I was lucky for, finding no other place for me, I was sent to help Old Turvey the shepherd on the Home Farm.

He was not best pleased to be saddled with a 13 year-old lad who knew nothing about sheep, except how to skin one quickly and hide the skin and meat. Living with the gypsies, had taught me that. However he became less angry when I showed what I knew about herbs and how they could be used as cures. And, I was a strong well set up lad quite able to work hard all day which earned Old Turvey's grudging respect.

Later I came to realise that, as more and more land became enclosed, farms often grew larger and more prosperous. Old Turvey talked about this, saying that it were progress of a kind. When I asked him what he meant, he told me how lots of labourers and smallholders had been badly treated despite the big landowners doing well.

He used to count the sheep in the old way: *Yan, Tan, Tether, Mether, Pit, Tayter, Later* , and so on. I asked him once why he counted this way. For an answer he tapped his nose, winked his eye and said:

"So only we know."

He added "Anyways, that's how my fadder counted so I do too."

So I learned from Old Turvey the shepherd's lore including dealing with scab and suchlike diseases, though I was less ready to accept the need to carry out some of the rituals that he swore were necessary to make the cures work, like waiting for a full moon then going widdershins at midnight.

He was doing one of his rituals one day when he just fell down and lay twitching. His breath came like he was snoring and despite what we did nothing seemed to help. When he died I realised just how much I missed him and all his advice.

Somehow, everyone thought Old Turvey was going to live forever, for most of them had never known a day when he had not been around. He walked everywhere, was afraid of no man and, because of what he knew, was ready to speak his mind. So it came as a shock to everybody when he ceased to come out of his cottage like he always did.

With the death of Old Turvey, they let me carry on as the Home Farm shepherd, and I even had a lad of my own to help me. I was about 21 then, having spent seven years looking after sheep. I had been introduced to ciphering and reading, so when I heard about a book written by a certain Francis Cater called "Everyman his own Cattle Doctor" I asked for it. By now we have a land agent running the Home Farm, for Mrs Jordan was often aways in London or Bristol. He hemmed and hawed about my request until I reminded him how we had lost a might of sheep and lambs to sickness the previous lambing season. After that he went away and did some figuring, the result of which was that he bought a copy for his-self. But, I was allowed to look at it from time to time, so I learned even more about sheep and suchlike.

Old Turvey had taught me how to count country style so that I could keep track of the numbers in the herd. But his grasp of reading was not so sound, and I had to wait until I met Mary Turndall, a singular young woman who I took up with to such an extent that eventually we lived together and I had a daughter by her. She improved my reading and writing, which up to then had been the little that a giant who were shown in the fairs had taught me. I had learned some too from a deserting soldier whiles we were both hid in a barn for a very rainy spell.

Mary were a real Spitfire of a woman. She'd been in the workhouse, both parents having died, then was apprenticed to a factory in the North from where she did run away to escape the unwelcome attentions of the foreman, eventually fetching up near our farm.

There, at first she just worked on any farm tasks, but as she could read and write a little and was as bold a lass as ever you were likely to meet, the bailiff took her on regular. I think he would have liked to do what the foreman in the factory never accomplished, but she managed to intrigue him without giving in.

Chapter 4

Amanda Jane

I truly loved my work. I was fit, well fed, as well fed as most any ways, and always had clothes to my back, even if they were merely coarse fustian fabric smock-coats and similar trousers; and I had been well taught by Old Turvey the shepherd. What he did not know about sheep was not worth knowing. And of course he knew all about plants. He knew all the regular plants such as Meadow Buttercup, Clover, Cow Parsley, Dock, Stinging Nettle, White Dead Nettle, Field Thistles and Hedge Woundwort. And later on he taught me about other ones that could be used as simples to treat animals and people. Plants like Boy's love and Southernwood, which were fragrant aromatic plants, and could be used to soothe and calm a body.

Right up to the day he died he had been up with the light and busy all day; and even when we were shearing, despite his age, he managed to do more than any of the others. It were the way he always worked, steadily, continuously. He never took a drop of spirits, confining himself to country ale and I wish to God that I had followed his example, which had I done so, I would have avoided a great deal of aggravation and grief in my life.

One day, we were in the Upper Meadow dealing with a sheep that had got itself so caught in some brambles that we were hard put to cut it free, when we saw her. She was leading her horse what had gone lame, and when she saw that we had spied her she stopped. She were well-dressed, well enough for us to guess what she were - a farmer's daughter. She asked was there a farrier or blacksmith hereabouts so we gave her directions. I was seized with curiosity; she were a comely lass with no trace of smallpox that so blighted so many young women. I asked Old Turvey what she might be a'doin. He seemed to have no interest, but I learned all from him later as he heard the tale in the ale house. He knew that he would hear all the gossip there.

Her name was Amanda Jane Pendall, and she had run away from home. Her parents, rich farmers, were distraught. She were an only child and had some money which she would come in to when she reached her majority.

Most of the story was got out of the two farm labourers who had been sent after her. Seemingly her head had been turned by a young officer, and she had run off to marry him. It was thought that she was heading for Portsmouth where his regiment was due to go to India.

A week later the labourers were back, empty-handed. Amanda Jane had found the officer and was living at his lodgings as his wife. A year later we heard the end of the story from a recruiting sergeant. The regiment sailed, but without Amanda Jane. For a while she lived in lodgings on a small amount of money given her by her officer, then her landlady had her taken up for stealing her property. Amanda Jane, desperate, had pawned some pewter plates that were in her lodgings, and her landlady had found out. Eventually Amanda Jane appeared at the assizes and was sentenced to be transported to a criminal colony.

Chapter 5

I meet Mary Turndall

It were at the hiring fair where I first met Mary Turndall. She looking for work and an officer was talking to her. This officer was a splendid fellow, All red coat and brass buttons, with a red sash around his waist and white gloves. Alongside his white breeches and black top boots he had a sword. He had a recruiting sergeant with him too, who tried to very hard to get the yokels, including me, to take the King's shilling. He managed to get a few, but not me. I was happy where I was, and didn't fancy fighting for my King and country, having heard that being in the ranks was not all that it was cracked up to be. I had also seen some of the men who had come back, having been wounded. Some were so wounded that they would never work again, but had to beg for their living. The soldier, who I told you about the one who helped with my letters in the barn when I had run off from the Romanys, told me enough about going for a soldier to put me off that for life.

Eventually Mary got taken on at the farm, and later, when I got to know her well she told me how she got to our part of the country. Orphaned of both parents who died of some sort of fever, she went into the workhouse. By the time she were nine she were working in the local mill, and by great good luck, having always been a strong lass she thrived. Then when she were thirteen she caught the eye of lad who took such a fancy to her that she got extra food as a result.

But when she was 16 she were 'prenticed to the mill. I asked her why she did this and she said she had no choice they were all 'prenticed once they reach that age. She resisted the foreman and his advances for as long as she could, then seeing what was happening to the other girls she ran away.

She begged lifts on carts and wagons going south and many a wagoner took pity on her. When I saw her at the fair she had resolved to get farm work; her feet were all bloody from walking barefoot, such shoes as she had had were completely worn away, and she could go no further. She were a strong passionate woman used to getting her own way, but she had to talk hard to get taken on at our farm.

Well, eventually we set up home together in my cottage, and lived there content enough despite it being rather rough. We had a daughter, and this made me think we oughter be married, but Mary said there was no need of that. Like I said, she were a strong willed lass so I said no more.

Chapter 6

I meet Roman Ted again and lose my wife and child..

Fair time had come round again and I went by myself as Mary was looking after Emily, our daughter, who had taken poorly. Emily was showing signs of being a real beauty, but had a pale complexion, and this worried me. Mary said as how I ought to go as it would take my mind off things.

So I washed myself and put on my clean smock to make myself look halfway respectable. Then I walked the four miles to Little Outhland and as I walked along my spirits rose as I listened to the bird's song, the Larks and all the other small singing birds.

Part of the way I rode with a wagoner who were taking a few sticks of furniture to a cottage in a hamlet near to. After I'd helped him unload, and we had been given a drink of ale, he became talkative, and as we ground along the flinty dusty road he told me that some tinkers and gypsies had come up for the fair.

I spoke to few at the fair for I were generally one to keep myself solitary, contenting myself with buying a few ribbons for Mary. I thought about the fairs in the past where I had spent my early childhood, then, as I walked around the booths, I suddenly saw a face I knew! It were Roman Ted, looking just as same as I remembered him when I were with the gyppoes. I thought that now I was growed that I might have changed and he wouldn't know it were me. So I quickly turned on my heel. But he came after me, and although I tried to shake him off, he spoke with me reminding me of all our old times together. I soon told him what I thought of our old times, how I had nearly finished up in prison for a really long spell. He simply laughed that off, but at least he left me alone. Then I saw him talking to the other farm workers before making off. I spoke to them and they told me that he had asked where I worked.

That unsettled me so I went straight off home not even waiting to beg the favour of a ride, and all the while thinking of Roman Ted who I hated for what he'd done to me. But I was to hate him still more later on.

The following Friday he came to the cottage where I was alone. I were in our one room with its simple table and two chairs that I had collected from the main house when they threw them out. I had mended them and was proud of the way they looked in our clean cottage with its scrubbed flag stone floor. Truth to tell those chairs were the best sticks of furniture in the place, but we had a table of sorts on which to set our vittles. We also had a stone floor thanks to the stone-mason who helped me lay it instead of the beaten earth floor that used to be in the cottage.

He walked right in as I sat by our open door watching our pig in the pen that we would butcher later in the year to make our hams and bacon. He simply sat hisself down smiling all the whiles and said he had a proposition for me.

He said the that as I were friendly with Anne Moston, she could let me into the house that night, and while I was keeping her occupied, he would creep in and steal whatever he could. I refused of course, for I had put those ways behind me. He smiled and said that I would change my mind, then he stood up pushed aside the chair and went off.

Mind you, I knew that Anne were still sweet on me. Several times, before Mary had come to the farm, I had walked out with Anne usually after Church on a Sunday. But when my Mary and me set up together in my cottage I thought that Anne would have forgotten me; she hadn't, and Mary made no secret of the fact that she didn't like Anne anywheres near to me.

On Saturday the Boots from the house brought me a note from Anne asking me to meet her in the barn. She said to destroy the note too, which I did. I tore it up and threw it into the pig's pen. I thought that she was coming to tell me about Roman Ted, so I went to the barn expecting her to ask me to help her resist him and his ideas.

Inside it were dark, but not so dark that I could see her over by the horses with a shawl over her head. To my surprise she asked what I wanted from her. Nothing, I said, totally at a loss. Then why, she wanted to know, had I written her a note asking her to see me in the barn? Roman Ted had given her the note.

Of course I denied that I had done any such thing. Then, before Anne could say another word, my Mary came in. She said that Roman Ted had told her that Anne and me were meeting secretly. She began to scream abuse at Anne who screamed back saying that everything had been fine before Mary had come to the farm.

Furious, I ran out leaving the two women together not thinking that they would do more than continue their argument.

I looked about to find Ted but he were nowhere to be seen. I began to ask around if anyone had seen a stranger, then we heard a terrible scream from the barn. We all ran there and found Anne lying on the floor in the muck and bits of straw, her hands to her throat on which there were livid finger marks. It were quite clear that Mary had completely lost her temper and strangled Anne, for she were dead.

As to Mary, there were no sign nor sight. She had run off. That night however she came back to me in the cottage. I started up meaning to embrace her. She held out her arms to hold me away telling me coldly to stand back, then she told me that she had Emily and would destroy her if I came after her. I called after her as she turned and left. She ignored me and ran off into the darkness.

Chapter 7

My wife is arrested and I renounce her and my and child.

Despite her threat I looked everywhere for Mary and for Emily, and in doing so I began to neglect my sheep. I took to travelling out to nearby places where I thought she might have gone. I were warned and eventually, because I persisted in looking for them both, I lost my job.

I didn't care. I took to roaming around still asking everybody I met if they knew anything of a young woman and child. I slept in ditches, or in barns and begged for my bread. Many poor folk gave what they could; I noticed that the poorer they were the more generous the amount that they gave me. It was no use begging in towns. If I had tried to I would have been taken up, but I needed to go to towns to seek Mary and Emily. I described them each time, but always got the same answer, until one day, in a nearby town I heard someone say that a young woman had been taken up and was due to appear at the assizes. I immediately asked what she were like and got the answer that she were young and had a child with her and was being arraigned for a most horrid murder.

They were wrong. It were Mary, but she had already appeared at the assizes before I could not get to her. I wanted as much as anything to ask about our Emily. Of course I loved Mary stil, despite anything that she had done, but my burning need was to see my child. I took to loitering near the lawyer's offices in the hope of hearing more.

One day someone pointed out a lawyer chap to me saying that he had defended Mary. I recognised him and tried to see him, and had a real fight to get into his office. I only got in because I used my knowledge of the criminal world to persuade his clerk to let me in. What the clerk did not know was that I had helped him in the past when he was a young lawyer just making his way. Don't ask me how I helped him, but he was obliged to me.

He told me that arrangements had been made for Emily to be cared for. You know him as Jaggers. He added that as he was going to speak for Mary, who had apparently lost her reason, it would be best for me to stay away as Mary had it firmly in her mind that I were the cause of all her trouble. He hoped to speak for her as she was sentenced, offering to take her into his household and being responsible for her.

Were I to put on an appearance she might run wild again and have to go into a lunatic asylum. I shuddered at this prospect, having heard nothing good of such places. The poor souls were treated abominably with no attempt to cure or treat them. He added that Emily were being well cared for, and, again, were I to find her I would put her future in danger. I had often seen children just like Emily tried at a criminal bar, then imprisoned, whipped and eventually transported or even hanged. So I turned my back on them. They were lost to me; in one stroke I had lost my wife and my child; I resolved never to speak of them again.

Don't think Pip that this was an easy decision. It were

hard, but I had to do it for their sakes.

Chapter 8

I go tramping and meet Compeyson, and I am sentenced to transportation.

So I kept away, and instead I took to tramping the countryside, doing some rick-building work here, some labouring there, and even a mending of the roads as coaches were fast needing much better ones. A strong man as I was then could always get employment, particularly as I had only myself to keep and was willing to sleep anywhere.

Being used to the countryside with a gypsy education of sorts I could also get myself some food from a rabbit or hare or suchlike when the opportunity presented itself. I was careful to avoid gamekeepers who were easily outwitted as they liked to stay in the warm whereas I was at home in the outdoors no matter the weather.

Now and again I were taken up for vagrancy, in fact I had just come out from Kingston Jail on a vagrancy committal when I fetched up at the Epsom Races hoping to earn some money holding the horses or such like job. I did earn enough for a night's lodging, sharing it with three other poor souls on the road, then I went looking for work. I were in a booth at the races asking did they need someone to help with taking it down at the end of the day, hoping by doing so to earn enough for a meal and a night's lodging, when the publican pointed me out to Compeyson, a really flash swell, telling him that I was just the kind of man that he was looking for. And he was flash, with his well-cut coat and fine linen and gold watch and chain. While I was nothing, just a drudge, a mere cipher in his scheme of things. Someone who could be worked on to do his bidding without too much effort.

I was exactly that. A poor fool who could be twisted this way and that because I had had enough of tramping and having no roof over my, nor bread to put into my mouth. Compeyson used me. He were a swindler, but because he were such a flash swell the people what he duped trusted him. His speciality were forged notes, but I think he also forged other documents.

I'm not saying that I were an angel; I was his leg man, his runner, who ran all over at his behest, not knowing at the beginning just what sort of villainy he was dragging me into. But later on I began to realise, and when we were caught we were both charged, and I was by then so enmeshed in his webs of deceit that it appeared that I was as guilty as he was.

Then, when we appeared at the assizes, he tried to blame me for everything, saying that he had been deceived by me, that I had led him astray! Unfortunately for him the lawyer who was prosecuting the case had carefully spoken to many that Compeyson had tricked, including several that had been relieved of their cash well before I had even met Compeyson. This lawyer chap really tied him up in knots in court, so the final upshot were both of us being sentenced to be transported. I turned to him then, promising him that I would not forget how he had tried to make it seem that I was the really guilty one. He drew himself away from me and complained to the gaoler that I was a danger to him. He were right of course. I wanted to be a danger. I intended to be dangerous.

In prison he somehow seemed to have enough money to be able to have his chains removed and to have a room and vittles.   Me he ignored.   I was in his past as far as he was concerned.   But all the while we was waiting to get sent to the hulks I nursed my hatred of him.   I had a little money which I hoarded as I planned to use it when I had the opportunity.   I would not waste it on myself; I had known privations 'a plenty so I was well able to live through these.

Chapter 9

I escape, and meet Pip, then get Jaggers to act for me.

As I said, during my time with Compeyson I had managed put aside some cash, as I had always thought I might need it. Then I hoarded it so as to somehow get at Compeyson. I managed to use some of it to bribe the turnkey on the hulk and when he turned his back I slipped over the side. I reckon as how he thought I would drown seeing as I had leg irons on. Then holding on to of baulk of timber I kicked out and came to shore.

My first intention was simply to escape. On the hulk I had tried to get at Compeyson for I hated him so bitterly that I wanted nothing more than to kill him, and I knew that I could do that with my bare hands, only given the opportunity. But after one try. when I managed to catch him a hefty swipe on the side of his head, I were dragged away and we were separated. After that he were too well guarded. He carried the mark on his face though where I caught him

At first I hid in the marshes because I were held back by my leg irons. Seeing you Pip, and you coming from a blacksmiths were a gift from heaven. And you were a rare plucky young lad. Your file and vittles what you brought to me at the old battery were the saving of me. All I wanted to do was get away. I thought as how I could go north where my face was not known and I could make a fresh start.

Then, when I knew Compeyson had escaped too, after what you said, I resolved to kill him instead; and I would have done so had it not been for the cold and wet, for my fingers were too numb to get them around his throat. If I had killed him then everything would have been different.

I expect you might remember what I said when the file of soldiers brought us back to the blacksmith's. How I wanted to prevent some persons laying under suspicion alonger me. I hope you might remember that I said that I stole some vittles; I did that because I didn't want you to get into any trouble. And besides I was already forming in my head a plan, something to hold onto when I was transported. I had nothing else, having abandoned all hope of seeing Mary and my child Emily. A man's got to have something to hold onto. I also wanted to know your name again. You did tell me it when I first came upon you, and I needed to know it for my plan.

As you know Pip, I were taken back to the hulks, where, after a few days, both Compeyson and me were charged with escaping and my sentence were increased to life transportation. Compeyson's were increased from the original seven to fourteen years.

After our appearance at court we were taken in chains to a dirty side room and Compeyson were taken away. I got up to go as well but the gaoler growled:

"Not you, stay here." almost as if I were a dog, so I slumped back only to be aroused by a large solid man whose over-large bald head and black untidy hair made me suddenly affeared.

It were Jaggers.

"You, Magwitch", he said, waving a white hand at me. I smelled some sort of perfume on it.

He seemed to sneer, as well he might, then he said:

"No names but someone dear to you is well, and well cared for. Are you content?"

I nodded.

"She will continue to be well cared for as we agreed, but she will never, ever know of you and this. Are you content?"

By this he meant my transportation.

"Jaggers ."I said:

He looked at me.

"You helped me once for which I was and forever will be grateful. I need some more help."

He stood quite still, just as I remember he used to in court commanding everyone's attention.

"There's a lad, a country lad as has been good to me, in fact he acted nobly. His name is Pip."

I told him all your details, and as I did so he stood there biting his white perfumed hand.

"You know how I was of use to you in the past."

He frowned, so I hurried on.

"Please just assist this lad for a few years, then I swear to you I will make good in Australia and send back money to help him become a gentleman."

Jaggers burst out laughing, then, seeing from my passion that I was in earnest, answered:

"I agree, but for five years only, and in my own way, and after that the boy must shift for himself."

Then the gaoler came back and I was taken off the hulks to await transportation to the other side of the world.

It were common knowledge on the hulks that not everyone on the hulks would actually be transported to Australia. Usually only those who had been found guilty of the most violent crimes or those whose excessive crimes had caught the public's imagination were finally transported. So me and Compeyson, having tried to escape, and having attacked each other were given no second chance.

Chapter 10

I am transported abroad.

Once in Australia, we knew that we would either be assigned to the government or to traders as labour; and we knew masters could not punish us themselves but could charge us and send us to a magistrate who would hear the case and decide the punishment. But we also heard as how lots of masters ignored the law, preferring to flog their labourers as a way of keeping them down. .

We knew that alcohol would still be available. It made punishment by the lash, a cat-o'-nine-tails, just about bearable. And, flogging, which was the way the army kept control of its soldiers, was still the main punishment. And we also heard about the dreaded chain gangs where survival was often in months rather than years.

So we all waited on the hulk, the prison ship moored out beyond the shore. We suffered great privations but they were nothing new to me and I hugged to myself the thought that you were going to get the chance that I never had and that helped me endure the vile conditions. Then one day that began like all the others, we were told to get our things together and to muster aft. We shuffled along in our chains and rags, a sad crew to be sure. There we went over the side into long boats and were all transferred to the shore where we were put on the outside of coaches that took us down to Portsmouth.

Getting down from the coach all stiff and sore we could see out to sea a ship. This was to be the vessel that was to take us across the world into a land full of savage creatures and God knows what else. Being rowed out in the fresh sea breeze however was good and I took it as an omen. I asked after Compeyson and learned that he had been kept back as he was trying to get a pardon, using our capture as a way of proving his good intentions to the judge.

I thought that once we were off the hulks and onto the ship that it would be easier for we poor souls. I were wrong. The minute they took us aboard at Portsmouth they took us below in such conditions where I would not have kept a pig. In fact, later that week pigs, screaming as if they were having their throats cut, were hauled up from lighters on to the deck where they were put into pens that the ship's carpenter had knocked together.

Sheep and rams were loaded too, but not for the like of us to eat; they were being taken to Australia for breeding, and I, as a shepherd, was put to care for them, and the care and attention they got were far in excess of what the poor convicts were afforded.

On the actual day that we set sail everyone were taken on board in an absolute storm of activity. Everyone was running around trying to prepare for the future. I had no tools of the trade, for being a shepherd, the only tool that I would need was my knife, and that was forbidden me. But a few carpenters and suchlike had somehow managed to take their tools with them. Later some of these convicts tried to deny that they were skilled men, for the government in Australia took all such, and kept them employed whilst the unskilled often went to other employers where they stood a chance of setting themselves up. In any case it were all a lottery where prizes arrived unconnected with anyone's merit!

I had heard tales on the hulks how some convicts did not get to Australia, dying on the way, and being put over the side. So I tried at all times to stay on deck with the animals, preferring the smell of the sheep and pigs to the overpowering stink of unwashed humanity below. I knew that fresh air was better than most physic so I tried to make sure that I had plenty.

After a few days out of Portsmouth a routine were established. Every morning everyone were roused and taken up on deck, where we were told to air our bedding, such as it was. The doctor would see anyone who asked to see him, but most never asked as he dismissed most complaints, or made you take such awful draughts that it seemed to me that he was making sure you only came to him when you were half dead. Most of us had lice, but I shaved off as much hair as I could so denied them the luxury of living on my poor body.

On Sundays we had the so-called Religious Instructor. When I asked where next we would land I got a shrug. I was told much depended on the weather; we were ruled by the winds. We would stop in South America I was informed. Now I had heard of the Americas, but could not for the life of me see how we were to go to America if we were bound for Australia.

Most days were the same at sea, only Sunday marking the week's end. A great deal of the time was spent in cleaning for our surgeon strongly believed in the saying "cleanliness is next to godliness", although he added whether it made us any healthier he had his doubts.

I fell into conversation with him when I held a seaman as he stitched up a flap of skin that had been cut out by a flying splinter of wood. A sudden squall of wind had caught us napping and a yardarm shattered sending nearly lethal pieces everywhere. I told him how when I were in the country we used honey on wounds, and cob's webs, to which he replied that that were mere superstition. He allowed that many herbs might be useful, particularly the purgative ones; he were a great one for purging and bleeding, holding these to be the foundation for a good medical care. But for all his ignorance, he were a kindly man and his kindness and holding to cleanliness helped many a poor soul on that there ship. We missed one landing at Rio because of contrary winds, so had to go on to Montevideo where the breeze from the land was full of strange smells. The Canaries had been a revelation that this new place was a complete eye-opener.

As we came into the harbour the heat increased and so did the smell and the noise. Before the anchors had even been dropped, fore and aft, little boats surrounded us full of every kind of coloured person from jet black to yellow. Most were youngsters who tried to sell us fruit. I could see all this because I were on deck minding the sheep and rams. I had been warned to keep a close eye on them as the natives would steal anything they could, and a live sheep would be a good prize to them.

As soon as we dropped anchor the captain was taken ashore in the ship's gig all dressed up, to pay his respects to the authorities. The surgeon went too, saying that he wanted to lay in more drugs. Both looked hot and overdressed, but apparently it were expected of them to cut a dash, so they did their best to impress.

To my surprise the women convicts were brought up on deck where they indulged in a veritable orgy of washing, themselves, their clothes, their hair. As they did so the saucy remarks flew about between them and the sailors. Then the remainder of the convicts were released so that they too could clean themselves.

All this cleaning were made possible by clean water being brought on board by relays of young men of all shapes and colours, all smiling, laughing and flashing the such white teeth as I had never seen before. Along o' them came more flocks of small boats with loads of children offering fruits of all sorts.

What with this sun, and the heat and the hustle and bustle of it all, along with the strange fruit and even stranger smells from off the land, everyone seemed to be pleased with life. You would never have thought that this were prison ship. Then to my greater surprise some of the convicts were allowed to go ashore. I asked what would happen if they ran off. I was told that they would simply be taken up by someone who would bring them back for cash. And, I were also told, that if they got beyond the edges of the city there were the natives who were not so friendly.

I found out later that the captain had done this trip several times, and each time had modified his attitude somewhat as he had learned that a certain amount of latitude helped him deliver healthy convicts. He had had enough of throwing dead ones into the sea.

I never got to put foot ashore at Montevideo, but the sailors that went ashore there came on board full of tales of drinking, eating and women. From the ship we could see a city what never seemed to be at rest. It were all hustle, bustle, lights at night never going out, and a continual buzz of sound, composed of laughter, singing, shouting, dancing, music and all sorts of movement. Movements of horses, carriages, carts, wagons and people. London were noisy but this were a different noise, more exciting, seemingly promising something, but I never did find out what that might have been.

In time, however, once we left Montevideo and called at Cape Town we really began to find the time on board much less pleasant I can tell you. It became colder, more stormy, and we spent much more time below cramped together. Even I were sent below as some of the storms meant that water washed over the decks to such an extent that it would wash you away in a twinkling of an eye. Everything became damp and mouldy and the stink of the bilges kept many being sick although most had got over seasickness as we came across the Bay of Biscay. This led to much ill feeling and fighting.

And after several fights involving women, the convicts were all chained up once again. It all began with an argument over washing water which one woman said another had stole. From argument it proceeded to insults, and then to screaming, and finally a pulling of hair and a scratching of faces. At first the sailors just laughed, then, as more women joined in, the captain ordered the sailors to deal with the unruly mob.

They waded into them with wooden fids, tools that they used for splicing ropes, giving many a nasty crack on their arms, until they managed to bundle them all below to the prison deck where they were confined behind bars, The ones that had begun it all were put into irons similar to the ones used in Newgate gaol.

Chapter 11

I rescue the ship's carpenter from drowning

And so we progressed. Each day passed, sometimes easily and sometimes not so easy. Life on the voyage was much less painful in some ways than life in the hulks. We had some food, and we sometimes had exercise in the fresh air. Mind you, I were particularly lucky as I had care of the animals. We were a motley crew of villains, with only a few fools, including one who saw visions. Some called him mad but some thought he could see the future.

Most days we had to man the pumps. I were horrified the first time that I saw the bilges. They were full of water and I were sure that we were sinking. The sailors laughed at me because they knew that bilges were always full of some sort of ballast, usually gravel which smelled something horrible. Then, because the ship were made of wood, it leaked all the time. The way we dealt with that was to pump, pump some more then pump again. At least it gave us some exercise.

If we ran into really stormy weather we had to batten down the hatches, that is to say fix them tight and snug to prevent more water coming inboard. Everything were often wet below, so wet that things became mildewed. If it blew hard for some time there was no way that fires could be lit in the galley. So there we would be, cramped together, hungry and stinking to high heaven. And thirsty, of course, because there were never enough fresh water. It were kept in barrels which were filled at every opportunity. Usually though when a barrel was broached the water was brackish. The few women we had on board were always demanding more water to wash themselves or their duds.

It could also be oppressively hot, particularly when there were no wind to work the sails. They would hang useless on the wooden spars and the sailors would all try to outdo each other at whistling for a wind; they were a right superstitious lot. But I remember that when I had had my future foretold by the gypsies I hadn't believed a word of it, specially the bits about me going across vast deeps and getting huge wealth. So it's best not to dismiss such ideas; who knows what exists in this world?

It were during one such lull when suddenly we just seemed to run into a rain cloud. Within seconds everything were drenched and the captain ordered everyone to come up on the upper deck, even those prisoners in irons, to stand or sit in the rain. Then he ordered the ship's crew to rig the spare sails to catch the rain-water. Soon all the water barrels were filled and we began to strip of our rags and dance about in the rain. That probably did more for us than any medicine that the doctor gave us, except perhaps our daily glass of wine! We were also give sauerkraut, but no-one liked it, despite being told that it would fend off scurvy

More often though we made our monotonous way along using what wind there were to keep the ship moving. Then every now and then we might get a brisker blow like the one that caught us all one time by surprise.

It were a sudden squall, a splash of rain along o' a sharp blow of wind which, though not serious enough for us to take in canvas, still made us heel over. Howsomever, it were enough to make a seaman who were aloft on some task to fall into the sea.

We all ran to the rail and the captain, cursing, gave orders to reef the sails. I fully expected the seamen to swim to the ship, not knowing that many such could not swim. Then seeing his difficulties, which were clear in the manner in which he thrashed about, I took off my white canvas breeches and went into the sea. My first thought was the sublime feeling of cool wetness as the water closed over my head. Then I struck out across the short distance for the carpenter (as it were the ship's carpenter who had been aloft and had missed his footing) and got him safely in my arms.

I told him to stop struggling and to rest easy and I'll pull him to the barque which is what he did, so saving his life, for had he struggled I would be sure to have had to let him go. To tell you the truth my feelings, as I pushed him into the many willing hands that were ready to pull him inboard, were how I was going to get back on board looking decent, for I had no underdrawers, and I knew the few women they were being transported would surely be watching. They would surely want to watch something so interesting in the monotonous passing of their days.

I need not have worried for another prisoner were ready with an old piece of blanket to put around me. Later I was to learn that the captain had almost had me shot in the water for attempted escape. Then seeing that I was a saving of the carpenter who were a valuable member of the crew, he relented. And it were this same carpenter, who later when we reached Sydney Cove in Australia, managed to get me employment with a gentleman, whose name I can't just remember at the moment, glossing over many of my imperfections!

Later I were on deck taking my ease among the sheep when the carpenter came to me thanking me most profusely. He had seen a similar occurrence on a previous trip when the captain had been unable to return in time to save the poor soul who had been left to drown. He added that he had been going to and fro for a number of years so knew what we were likely to expect once we arrived in Australia. He said as how there was a probation system and convicts were eventually assigned to a probation station. He did not know what this looked like, but thought it were probably an office of some sorts. Those convicts sentenced to seven years could apply for a ticket-of-leave much sooner than those with life sentences, who had to serve eight years before being eligible for the ticket-of-leave.

He also said that skilled artisans were in such demand that on reaching our destination the government usually immediately took them all. But he was protected by the fact that he was employed by the Royal Navy so he came and went as he wished on shore once he had made all such changes and alterations as were necessary to the ship. In gratitude he made me assist him in order to improve my simple carpenting skills, saying that he would speak for me when we arrived to get me a good billet.

It was thus that I met with that gentleman, a Mr Wentworth, who, having considerable wealth, needed repairs to his house. My carpenter persuaded him that I should be his mate, saying that I had acted in such a capacity on the voyage.

But I must first tell you how on our arrival at Sydney I was ordered to help unload the sheep what we had brought. I had cared most pertickler for these animals so I were pleased to be able to hand them over to their Australian owner. To my surprise this turned out to be a woman! And, as she cross-examined me about them, something turned over in my brain. It were the way she held herself and her tone of voice. Then it came back to me. Another young woman slipped into my thoughts, a woman with pluck who had come my way when I was a' working with Old Turvey.

"Excuse me for asking", says I, "but did we never meet?"

She looked hard at me and said we had never in this life met afore to her best recollection.

"Then," I said "perhaps you recall a certain time when in England a certain young woman needed a farrier, and a couple of shepherds, one old and the other younger, did tell that young woman where to get one."

She looked at me harder, saying that she knew of an occasion when such a happening occurred, but still knew me not.

I took her to one side so as not to give any offence in what I was to say, then told her all that I knew of Amanda Jane. She nodded as I told her about on officer and a lass deserted when that same officer had gone to foreign parts.

At this she told me that she still did not recognise me, but had no doubt that I knew her.

We went to a miserable lean-to where over a dram or two she told me her story. After she were sentenced at the assizes she were first sent to Newgate prison where, along with prostitutes, thieves and all sorts of human flotsam, she was kept until a ship were ready to go to New South Wales.

During her time in the prison her parents desperately tried to get her pardoned, visiting her very regularly. It were their visits when they brought food and clean clothing that sustained her. One young woman simply turned her face to the wall and died; others sold themselves, saying that that were all they were used to anyway. In time a parcel of them, in chains, were taken by coach to Portsmouth where Amanda Jane, whose time on the farm had taught her about birthing animals, helped the surgeon with several child births on board.

This sealed her future. All through the voyage she were appointed to assist the surgeon, while the other women were taken up as "wives" by the men. Some almost immediately became pregnant, but Amanda Jane steadily refused to enter into any liaisons, saying that being deserted by her officer had taught her a lesson that she was not forgetting very easily.

At Sydney she were immediately assigned to a household where eventually she married the owner, whose wife had died the previous year. Then he died leaving her a rich widow with lots of land. So drawing on her experience as a farmer's daughter, she made her spread prosper. She sent to England for more breeding stock, and it were the rams and sheep that I had cared for during the voyage. She were mortal pleased to have them arrive in such good shape, and on hearing my story gave me some money which I immediately gave to my carpenter to take back home to give to Jaggers.

Most convicts simply survived, but some became landowners, improving New South Wales for future generations. To be fair to the authorities, they tried to raise some of us out of the dirt and dust, and some of us did. But you don't make silk purses out of sow's ears, which are ever the case.

Some were such simple souls that they ran off at the first opportunity thinking as how to get to China, having heard the seamen talking about that place. The ones that were captured were the lucky ones, despite being brought back into virtual slavery, for the others simply died of hunger and thirst or were butchered by the black savages.

Of course, these were the black heathens who tried to resist the white men, but they were often hunted down or simply went off further into the bush, only coming out occasionally to steal our sheep. They seemed to have no idea of property. If an animal were there, they thought they could take it despite it belonging to someone else.

Amanda Jane were lucky, and she knew it. Most female convicts in Australia were treated as inferior beings, a hangover from England's ideas about women as an inferior sex. It were only exceptional women like Amanda Jane who were able to rise above their circumstances.

She saw as how I had fallen on my feet so thanked me, said goodbye, and said that I was not to forget that if I needed help I should come to her.

Chapter 12

I make my way in New South Wales.

The carpenter told me that he was to do some work for a Mr Wentworth in Vaucluse where he was to help enlarge a house. He told me that his joinery was to be done in local wood, then painted to resemble English Oak, a conceit that was soon to be copied elsewhere. The carpenter was in demand as he had worked on houses in England before going to sea. He said that he needed me as a mate as the government had taken all the skilled carpenters to work for them. This Mr Wentworth owned several sheep stations, an item of information that interested me as I thought that if I could work on one of them I would surely be able to prove my worth.

Of course I weren't a skilled man, but having worked on a farm where I was used to knocking up odds and ends I could use an adze and a plane. My work with a chisel weren't that good, but I could saw straight enough. Mainly though I just carried things around and gave a hand where necessary. I didn't drink, that is to say I kept off the rum, and that made me more useful.

At first I was housed with the other convicts in the barracks nearby, but soon my friend arranged for me to assist him and pressed for me to be housed upstairs in the stables of the house that he was working on. Within a fortnight I was told to get ready to leave the barracks with my small bundle of clothes and to go over to the house along with a cart taking provisions.

There I was taken upstairs in the stables to a small attic room, where after climbing an exceedingly steep staircase I was shown a bed with a hook where I might hang my clothes. Hung across the corner of the room was a thin piece of material that provided some privacy when I washed, and to my delight there was a basin in which to wash along with a jug of water. This was real luxury after the crowded noisy barracks.

Working on a house such as Vaucluse made me even more aware of my station in life and the station to which I wanted to raise you Pip. I ate off pewter plates, and although the food were enough, it were rough stuff.

Finding suitable staff in this new country was a constant problem so I was put to work on helping to assemble shutters for the outside of the windows, though I do not know if my work ever got completed as I was taken away from it almost as soon as they learned that I had been a shepherd.

My carpenter friend was not very cheerful about the work that he was doing, giving it as his opinion that:

" Those blasted termites will destroy all my best endeavours".

"The best wood for joinery", he went on "was Australian Cedar."

He told me too that in his opinion the floors should be made of Australian Blackbutt. I must say that I scarcely listened to him. It were all the same to me whatever wood they were using.

Just once I were taken down to the sea nearby through such heat and such vegetation that made me stare. I had never seen or felt anything like it in England, but the beach were sandy just as I remembered a beach in Dorset when I was with the Gippoes. It made me homesick I can tell you as I felt the wet sand between my toes. I would have like to go into the sea to get cool but I were mortal affeared of sharks and suchlike, and in any case I could not be sure that they might think that I were trying to escape and I would get a musket ball in my back. I was to help unload small items of furniture that they were landing from a small boat what had brought them from around the coast. Mr Wentworth was keen to spend his money on furnishing his house so that it looked like a gentleman's house in England

One morning I started work as usual, then during a break my carpenter came to with a well set-up gentleman. He looked hard at me as the carpenter told him what a good worker I were. Eventually he said he would take me on which was lucky for me as my carpenter was about to return to England so I might have been employed anywheres, maybe simply in a labouring gang clearing the bush. Many were used in this way and they had a mortal pitiful time of it too.

This Mr Jackson said that everyone deserved a chance, but his attitude changed when he heard that I had been a shepherd.

"Were you now! " he exclaimed, then put me through a reg'lar catechism of shepherding.

Did I know how to deal with scab?

How do you deal with worms in the wool?

And so forth while all the while my carpenter stood behind him a nodding and a winking fit to bust because he knew that Mr Jackson had many acres and a fine flock of merino sheep.

Eventually I told Mr Jackson that the best way for me to show him what I knew was to let me start work on the flock, and I offered to be sent back if he were not delighted with my efforts. This pleased him so I said goodbye to my carpenter, collected my duds and was taken off inland for the longest journey I had so far taken in this strange land. It were by foot as I had to follow my new master who rode a solid looking bay mare.

But my heart sank when I saw the flock, and I asked who had been a' shepherding them, for the flock were in a truly sorry state. I got no answer except a nod to a scare-crow like figure who stood watching me. This I found out later was John Beckett who had been transported for seven years for stealing a loaf two years afore me. I quickly determined that he were a half-wit for he could scarcely answer my questions. I found he had worked with sheep in the old country, but in no way shape or fashion could anyone claim that he were a shepherd. At first he seemed angry at my taking over his work, but once I had snatched his shepherd's crook from and given some orders he did what I said quickly enough, particularly as I waved the crook at him to make him think that I would use it on him. I might have too, but only were I to be driven to it. The poor lad needed help and I found out later that he had been beaten enough in the past.

Chapter 13

I start work as a shepherd in Australia.

Within a few days I had established some sort of order in the flock, only having to kill those few who were too sick to be left alive. We butchered these for meat, and by were mighty pleased to do so, for which it gave us enough meat for several days, not only to feed Mr Jackson, our master but also his housekeeper, Ada, who were only a black heathen woman, but kindly enough for a heathen, and for our own use. We also dried some of the meat to use later on, which was a good thing seeing as John and me were sent out into the wilds with the flock with only the dried meat and some meal to feed us, there being no other vittles available.

Luckily we had a black heathen boy with us who spoke not one word of the King's English, but managed to convey to John where we were to go to find water and it were truly amazing how he and John got on with nary a word between them, using only signs that they made with their hands, signs that I began to learn. Indeed if I had not I would have been in a state

I later found out that this poor creetur were dumb and had been since a baby. He had been abandoned by his tribe who thought he had been cursed, particularly as his mother had died when he were three years old, or thereabouts. Ada had taken care of him at the request of Mr Jackson who, although a stern man was a complete Christian. How much of real Christian I was to learn later. He took to me as I quickly learned some basic signs where he and I talked together, and was kinder to him seemingly than the others had been formerly. I tried to get him to wash like a Christian but he would have none of it, and to tell truth the flies and other insects didn't seem to bother him as much as they bothered us. So In time I often plastered mud on myself like he did, at first because it were cool. Then I found that I too was less worried by the insects.

We three slept out under the skies huddled together for warmth if it turned cold. Some nights there were only sacks to cover us. This was no real hardship to me. I had spent many a night out in the fields back in England. Mostly though the weather were warm. Warm and dry, and not nearly enough rain to make the grass grow, so we had to let the flock range further afield in order to get grazing.

Our rations would be brought out to us every week. And sometimes we had to walk miles to get them, the flock having strayed all over the place. I asked John how much land Mr Jackson had so that I could determine where to take the sheep. Both John and the blacky pantomimed to me that there were no limits. Apparently Mr Jackson had been granted so much land he could pretty well go anywhere as long as he did not stir up the natives who had some funny ideas about some rocks and trees that they thought were holy. They're a funny lot.

At first I was shocked at the way they behaved, then, realising that they were heathens who could know no better I ignored their nakedness and their smell. Mind you it were best not to ignore them altogether. When they were roused up they could be a bloodthirsty crew as I was soon to find out.

Some of the things that they made were a wonder. They would take a piece of wood and work at it until it were a fearsome spear; but that weren't all, the spear would be decorated in such an elaborate way that it became a marvel.

Of course they were bone idle, sitting around most of the time until suddenly for no reason at all they would take off and you might not see them for weeks.

Chapter 14

My days on the sheep farm.

So I gradually got used to working in Australia. We shepherds had to bring our flocks of sheep eventually from miles inland into Port Phillip. This was easier said than done, and I really more enjoyed staying out in what they called the bush looking after the flocks. I had to put up with bad food, and lots of times being thirsty. And there was always the fear of being attacked by the black natives. But I was used to loneliness and extremely hard conditions. These hard times in the bush were just about bearable because like others what had been transported I had suffered worst on the ships. At least I was on dry land!

For many men the absence of women were a real trial but, as I told you Pip, I thought that I had left that side of life behind me for good. Being married then being mixed up with women had been a blessing then a curse.

I found out later that many like me, having served their time out, got themselves some land, and the fact that they were now working on their own behalf enabled them to carry on. They also knew that those convicts that ran away into the bush often died it of hunger or thirst or at the hands of the savages, who were always ready to attack any white man on his own.

Sometimes, for no real reason that I could think of, the black heathens would attack us even when we were together. One day in the middle of the afternoon as we were drinking tea from metal cups, having stopped in the shade of a large rock all covered over with strange pictures, a group of them approached us. They were daubed with white clay and carried spears. John had been scratching at the pictures, something that my master had told him to stop doing. On this occasion though John, who usually did what he was told, saw fit to ignore him. He carried on scraping at the funny figures muttering under his breath about bloody savages.

I stood up. The heat was intense, dry, and, despite the

shade we were in, overpowering. It pressed down on me and I

knew something bad was about to happen, I just knew it.

"Stand up", I said, "and move back beyond those rocks". My master looked at me in surprise. Then he saw the blackies and saw the look on my face. Do as he says, he added quietly.

"Why"? asked John.

"Don't argue just go", replied my master.

We all turned and scrambled over the broken rocks but it were too late.

Chapter 15

I rescue my master.

They rushed after us a' whooping and hollering, stark naked but daubed all over with clay and such. John beside me called out " Oh Gahd" and fell over with a spear stuck right through him. My master grunted with pain having received a spear thrust. Luckily though he always went prepared for such attacks, and he immediately shot dead the biggest of the savages with a single well-aimed ball from a musket. They fell back then looking affeared, but soon enough they starting their chanting and making little rushes at us. I pulled John back to where we had some rocks between them and us but it were clear that he were dead. I had seen too many dead men not to know one when I saw one.

My master thrust into my hands another gun, a horse pistol, saying

"shoot, shoot".

I had never handled such a weapon before, but having seen them used, I knew enough to cock it and to aim low and pulled the trigger. The noise startled me as did the kick of the pistol. I hit one who fell sideways and as he did so he called out something in his heathen language. The black heathens had paused when their leader had dropped, then when I had fired too they howled and fled, leaving two of them on the ground. The one that my master had shot was dead, his mouth still open with flies already settled on his mouth and eyes and his bloody wound. The other wounded savage that I had hit jabbered at us. I could see that he was bleeding, and was very surprised when my master said

"Come away, leave him."

I had expected him to kill the savage but as he explained it to me later as we struggled back to the farmhouse, he would tell the others about our guns. They need to know that we are armed. That way, they might leave us alone.

It was only then that we realised that my master was badly injured, for he staggered to his knees cutting them to the bone on the sharp stones on the ground. A spear had severed something in his arm, and the blood was oozing through his rough cotton shirt. I tore some of the shirt sleeve off and bound up his arm and supported him as we moved towards his horse.

" I can't make it lad", he said, "I can't ride."

I lifted him up until he hung across the horse, then it led it all the twelve miles back to the homestead. It took me most of that afternoon and evening, and constantly on my mind was the fact that we had left John dead behind us. But we got back eventually to the homestead where the woman, Ada, washed his cuts and bound them up before putting him to bed. I watched how she included some herbs in the rags that she put onto his wound. They seemed like to ones that I had seen the Gypsies using.

Just as I were going to bed too he called me in looking mighty solemn. He told me that he would have died if it had not been for me looking after him. I said I might be a convict, but I hoped that I was a Christian too. He took my hand and told me that I was a good fellow, and that he would not forget me at the right time. Nor did he. He were not only a Christian gennelman, but a man who kept his word.

Chapter 16

My master dies and I inherit the farm

In Australia out of Sydney if you were took ill there were mighty little you could do about it. Although we had our remedies, they were crude. So when my master suddenly developed a fever and Ada nursed him, she knew, from having dealt with kind of fever before, that he had less than a sporting chance to pull through. She sent for me out in the bush and I came riding back on his horse, that he let me use, to find him almost gone.

He was asking for me, Ada said, and were insistent that I had to be brought home back to our three-room shack that stood under a stand of trees. I went into him and realised immediately from the smell that he were a very sick man. I knew that smell from the hulks and the barracks. It were the miasma that gathered around a body when he was about to leave this world. We all prayed, each in his own fashion. My prayer was for him to have a few more years so that he could see the fruits of his labour for we were just about pulling through and making something of his land. We sat with him trying to keep away the flies and wringing out cloths to wipe him to try to keep him cool.

It was not to be. He called me in and took me by the hand telling me that I was a good and faithful servant and as such I would be rewarded, and he added, not in the next world. He told me to look in the old sea chest where he kept his papers. I was to find a bundle of papers tied up together and bring them to him. I found them and he made me unwrap them only to find that he had made a will.

I knew that he had done something of the kind on one of his infrequent visits into Sydney. He had hinted as much to me and I thought as how he would be leaving everything to a relative. It turned out that he had no-one and that was why he had come to Australia. He told me that when I read it I would find that he had left almost everything to me. Apart from a bequest to Ada I was to have the bulk of his estate.

He died that night as I sat with him, slipping across to somewheres where I hoped he would be happy. Ada gave great cry and threw her apron over her face and keened when she in and found me sitting with him, and he all cold as a clod and stiff. I tried to comfort her but that's not a job I'm easy with. Later on when I asked the others they said that she had gathered some things together and walked off into the bush. We never saw her again

Now I really had my hands full, I can tell you. I set everyone to work and rode into Sydney to see the authorities about the will. I half expected trouble as I was a ticket of leave man, but they had trouble of their own and so a convict who could read write and cipher took the details and copied them into the rolls. He said that I should register my master's death which I did and that were that.

I rode back to the shack thinking all the time about what I should do. On getting back I sat down and wrote down what I needed to do and what needed to do it. It frightened me some as I realised that I was a'going to need a deal of things to make a go of it.

Chapter 17

I get news about Pip.

What I principally needed were cash; I needed money to do all the things that I knew from my experience needed to be put in hand, so I went to Sydney where I looked for Amanda Jane.

I had no difficulty in finding her as she had become a well-known lass. I explained to her what I needed, and to her eternal credit she gave me a banker's draft what enabled me to shop and buy essential things like shears and suchlike things. I also needed chemicals because Scab and catarrh had started to appear in my sheep. The fencing of property boundaries, particularly along roadsides were also necessary if I were to keep hold of my land, and that cost money too.

I was allowed to use convicts, and because I was a good employer, they worked hard for me, despite the fact that for many of them the only contact with a sheep before coming to me was when they ate mutton broth. Soon I had made enough money to pay back Amanda Jane, and I might have married her except for one thing - she would not have me. And who could blame her? Who would want a varmint like me, even with my money. In any case she had become involved in politics, supporting someone who was a real gennelman.   The talk was of emancipation, something that I steered clear of. I'm sure it were not for the likes of me anyways.

Of course I could have married someone else. I would have liked that. I might have enjoyed the pleasure of a female's company, like I had in England. There were no end of women available and ready to be married, but I had heard tales of many a marriage contract being broken soon after the wedding, and that put me off.

Men would go to the Female Factory, a desperate place at Paramatta, where the women would be lined up, poor souls, as soon as it were known that some man had come a'lookin' for a bride. They would do what they could to make themselves attractive, though that were an impossibility for some of them as they were so broken down by their experiences. After wandering up and down the man would choose his bride to be, more often based upon what he thought of her health and strength, rather than looks, though a full set of teeth were preferred as the new wife would have to make do with some pretty rough food. Then they would be married straight away, despite the fact that one or both of them might have a spouse in England or Ireland.

Some of these marriages would be a success with the new wife being a strength and a support to a man in his struggles in this strange new world where everything seemed to be the opposite of what all remembered from home. But equally some soon fell apart as the trollop, either realising that she had exchanged one set of nasty conditions for a similar set, or never having intended to make a go of it, took off for Sydney and led a riotous life in some of the areas where she would be welcomed as much as the rum that were consumed.

And so I went on getting more and more successful, little by little, it's true, but I was a success in my eyes anyways. I could just about read and write and I could cipher well enough to know that I were making profit. I thought that I had done pretty well, thanks to my master; so when two high and mighty so-called rode by on their thoroughbreds and I heard them say that I might be rich, but no gennelman, I thought to myself that I could buy and sell you two. And I thought too that I was the makings of a gennelman back in the old country. I hugged that thought to me.

All this time I was sending money to Jaggers by my friend, Arthur the carpenter. Of course I had to tell him about you. He came regular to Australia as a ship's carpenter, but I knowed as how he also brought cargo with him, things that you couldn't easily get in our new world, so he made hisself a great profit each time.

When he came again, looking much older, for the journey had been a difficult one, he brought news of the famines in Ireland and told us that as a consequence the Irish were going to America. Lots thought that no bad thing as everyone knew as how the Irish were a wild lot, leastways the Irish convicts certainly were, particularly those who were sent for being rebels. He also told us about Queen Victoria, but most said having a queen were no different to us poor souls; we would get no pardons from her.

But more important to me were the news that he brought of you Pip! He took my arm and led me to one side and told me of having seen you arrive in a carriage at a house where he was doing some work. You were at some swell's house in Richmond in Surrey looking as high and mighty as any of them. My heart swelled when he said that, and I resolved that very night that I would travel back to see you. Of what use was it, I asked myself, to have made a gentleman if I could not see him myself with my own blessed eyes? I also managed to persuade myself that you would want to know how a mere convict, a mere varmint, what you helped so nobly so long ago had raised you up to what you had now become.

Both Arthur, my carpenter and Mary Ann counselled caution when I told them as how I planned to return. Others had tried this and been caught and been returned. Worse, one or two had been hanged. But I were not to be turned from my resolve. I burned to see you again as well as some cool green countryside where sheep could graze and move about without raising clouds of dust. Finally Arthur warned me about Compeyson who had already managed to get to England and was making a living by acting as an informer. He gave me the details about how Compeyson had accomplished this, and begged me to think again. I said I were resolved so he simply said that I should take care.

Chapter 18

I leave Australia

Eventually both, seeing how firm I were in my intentions, agreed to help me. Mary Ann, after lots of attempts to make me change my mind, agreed to buy some of my land and to transfer the money into the New South Wales Bank. She knew the cove what kept the records on land sales. He was, as you might expect, a convict; and he were ready to falsify the accounts for a fee. This was necessary as I might be missed. It were recognised that most accounts in the colony could be set to rights for a fee, and so I profited from both being honest and not so honest, but what else could a poor varmint like me do?

Then Arthur made arrangements for us all to go aboard a ship that were due to sail soon. It were standing out to sea at anchor though it could have come further in and tied up to the newly constructed jetty. It seems that the captain was a might nervous of being too near the convicts. I later learned that not a few of the convicts tried to stowaway on ships. I also learned that some even stole boats and made an escape. We went on board seemingly only for to have a dinner with the captain. We did eat a really hearty meal washed down with some rum and sat about until it were good and dark. Despite it being night it were still hot and the insects still buzzed about us. Then, when it were really dark, we all left the ship. Leastways it seemed that I did for although my hat and cloak went ashore it were not me in it!

My hat and cloak, worn by one of my workers, went straight back to my biggest farm, where, as far as anyone could tell, I were there too. Although I were well known in the

70

country we imagined that it might be some time before I were missed. My hands had instructions to put it out that I had the ague from being at sea and that was why I was not overseeing the work as usual. It cost me more money to get all this done, but my friends insisted that I go through this masquerade as a way of getting me clean away. They knew that they were putting themselves in danger too so taking all these precautions helped them as well.

So that night after dinner, and after all had left, I went straight to my cabin. I might tell you that that small cabin cost me dearly as space was not got cheap. But it were cash well laid out for it meant that I was another man, do you see, when I emerged from the cabin once we had got under way. This Mr Provis was every inch the seasoned traveller; the very picture of a man who had tried his luck abroad and had made some money and was going home to England. And that were the beauty of it. I really were that man. I practised at this deceit and it reminded me of the deceits that I had practised in the past. I thought about Compeyson who I knew had wormed his way into the confidence of those in Sydney who considered themselves better that all the rest of the poor souls who sweated to support them in that damned place.

And the trip to Cape Town as Mr Provis was nothing like the trip that I had made to get to Australia. No mustering to the sound of a drum; no having to knuckle my forehead; no short rations and warm brackish water. No sleeping on the deck among the animals. Instead I had a bunk to sleep in with my pocket book always under my body alongside my primed pistol. That cost me a pretty penny too and some marine officer were quite well rewarded for enabling such an article to go missing; of course a convict scribe had to be bribed too so that the records all tallied. Oh! ain't it pretty what money can do!

I broke bread (still hard tack once the soft tack were finished) with the captain, an entertaining man who knew to make conversation without asking awkward questions, something I appreciated. He were going straight back to England, not going by way of China for a freight of tea. He had some sort of arrangement hisself that meant that it were more beneficial to go direct. I never asked him about this, and he did me the favour of being as delicate over my arrangements.

At Cape Town I changed ships; and by now I were ready to put it about that I were on my way back home from Australia having made enough from my trip there to go home to live out my years in England. I bought seaman's duds for I did not want anyone to think that I were that rich, but I had a full pocket book what I were ready to defend with that loaded pistol, if I had to.

Chapter 19

Coming home

I knew that I was taking it a terrible risk in coming back to England, but I had to see the young gentlemen that I had created. I also thought that by coming into England from France on the regular packet that I would not be drawing attention to myself. I reckoned that if I landed in England from the ship from Australia even if it came via China, I would be a marked man. There was not much I could do about my appearance. If they were looking for me they would know that I looked about sixty, had iron-grey hair, was a muscular man, strong on my legs, and that I was browned and hardened by exposure to all sorts of weather. But that description could fit a dozen men, particularly if he were dressed in old slops.

So I took care to embark on a ship from Cape Town that let me off at Cadiz, then I travelled by coach across Spain and into France, staying sometimes in small inns on the way if there were no coach immediately available. All the time I were doing this I fretted about the journey and the waste of time that it was causing me. I daydreamed in the coaches about you and what you would say to me once we met again; sleep in the inns were pretty near impossible. They were dirty and the food was rotten foreign muck. I longed for some roast beef or lamb.

But my luck ran out for during one part of the trip in France we were held up by two highwaymen. One man rode straight at the coach and make it stop, while a second, all muffled up in a riding coat, came alongside and put his pistol through the window jabbering in Frenchy lingoe which of course I did not understand. I understood his pistol though, so I took out of my pocket a small cloth bag in which I carried a few gold coins what I had prepared for just such an occasion, and as he took the bag I put *my* cocked pistol to the Frenchie's face. It was at that precise moment that the coachmen, unable to restrain the poor horses what he was hauling back with his reins, let them go a little which shook the coach, but this made me pull the trigger. I swear to God that I only meant to frighten the poor devil who was holding us up and get back my gold if I could.

Immediately the highwayman fell backwards dropping my gold coins; then his horse bolted, dragging him by one foot in the stirrups into the nearby woods where we heard him crashing through the undergrowth. The other man, startled by the shot, simply turned and galloped away. The coachman cracked his whip and made the horses start off so I called to him to stop a moment.

My first thought was to retrieve my bag of coins what the highwayman had dropped, so I hopped out pretty smartish, picked it up and got straight back in. I were sorry, of course for the poor fellow what I had shot, but it were no use dwelling on what might have beens. Then I told the coachman to go on

I was the hero of the moment! The ladies, once they had got over their hysterics, wanted to kiss me, and they all called me their saviour; while the men all wanted to wring my hand. Just fancy Pip, they wanted to shake the hand of a convicted felon!

At the next stop, for we did not stop to ascertain whether the man had died that I had shot, as the horses were being changed there was an excited babble of languages, then an official approached me. His English was as a non-existent as my

French, but he gave me to understand that I had to give an account of myself to the mayor in the town. I said that, once I had taken some refreshment I would do that. But instead I slipped away and ordered a post chaise to go immediately. I did not want to be involved in any official business. And that was my mistake, for what I did not know was that the French have a system of Telegraphs set upon hills which meant that word of me and my doings were sent on ahead of me. No-one knew my name of course, but there were enough who had seen me and could give a description of me, the hero of the hour, to a remarkable detail.

I still intended to board the packet from Calais, and to land in Dover. Then I heard them talking about me in the Inn at Calais while I waited for it, so I changed my mind and headed for Le Havre where I took a boat to Portsmouth. All the while I kept a sharp eye out in case someone was going to try to take me.

Chapter 20

Nearly home and dry

You would have thought that after coming clear across the world that just crossing the English Channel would have been easy. Arter all, it's a small piece of water. But, suddenly autumn storms blew up and the packet were delayed for days leaving me to fret in Le Havre, kicking my heels and, unbeknownst to me, attracting attention.

Eventually I was able to board the packet and after a rough crossing, managed to land in Portsmouth safely. Howsomever, from there I must a' been shadowed all the ways to London. I wanted to travel in a regular coach, taking an outside seat as I did not want to attract attention by paying for an inside seat. Everything had changed though and I were directed to take a steam train on the London and South Western Railway. I did not like the sound of that, particularly as it had only just begun running, so I hired a coach instead.

I had to wait awhiles because I wrote to Jaggers from Portsmouth asking for the particulars of your address. By return of post, Wemmick, Jagger's clerk, sent me the details and it was only then that I was able to continue my journey. It were a cold miserable journey too only relieved by the knowledge that I would be seeing you so I passed some of the time in reading a newspaper, the Portsmouth Telegraph, what I had bought. I were amazed to find the changes that were happening. Maybe I should have kept a sharper eye out rather than reading the newspaper but what I read amazed me. When I were in Australia I were either concerned to stay alive or working hard to improve my farming so I had little time to sit and read about events far away from me. Of course I heard occasional snippets of news particularly when my carpenter came again and I met up with him to pay him money for Jaggers. I had heard, as I previously said, about the famines in Ireland and Queen Victoria and I also knew that there had been trouble over Cholera. Now I read about a proposed Railways Act and an Act to make factories safer. All to come about because Members of Parliament were troubled by the bad way of things. They never had before to my knowledge. But what really amazed me was the news that people were emigrating to Australia in large numbers. I read that in April 165 men, women and children emigrants had embarked at Deptford on board the St Vincent, bound for Plymouth, Cork and Sydney Australia. They even set out their allowances for the voyage. I made a note of it. Here it is:

The weekly allowance, given in proportion daily, to each adult during the voyage is 4½ lb of Bread, 1lb of beef, 1 lb of pork, 1lb of preserved meat, 1¾lb flour, ½ lb raisins, 6oz suet, 1 pint peas, ½ lb rice, ½ lb preserved potatoes, 1 oz tea, 1½ oz roast coffee, ¾ lb sugar, 6 oz butter, 5 gallons and 1 quart water, 1 gill pickled cabbage, ½ gill vinegar, and 2 oz salt.

Imagine that, all these poor souls sailing voluntarily to a place that so many of us had striven to get away from.

Anyway, I came to London and, like so many others, I peered around at the sights which for others might have caused no harm, but in my case were mighty dangerous. Dangerous, as Compeyson had already returned to England after a particularly nasty bitter business in Port Phillip where he had pretended to go along with a riot by the convicts, but at the last minute had blown on them all to the authorities.

Some were hanged; he were released and sent back to England for his own safety, because if any of the convicts had got to him, his life would have been forfeit, and his death brutal in the extreme. I had heard about this episode, how at a word some convicts had overpowered the soldiers, seizing their arms, but because Compeyson had already betrayed them they were seized immediately.

I say that I had heard of this but didn't know that Compeyson had been the betrayer.until Arthur, attempting to persuade me not to return to England, had told me about this again saying that Compeyson was the Judas.

Up to then in Australia he had tried some of his former tricks, being as how he was clever with the pen, but he had not reckoned on the other convicts who were unwilling to let him into any of their stratagems. They already knew how to swindle. He tried to pass hisself off as an architect, and for a while had some success, using a real architect who had been transported as his assistant. Then he was unable to sustain the role, though there were some buildings put up as a result of his work. Back in England he acted as a petty informer, particularly on returned transported convicts like any such as me

I tried to get to you quietly once it were dark. It were certainly wet and windy when I came to your lodgings, and you were so cautious when I first sat down. You treated me just as I imagined you would. A real gennelman you were and that so pleased me. And you were so ready to ask what precautions could be taken to avoid me being recognised and seized, and that so pleased me too. But you were right to be so extra cautious. When you asked me as I came in was anyone with me I said no; then after some thought, I told you that I didn't take particular notice but I thought there might have been someone.

That caused you some disquiet I could see. You thought that I would be taken if you didn't help me. And you were right. I could see that. So I left you to make such arrangements, smoking peacefully in the meanwhile. Then you and your comrade got me clothes and lodgings and in the end got me here a'waiting for a boat to get me off to Germany safely, and the rest you know Pip, but at least whatever happens to me I have made you a gentleman. Not bad eh! for someone who was sold for five shillings?

Epilogue

We now know that Pip and his comrade did not manage to get Magwitch away safely. They were right to be suspicious. Wemmick thought that Compeyson must have used his network of disaffected men to keep himself informed. So, despite Pip and Herbert's best effort, he was always hard upon their heels. Pip knew that two men had been seen whilst he and Herbert were with Magwitch at the Ship Inn. Were they Compeyson's men or were they part of the London Police?   No matter. It was clear by then that plans had been laid and would be carried out with a dreadful and deadly inevitability.

The attempt to arrest Magwitch, when Compeyson was finally revealed in the stern of the cutter, led to Compeyson's death. It also led to the death of any efforts for Magwitch to pass to Pip his money, for, as an arrested returned transported convict, his possessions were forfeit to the Crown. This truth was kept from Magwitch.

Why were Pip and Herbert not arrested for their part in assisting a returned convict?   Their non-arrest was due to Wemmick who spoke to the authorities and persuaded them that, both Pip and Herbert had been gulled by a notorious crook Magwitch, and he was able to point to Magwitch's convictions to bolster up his evidence.   Magwitch, he averred, had lied to them that he was a rich Australian seeking to settle in Europe and so convinced them, that they were totally taken in by the rogue. Jaggers had gone along with this fiction having carefully kept himself free from any involvement that might be to his disadvantage.

But why had they helped him? Wemmick explained that Magwitch had conned Pip and Herbert by telling them that he had come to London to seek his relatives, but was being chased by a convict who was trying to steal his money. When Compeyson's body was recovered from the river later on they found notes in his possession that included the name of a banking house in New South Wales where indeed money and land was registered. So Wemmick cleverly wove the truth into a different version that satisfied the authorities; something incidentally that he had seen done many hundreds of times in his occupation. But that seems to go on now; nothing really changes.

By dying before he could be hanged Magwitch cheated the law, a victory of sorts for him. But his final victory was told to him by the "gennelman" that he had made. It was the news that that his daughter was alive and well and was now a lady. So, ironically while his efforts to create a gentleman had apparently failed, his wife's desperate actions following her arrest for murder had led to her and Magwitch's daughter becoming a lady.

Can we really say though that he failed with Pip? Maybe Pip lacked Magwitch's money and land at the end, but he certainly behaved like a gentleman when he agreed with Herbert that they would try to save Magwitch by getting him out of England. So it was deeds as well as words that give us the final proof.

Part two

Made a Lady

Amanda Jane's Story

Prologue

The scream pierced my ears and the knife flashed in the late autumn sun; I braced myself for the blood. As it jetted out, pouring into buckets that had been set to catch it, I knew that eventually the body would be hacked into two having been hung up on a meat hook for this very purpose. And this was the body that I had helped nurture.

I turned and ran from the scene in tears. Later, my mother wiping away those tears with the corner of a rough blood-soaked apron soothed me saying that our pig had to die for us to live. As a farmer's daughter I had to understand that the cycle of life included death. It was then that I began to really grow up, but it took me many more years to become mature.

So begins Amanda Jane's story. The story that Pip travelled half way around the world to Australia to collect. The story told by one of the good friends of Abel Magwitch. Pip travelled more comfortably in The Symmetry to Australia than Magwitch did when he was transported in 1830; and he travelled more comfortably than Amanda Jane did in 1815.

He embarked in London on The Symmetry on 24th June 1845 and arrived at Port Adelaide on 7th November, journeying on in the Antipodean heat to Sydney. There he found Amanda Jane, who was now Lady Amanda Jane Spens.

Readers who have read "Made a Gentleman" will know that that book tells the story how Abel Magwitch was able to support Pip while he was in Australia. Pip heard from Abel how various

85

people helped him, so he determined to go and meet one of them who was instrumental in Magwitch's effort to make Pip a gentleman.

I came across this history, obviously set down by Pip, in an old manuscript and decided that it merited being told, just as Magwitch's story that was told to Pip also merited being published. However I could find no trace of Pip when I examined the passenger list of the Symmetry for the journey that took place from 24th June 1845 to 7th November from London to Port Adelaide. It occurred to me though that Pip would not wish to travel under his real name after all the problems that he had had in London. He must therefore have travelled incognito.

Amanda apparently welcomed him by saying that she was truly sorry to hear about Abel Magwitch's death as he was in her eyes a good man who did much good in his life, certainly a lot more good than any ill that could be put to his account. She went on to say that as Pip had already heard from Abel's own mouth how first she and he had met, and how subsequently their lives had come together in Australia she would now relate her own story. She had long wished to have this set down and having Pip there gave her the opportunity to do so.

Chapter 1

My early years

The scream pierced my ears and the knife flashed in the late autumn sun; I braced myself for the blood. As it jetted out, pouring into buckets that had been set to catch it, I knew that eventually the body would be hacked into two having been hung up on a meat hook for this very purpose. And this was the body that I had helped nurture.

I turned and ran from the scene in tears. Later, my mother wiping away those tears with the corner of a rough blood-soaked apron soothed me saying that our pig had to die for us to live. As a farmer's daughter I had to understand that the cycle of life included death. It was then that I began to really grow up, but it took me many more years to become really mature.

I was born in Shropshire to elderly parents who having lost one child treasured me as a gift from God. This was in 1796 on a farm that was not far from Oswestry; a farm that had made my parents rich as they used the most modern methods to increase their harvests. As a consequence their harvest homes each year were jolly rollicking affairs and, as my father believed in treating his people with care, him being as devout a Christian as you might meet in all Shropshire, all were welcome to partake in what the Good God above had provided for his children below.

My first real memory is being frightened by a ram that suddenly charged me and tumbled me in the muck. Our old shepherd laughed and picked me up whereupon I stamped my foot and said that I hated the silly ram. That made him serious and he told me that it was the ram that put bread in my mouth and clothes upon my back.

I have never forgotten that. I also remember how they brought the news of Lord Nelson's death and I remember it as that year I was five and had a doll with a porcelain face that I called Sally. I also remember my father holding his watch to my ear so that I could hear time as it went by. He would tell me that it waited for no man.

In time I grew and put away dolls and by the time that I was a strapping comely lass I could wrestle any ram upon its back if I so needed to do. I lacked for nothing, including boundless belief in myself. I could write and cipher tolerably well and as to reading, I was ready to devour any thing that came my way which made me all the more ready to express my opinions, which I must own were mainly those that I had taken unto myself from such books as I read.

I could also ride, and because my father, who would have dearly loved a son, encouraged me I became a regular tomboy. That is not to say that I was not useful in our dairy. I helped the maids there in all their work, churning the cream to make the rich country butter that we were famous for, and helping to make both the hard and soft cheese that we took to market in nearby Oswestry. My father would show me his watch and say that as he had no son he would leave it to me.

Chapter 2

More early years

How I enjoyed market days. We all had to be up betimes so I as a consequence was often asleep as we returned on our farm wagon pulled by George and Hannibal our patient farm horses. Sometimes before I dozed off I would hear the maids who sold our butter and cheese chattering softly about their so-called admirers. Most of what they said went right over my head; then, as I grew I began to understand more, and at thirteen after a much longed-for event arrived, which I felt made me much more important, they drew me into their feminine world and much of what had been mysterious was now clear to me.

I began to speak less of my thoughts and to keep them to myself. I dreamed of someone who would come to carry me away from what I began to consider to be an humdrum existence.

I was not unhappy but at times would go to the ice-house that we had at the back of the farmhouse and sit there quietly in the cool. The ice came from the pond at the end of Ten Acre meadow and was collected every year and hauled in our cart by our patient willing shire horses. Father said that these horses were the direct descendants of knights' horses that were ridden by them in old battles.

I dreamed of these knights in richly worked armour, a bit like the knight that was stretched out on his grave in our church where we went each Sunday. Someday I told myself one such would come to rescue me from this dull dull existence. I longed for adventure, for romance, for excitement.

It was in the ice-house that I made a momentous decision that changed my life. In the ice-house where it was cool I dreamed of another life that didn't include going to market and going to church and listening to my mother forever fussing over me and insisting that I acted properly, kept my bonnet on and behaved like a lady.

In vain I pointed out to her that as the daughter of a farmer's wife, no matter how rich, I was still a farmer's daughter and could hardly aspire to be gentry. She would shake her finger at me telling me that I was as good, if not better. nor all those folk who gave themselves such airs despite the fact that they were often as poor as church mice. Handsome is as handsome does was her motto.

Father in his bluff homespun fashion would insist to me that she was right. But, truth to tell she was a complete mystery to him, as all women were. My mother had set her cap at him and snared him like a hare in a gin long before he rightly knew what was what. Not that he regretted his marriage.

"Best thing that happened to me", he said on more than one occasion.

Then, over the years I gradually got the story of his youth. Usually when he was at ease in the evening having a pipe of baccy.
In his time he had roistered and played merry hell so that his parents lost all patience with him. In time they threatened to cut him off completely so when my mother appeared on the scene and captivated my father they were overjoyed and

encouraged the match. She had a little money and they a large farm that eventually came to both my parents. To my surprise I learned one day that my father had been to college for a spell, enough time to appreciate the way in which the world was moving. He read books on agriculture despite the scoffing of such la de da ways by his neighbours.

"It's a science, Amanda" he would tell me.

"You add something and something happens; you can do it again and it happens again; it's not just magic and moonshine."

So he rotated crops, added things to the soil, grew crops then ploughed them in, much to the amusement of his farmer friends. But he got results.

"I don't mind their chaffing", he would say.

"I do mind having good yields and healthy stock, and that's what I have got."

Despite all that he was still superstitious, as was my mother. They held firmly that hare-lips were the result of being cursed by hares, that when cows became infected that was the result of some malign person casting spells and that the moon was ever important in the planting and harvesting of crops. They may have been good Christians, but the land held them in its grip exerting an age-old influence that made them celebrate Christmas more as a pagan farewell to an old year and a greeting to a new one. Whilst Easter was simply rebirth and fresh growth.

Harvest time was the result of the ground being fecund and bringing forth fruits of its womb and yielding up its fruit and riches to its servants. Yes, they did go to church, but no, they didn't forget the old country ways despite the disapproval of the parson. His disapproval, I noticed as I grew up, became less strong after a gift of a dark brown smoked ham that had hung at the back of our huge kitchen amongst the others that would see us through the year. Those hams had once been hogs, and I had cried once to see one die. Now I relished the sweet meat that their deaths provided. I had learned to appreciate that death comes after life, but I still had a great deal more to learn about what filled up the space between.

Chapter 3

My beloved spurns me and Lieutenant Paffrey appears

Then in an instant my life changed. James Olifant Strangatte appeared. Who was he? A god, a veritable god. No-one that I had ever met before was like him. He was tall, had fair curly hair and the straightest nose that went with such a dashing air that all the milkmaids adored him, as indeed I did too.

He charmed them all, chaffed them about their beaus, buttered them all up with his quicksilver tongue, not favouring one over another and left them all ready to neglect their work for just a smile from his brown eyes.

Me, he ignored. I was just a girl. I later found that he was under the strictest instructions from his pa not to pay me any heed. This was because his father was deeply suspicious that my parents would inveigle him into some situation with their daughter to their advantage. So I moped and made eyes at him and cried at night and did a hundred silly things to make him aware of me. I was buxom, I had good hair, a fair skin untouched by smallpox, I cleaned my teeth after meals, kept my apron spotless and I told myself that I loved him.

I set my cap at Jos, which was what everyone called him, but to no avail. As a rich farmer's son he had plenty of time to spare and would often spend it at our farm. I plotted to be in his way when he came calling. I would purposely ride over near King Harry's Wood where I knew he would often ride too. Nothing proved to be any good. In fact it did some harm, for one day I chanced upon Jos as he chatted with Elaine Ardath from across the river.

Even I, unused as I was to the ways of men and maids, could not mistake the way in which they spoke and the way in which they exchanged looks.

I turned my horse around and let it trot back home, furious with the world, with Jos and most of all with that stuck-up madam Elaine, only to be hailed by a young officer who from his horse saluted me and asked the way to the village.

"Please allow me to introduce myself," he went on once I had given him the information that he sought.

"Lieutenant Paffrey, Frederick Charles Paffrey of the 53rd (Shropshire) Regiment of Foot at your service."

This was delivered with the raising of his hat and a bow, somewhat marred as his horse, a large bay, chose this moment to skitter a little.

Nevertheless I was charmed to be so addressed and immediately took my soldier home to meet my parents, who having found that he came from Bridgenorth, where we had relatives, they made him welcome. I think that they were pleased too that I had someone else upon whom to practise my feminine charms, having observed my obsession with Jos.

Unfortunately for them, practising my charms on a new beau did nothing to get Jos interested in me so I spent more and more time with my gallant officer and we soon became Amanda and Freddie. We were often to be seen on our horses. Freddie was a consummate rider and what I lacked in ability I tried to make up with daring. We would come back from our ride with our faces glowing and on one occasion mine glowed exceptionally as Freddie had kissed me.

We exchanged details about our upbringing, mine so dull, his so romantic. I know now that he embroidered it to enchant me even more than I already was.

I was impressed when he spoke carelessly about his family who, he implied, were related to royalty on his mother's side. Only distantly he would insist, charming me even more at his modesty. Of course I told him about my inheritance and the fact that I could at present lay my hands on some of it as my father had indulged me by making it available before I was strictly due to receive it.

It was a shock though when Freddie, meeting me in the ice house, asked me to run away with him. He pleaded with me saying that such a beautiful girl as I so patently was should have a larger milieu in which to be seen. Did I want to spend all my life with these turnip munchers? Wasn't I eager to see more than a small town or two? Didn't I want to travel? Wasn't I ready for adventure?

To all these questions, except the first, I answered with a "Yes!" Who else had offered me such a menu of opportunity? No-one. What else was there to hold me back? Nothing. Freddie played me for the little fool that I undoubtedly was with the result that I said yes, I would run off with him. If you cannot imagine how I could have been so stupid, you don't know much about young girls who are ever the author of their own undoing.

Chapter 4

I run away

Freddie said that he would leave to join his regiment the following day and that I should follow in a few days. Do not go to Portsmouth but go instead to the sign of the Green Dragon in Petersfield where I shall be waiting for you. You can use your horse and if you slip away early you will not be missed until you have had time to make your escape. Sell your horse to get some money once you have gone part of the way and you will be able to pay with that for an outside seat on a coach.

He made it all seem like an adventure, a way of getting my revenge on Jos. I was just another silly girl whose head was turned by flattery who did not think for a moment of the pain that I might cause my dear parents. I had seen other young girls get married and it all seemed so romantic especially running away with my lover.

I might have been influenced too by what I had heard some of the dairymaids say about their beaux. And, of course, they admired Freddie so I would be making them jealous too.

Freddie duly made his farewells, leaving all with their good wishes to speed him. He looked magnificent in his uniform and I hugged myself as he went off telling myself that we would soon be together and that Jos would be so sorry to have lost me. I told no-one of my plans as Freddie had told me that I should conceal my intentions from all. He advised me to carry on with my life as normal until the morning that I left.

The following days were difficult ones for me, as I desperately wanted to tell someone about my big adventure. On the Thursday following the Tuesday that Freddie departed I rose early as usual, saddled my horse as usual and rode out as usual, but instead of heading for the woods I turned south and headed for the main road down to Winchester.

This was where I intended to sell my horse and with the money pay for a seat on a coach to Petersfield, which was where the coach stopped at the Green Dragon.

All went well and I was well on the way when disaster! My horse threw a shoe. I got off it and led it until I espied two shepherds trying to cut free a sheep from the brambles. They saw me so I stopped and, ignoring the inquisitive look that the young man gave me, I asked was there a farrier or blacksmith thereabouts. I got civil answers from the young man; the older shepherd seemed uninterested.

Following his directions I found a blacksmith and with a fresh shoe on my mare I was able to continue my journey. I made no secret of the place where I was headed. To all I said Portsmouth, not revealing that Petersfield was my true destination.

In another few hours I was able to reach a small village where I sold my mare and, after carefully tying up the money, only half of her real value, in a handkerchief, I begged a lift from a friendly talkative carrier who kept me entertained until we reached a town where I could take a coach.

Before he drove off and left me he said:

"I hope he's worth it."

Then he tried to crack his whip, and failing in that endeavour, flourished it instead and raising his weather-beaten hat said:

"God be with you."

I almost turned and started on my journey home at that point. What was I about to do? Interrupting my thoughts came the sound of a trumpet and I knew that the coach was about to start so I hurriedly paid for a ticket, mounted to an outside seat and we were off.

At Winchester I got another coach that took me to Petersfield where it stopped outside the Green Dragon. As we approached the town I became apprehensive; would Freddie be there? I was sure that he would be true to his word but was I too late? I had taken longer over my journey than I had expected.

I entered the inn hesitantly never having ever been in such a place before without an escort. To my intense relief I immediately saw Freddie who strode towards me embracing me so violently that I had to rebuke him. He spoke to the innkeeper who replied and guided us both to a door that to my surprise led to a tunnel along which we walked. At another door when Freddie knocked, a nun opened it and we went inside. The nun left us.

"Where are we?"

"In a convent where you can reside safely until we are married."

"When shall that be, dearest?"

"Tomorrow. I shall return to take us to Portsmouth to our lodgings. I must go now as I have regimental duties to attend to."

The following day he returned and we went to Portsmouth where we took up residence in a poky set of rooms above a tavern not far from the harbour, where every night there seemed to be some celebration as drinking and carousing never seemed to stop.

Despite Freddie's insistence on getting me to Portsmouth to be married it took some days of effort on my part to achieve this. Eventually he relented saying that we must do it in secret so as not to broadcast our whereabouts to all. A rather dirty and unshaven clergyman came along with two of Freddie's officer friends as witnesses and the whole ceremony was over in minutes. It was not very romantic, but I did not care as Freddie promised me that we would be moving soon into better quarters.

We moved within a week.

Chapter 5

Life in Portsmouth

Now a respectable married woman and having moved with my husband to more salubrious lodgings I could duly sally out when my husband was attending to his regimental duties. I had some money but husbanded it carefully as I began to see that my husband was rather too free with any cash that came his way.

I comforted myself with the thought that once we were in India and he was on full pay we could live like a prince and a princess. My head was also full of the tales of "shaking the money tree" having heard such stories of Clive of India who won the battle of Plassey and returned to England to became MP for Shrewsbury and become an Irish peer. Before he came back he was made governor of Bengal where he amassed a fortune.

I knew of this because he came from Shropshire and I had heard my parents talking about him. Apparently Parliament had become dissatisfied with him, despite his military prowess and there was some sort of enquiry about him that they read about in the newspaper that came to us. It was always out of date, but we read it all, savouring bits of news about London and other, to us, foreign places.

One day not long after my arrival Freddie came home with a grand piece of news. Following Napoleon's defeat there was to be an enormous celebration with his Royal Highness the Prince Regent, accompanied by his Royal Highness the Duke of Cambridge in Portsmouth town. Freddie was to be in charge of some of the soldiers who would line the route where the Prince Regent and the Duke of Cambridge would pass along. To tell you the truth I was more interested in whether there was to be a ball or some other occasion where I could appear on Freddie's arm.

For some time I had been worried as I saw less and less of him, due, he would tell me, to the immense amount of work that getting the regiment to India entailed

On the day in question I was at Portsdown Hill having been told that this would be an excellent vantage point. It was indeed but my shoes and gown were muddied as a result of climbing part way up the hill. There, when the royal visitors were received with a royal salute from a brigade of Royal Artillery, I was quite deafened. Almost immediately, out at sea, another royal salute was fired from all the ships and vessels of war that were lying at Spit Head. The soldiers and sailors do love shooting off their cannons.
I said this at some point, and this was received as a bon mot! and reported to Freddie's Commanding officer, and as a consequence later that week Freddie managed to get me an invitation to Government House. I had to clean my own shoes and gown, having only the one that I could wear on such an occasion, there being no-one to do this work as we could not afford a servant.

There, by craning my neck and pushing forward, I saw the Duke of Wellington, who had arrived (whilst his Royal Highness was at sea) in a coach and six; he had had the horses taken from his carriage and was drawn to Government House by a crowd of people with everyone shouting. Freddie got his soldiers to present arms (that was why he was there and I was invited) while the band played " See the Conquering Hero comes," by Mr Handel.   He passed me on his way to the balcony and I thought how thin he was, but very brown from the sun. I could not help supposing that underneath his shirt he would be as white as Freddie. I blushed at the thought of seeing him naked while the Cavalry whirled their sabres round about in the air over their heads as everyone shouted out:

" Long live Wellington!'

It was all so exciting for a young silly thing as I was then. It went to my head and I began to imagine myself to be grander than I really was.

That evening Freddie and I quarrelled because I accused him of not getting an invitation for us both to attend the Prince Regent ball and supper at the Crown Inn. I later found out that, while many were there, his Royal Highness was not present himself. So I forgave Freddie. My word! What stupid things concerned me then.

Chapter 6

The regiment sails

As time went on and it got nearer to the time that the regiment was due to sail I knew that I was with child. You don't live on a farm and not know about such matters but for some strange reason I did not tell Freddie. Perhaps I was aware of the difficult times that were ahead of me. My family had always had at least one relation that had "the sight", an ability to see forwards. Maybe I shared this ability.

One day as I sat in our lodgings I suddenly felt the most excruciating pain. It was like nothing that I had ever felt before and it made me call out for our landlady. She being out did not attend me and so I tried to make my way downstairs but had to go back into our bedroom.

I had just entered the room when the pain in my belly became so intense that I screamed and gasped and fell upon the unmade bed where I sobbed into the pillow and called for my mother.

Of course having been raised on a farm I knew all about birth and I also knew about miscarriages, but at first it did not occur to me that I was miscarrying. Then as the pain increased and I began to bleed I knew what was happening to me was what had happened to Beth, one of our milkmaids.

By this time I was quite distraught and my screams now brought Mrs Overley, our landlady, to me, she having returned. She immediately saw what was going on and taking me by the hand she sought to comfort me as by now I was at that point where little could be done to save what would have been my baby. She called for Dorcas, her maid, who brought cloths and water in a basin. It was this same basin that she later used to remove all traces of what had previously been inside me.

Following the loss of my child Freddie became all attentive, bringing me broth reinforced with eggs, and strengthening cordials along with dishes of cooked meats that he brought from a nearby tavern.

When I had recovered sufficiently to walk out he went with me and as we walked along he suggested that I should go into the country to avoid the miasma in the town and regain my strength. He said that the good nuns in Petersfield could care for me.

So I went there and was for a time at peace in a small cell where I spent the time reading. When I went out I helped the sisters in the gardens where, as they grew many herbs, they taught me about them and their use using Culpeper's English translation of the Pharmacopoeia Londonesis of the Royal College of Physicians. He was convinced that as everyone enjoyed the gospel in plain English the same thing had to happen with prescriptions and all medicines.

This idea was embraced by the nuns who also had a copy of Culpeper's work on midwifery entitled A Directory for

Midwives; or a Guide for women in their conception, bearing and suckling of their children, etc.

Remote and removed from the bustle and trouble of town I reverted to the bonny country lass that I had been previously. Although still only nineteen, I felt so much older and deluded myself that I was also much wiser.

One day as on my knees I weeded the herbs in the garden, carefully making clear spaces around the borage, fennel and parsley as I had been taught to do, an old nun came to me to tell me that the regiment had sailed! I thought that she must be mistaken, but she showed me the newspaper and there it set out the news that it had indeed sailed and only left a small rearguard in the garrison.

Then Freddie will be part of the rearguard, I determined and went to see the Mother Superior to tell her that I must go back to Portsmouth. She blessed me when she heard that I intended to leave and called for one of the nuns to bring me some books. She said that they would be useful to me in India where she had heard that there were savages who worshipped false idols. She said that she had also heard that they had different plants, but I could show them the ones in this book and they would be able to show me equally efficacious ones in that far off world. They were both Culpeper's books and at first I declined her generous gift saying that I could not deprive them of the volumes that so inspired, along with the love of God, their work.

"Take them, my child", she said, "for they are copies that we have made over the years so that we can spread knowledge as well as the love of Jesus Christ our saviour. I thanked her and returned to my cell where I had regained my health and looked around me. It was bare but clean and the bed, though hard, was sufficient to my needs as I went to it each night tired from my labours. I little imagined how soon I would sigh for such simple comforts.

Chapter 7

Abandoned in Portsmouth

I hurriedly put together such items as I had with me at the convent and returned to Portsmouth with all speed. Not even going to our lodgings I went straightway to the barracks where I found the soldiery of Freddie's regiment who told me that they were the rearguard and were due to sail soon. They were standing around smoking and chatting.

"But where is Lieutenant Paffrey?" I asked and heard someone snigger and say: "Not another."

"He is sailed with his wife." Replied a corpulent officer who had come out and whom I recognised from the night we saw the Duke of Wellington.

If the officer had struck me a blow across the face I could have felt worse.

"But I am his wife, do you not know me?"

The officer stiffened and said: "Take this woman out; she is obviously a trouble maker, one of the town doxies."

I tried to protest but somehow the words would not come out of my mouth in the right order. I slumped against the post and would have slid down into the street into the muck of mud and horse manure had not the sergeant attending the officer caught me and escorted me out.

"Got yourself a right one there", said someone as the sergeant supported me.

"Shut your face!" was his reply, then to me he said:

"Come back tonight. Major Baker will be here then. Only be sure to bring your marriage lines."

He turned to go back to his duties smoothing his ample moustache.

"Alas, I have them not, Freddie kept them."

The sergeant paused, turned back and belched. I smelled rum.

"Tell me, who officiated at your marriage; which church, or chapel and who were your witnesses?"

"None, for we were wed in secret."

"Then give him up," he said bluntly.

"I dare swear that you are not married at all, and you are not alone in this. Go home to your family if you can."

This second blow nearly robbed me of any ability to go on, but I dragged myself through the streets to our lodgings where I found Mrs Overley who grim faced and with pursed lips handed me a small packet. I tore it open and some money fell out. I ignored it and concentrated instead on the few words the Freddie had seen fit to write.

Chapter 8

Desperate Measures

Mrs Overey told me that the rooms were paid for until the end of the month and waited hoping, no doubt, to hear the contents of the letter that was in the packet. I thanked her and as she left I shut the door and sank down upon the bed. Then I got up again quickly and gathered together the small amount of coins that had fallen from the package including the few that had rolled beneath the bed. I remembered the passage from the Bible about the woman who looked for her lost coins.

What was I to do? Freddie had merely said goodbye in the letter and advised that I should go back home. No tender words, no intimations of having wronged me in the cruellest way. He might have been writing to a servant. Perhaps that was how he saw me; someone to serve him and his base needs.

I could not go home. I was ruined. Everyone would know of my shame, and even if my parents were to accept me I would be held up to ridicule, the more so as I was held in such high regard formerly.

So I put away my few possessions safely and went out to seek employment, for I realised that the small amount of money in the packet would quickly go. I now tramped the streets that formerly I had trod so joyously with Freddie, seeking work of any kind. Before I had been met with smiles. Now if I had expressions of regret I was lucky for, more often than not, it was indifference or outright hostility that I received. I went back to my rooms utterly dejected.

I lapsed into a state of indifference for several days until I realised that I had practically nothing left. I roused myself. I went out and tried to pawn the books that I had been given, but the sum that was offered me was so small I declined it. The pawnbroker, seeing my distress, said that if I had something more saleable he could advance more.

So I returned to my lodgings and took some of the plates and glasses. Freddie had often done this, saying that as he returned the items later it was not stealing.

"That's better", said the pawnbroker, but the sum he advanced was still very small.

I lived frugally and made the sum last as long as I could. Eventually even that was gone and was in my room in despair when Mrs Overey knocked and came in. She informed me that as I was now behind with the rent I should leave. Her frosty demeanour became even frostier as she asked about the plates and glasses that were plainly not there any more. I admitted that I had pawned them and that I would redeem them immediately and would then leave.

I went out as if to go to the pawnbrokers but hid instead outside in the yard until Mrs Overey had gone out whereupon I went back in and bundled up my things and crept out. I would have got clean away but Dorcas saw me.

"Oh! Amanda, she cried, "Whatever will you do now?"

For as I had poured out my troubles to her she knew of my ill usage by Freddie and subsequent desperate situation.

I replied that I would go to London as I was sure that there I would be able to find someone to employ me. She told me to wait and then came back with a small sum of money that she pressed into my hand. It was to be for a gown to attend a Christening. She said that it was surely more Christian to help a poor soul in trouble than to array herself in pride in God's holy church.

I thanked her and made off as soon as I could. With the small sum of money that she had given me I bought an outside seat on a coach that was advertised as going to London. The final destination in London was The Angel in Islington, a place that I had never heard of. I thought however that this might be a sign that my guardian angel was watching over me.

As soon as I alighted I was accosted by several men and women, but I knew enough to avoid persons who cried that that they would lead me to good clean lodgings. Instead I walked into a dairy where, asking if they knew where a poor girl could lodge, I received the welcome reply that they had such a room. They indeed had a frowsty room at the back where it looked out onto as dirty a yard as I ever did see, but it was cheap.

I thought that I was now safe. Surely I would not be pursued to London. Then, when I thought I would lose myself in that great metropolis I looked for cheaper cleaner lodgings and employment. But I had not reckoned with my landlady's knowledge of the law and her tenacity.

She had laid an information against me immediately that I had departed saying that I had stolen her plates and glasses.

This meant that as soon as I was in London and as I sought lodgings and employ, I was being looked for.

Ignorant of this turn of events I walked out freely never imagining that I would be arrested. Suddenly I was grasped and despite my cries for help I was bundled into a vehicle and brought before a magistrate, He, on hearing the evidence against me, committed me without another word to the next Assizes. And so I was placed in Newgate to await trial.

Chapter 9

Sentenced

In time I appeared at court where I heard that I was a most wicked and degenerate young woman and that I was to be hanged for the felony of four plates and six glasses to the value of ten shillings and six pence. My sentence was passed in a bored voice by one of the ugliest men I had ever seen, on a beautiful spring afternoon when the bright sun and fresh leaves on the trees outside mocked my misery.

In Newgate, several of us clung together for support, and I dared not think of how we would face the mob that still accompanied public hangings. I think it was that as much as anything that troubled us, when to our intense surprise we heard that the king had granted us all his clemency and we were to be transported instead!

So there I was with prostitutes, thieves and all sorts of human flotsam and debris, and all in one room together, when, along with some visitors to my new convict companions I spied my mother and father. I had lost all hope of ever seeing them again and immediately went to them weeping and asking their forgiveness. They said that there was no need to ask for that as I was their child and of course they forgave me. My father then went on to say, once my mother and I had sufficiently recovered from weeping over each other, that the next thing was to get me out and back to Shropshire. They gave me fresh clothes and food and said that they would return as soon as they could. In the meantime they had to continue with their petition to obtain a lesser sentence for me.

Within a day they had came back bringing more clothing, some of which I gave to the other poor souls that were incarcerated with me, and money for the turnkey.

This eased my plight somewhat for it is ever the case that money is the grease that can be used on most things that human beings have established in this world in order to make them work.

I was now able to buy food and even to have clean linen, as well as a more comfortable bed. Before they came again however, I gave up my bed to an unfortunate young woman who had suffered as I had from the hands of a soldier. She was a beautiful young thing who simply lost her will to live and said that she was determined to die. I felt that if she were to die at least she should have the comfort of a bed in her last hours.

As she died other women were using themselves to stay alive. They jeered at her, calling her soft. I think she was too well bred to follow their example and lacking parents such as I had, simply gave herself to a heaven that I dearly hope exists.

The day came however when my mother had to tell me that all their efforts had come to naught.

She told me that my father had laid out "a mint of money" in several directions but to no avail.

"Simple country folk as we be can look for no assistance", was her parting remark after blessing me and praying that God would keep me from harm.

My father stood to one side after embracing me, saying nothing. I could tell that his heart was breaking as he stood there in his broadcloth and stout boots, the very image of John Bull, according to my new convict companions. It was rumoured that a ship was nearly ready to sail and that a colony across the seas was ready to welcome females of all conditions. This was why impediments had been placed on all attempts to get me a pardon or a lesser sentence, and I was not alone in my failure.

Then, ironically, we were all taken in chains to Portsmouth where the sweepings of other prisons were added to our company as we boarded the Northampton.

Chapter 10

At Sea

We were one hundred and ten women prisoners, convicted of many simple crimes for which society had found a simple solution: transportation. The only trouble though was that transporting people took money, time, effort and ships. And, in time these simple prisoners, once they had arrived and were out of sight, could not be forgotten. But I am getting before myself. We still had not arrived and it would take us many months to do so.

Because my parents were able to provide me with food, clothing and money I embarked on the Norfolk in good health after an humiliating drive in chains where the whole world and his wife seemed to take a delight in our situation.

Unlike many of my companions in woe, my upbringing had been sound and instilled in me that I should use all my talents that God in his infinite wisdom had seen fit to bestow upon me. Many of the one hundred and ten were bawds, forced into such a career having lost their places as servants. A few were hardened in this occupation and I gained the impression that they would ever be making their way in life in this debauched fashion no matter what might be done to move them from it.

Some were plainly half-witted and one at least was of such an age that I held serious doubts that she would survive. I was to be proved wrong on that score. Several had skills that I could see might be useful; there were clever seamstresses for example. A few, like me, could turn their hands to anything related to farming. Were there to be cows in our new world, we had dairymaids to milk them, and I dare swear they could make butter and cheese. I knew how to hoe and to make hay and were there to be corn, with someone to grind it, I could bake bread.

But nothing in my life so far, up to the point when I was rowed out with the other women and assisted to scramble aboard, could have prepared me for what was to be six months in a floating prison. It is true that I had been incarcerated in what is probably the most notorious prison in London, but this thing of wood, ropes, tar, brass and canvas was such a novelty to my senses that I could scarcely comprehend it. I had, of course, seen ships out to sea but to be in one, in the noise, smell, confusion and strangeness made me quite faint.

To begin with, it was so small. We were a company of more than a hundred women, some sailors (I never really found out how many as while some were working others were resting, and the only time they all came out together was in bad weather when we were all imprisoned below and the gratings had hatches placed over them to keep the sea from entering), some marines and some officers, including our surgeon. Yet all were crammed together as close as pickled herrings in a barrel. This meant that any notions of decency and true propriety were not available to us; and like herrings we stank.

Next, it was a ship made expressly to float, to withstand and indeed to use winds, and to move great distances. So everything about it was designed with those ends in mind. Wherever the eye lighted there were ropes, strange blocks, canvas sheets, brass implements and such things as cleats whose true use I never did ascertain, but found them useful as we moved through the water for I needed to hold onto something to retain my balance. I would also say they were necessary to retain my dignity as a tumble with ones skirts a' flying provoked much crude comment and merriment.

This ship, although designed to carry cargo, was not designed for such a cargo as we were. You have to remember that the cargo in this case had to be fed and watered. We were not cases of furniture, nor loads of iron fittings nor casks of spirit, although this sort of cargo was carried too. I was also told that some of our ballast, something that had to put in the bottom of the ship to keep it upright and steady, was bricks. When we got to the colony they would be taken out and used for building.

On deck we had two cows, several chickens and a rooster that cheered me up as it saluted each dawn and called on us to wake up and see the sun. Alas! His crowing lasted for several weeks only. His end was occasioned by the lack of fresh meat and the antipathy that his crowing engendered. He made a change for someone as a contrast to the everlasting dried peas that accompanied the salt pork every day.

Somewhere in the ship there was someone screaming, but it faded away as we were led down to what the sailors called "below" where my spirits sank. The dark, dirty, dingy area that had been set out for we women was confined between what I learned to call bulwarks. There under the deck head, not ceiling, so low that most of us were forced to move around permanently bowed down as if to pay eternal homage to King Neptune, we were welcomed by such a stench that I almost vomited. It was not only the smell of unwashed confined women who were already there, having come from other prisons, but a permanent smell of rotting wood that rose as a miasma from below us.

We were the last women to join the ship so had the worst positions. I took mine but immediately was called upon to remove myself to the upper deck. There stood our surgeon who having conned through the lists of women spotted that I had had some experience of childbirth.

He had my chains struck off by a blacksmith and I was led to where a young woman lay in the last stages of labour. To the surgeon's amazement I demanded that before I even approached Emily Crake, as I later learned she was called, I wished to wash.
"It's a messy business, childbirth", he said " Won't you wish to wash afterwards?"

I stood in adamantine posture until some water in a bowl and a linen towel was brought me. I then set to work. I scrubbed my hands with a piece of cloth all the while ignoring as best I may the howls of Emily. I had no soap so I concentrated on rubbing and rubbing until my hands were red. I ignored the looks that the surgeon directed at me.

Then with a prayer for all the aid that heaven might grant me I encouraged Emily by rubbing her back and using low comforting words to produce a beautiful girl child with the most astonishing head of dark hair, which I might add she later lost entirely. Emily was just eighteen, well nourished and healthy, and her little girl, whom she called Ann after her mother, was small, so the birth was not that difficult. Emily, frightened almost out of her wits, had wailed incessantly until I had appeared. She wanted her mother and I was the next best thing.

Nevertheless, my apparent success was taken by the surgeon as proof positive of my sovereign value as an assistant, he having found so far no other woman on board with experience and steady common-sense that might fit this position. This angered some of the women, several of whom spoke of me in the most vile language to the others, seeking to poison their minds against me.

Some I managed to win round as I treated them with such care as I could summon up to show them that we all shared a similar fate. Even so a few maintained such enmity against me that I displaced in their minds those officers that ordinarily would have been the target for their abuse.

Their enmity grew as I was perceived to be one of the damned class who trod on them pushing them back into the muck. This was the direct consequence of my exchanging with the surgeon matters to do with health and childbirth, the latter subject I found him to be quite knowledgeable about as he had considerable experience and had studied under the famous Dr Smellie.

I had to return to our noisome quarters but as we left land and were encouraged to scrub and clean our living space it became infinitely more wholesome than the prisons that we had quit.

And, I must say several women told me that had they remained in England they could not be sure each night that they would have somewhere to rest until dawn brought the next weary round of whatever they had to do to live.

And the things that many had to do in order to put bread into their mouths and to find somewhere to lay their heads were a shame to the remainder of England.

I was astonished at how diligent the Master and surgeon were at driving the convicts to keep clean until I heard how previous ships had not done this and paid the terrible price of sickness and death. I was reminded that the safe deliverance to Australia of we poor women, never mind that we were convicted felons, meant an increased payment. I had thought that it was common concern for us, but it all came back to money.

The surgeon was particularly encouraging of washing, fresh air and exercise; I had however to remind him that he too needed to wash before he dealt with any of the women and their constant stream of ailments. As you might imagine not a few had such ailments as come as a result of dalliance with Venus. Despite this, several took up with the sailors and began to lead almost married lives.

I too received many offers that I steadily rejected, earning the opprobrium of a small hardened coterie of women led by two particular ringleaders. These two, until my arrival, had been almost unchallenged in their opinions and actions that they expected the other women to follow. I cannot bring myself to repeat the language that they used to vilify me.

Sufficient to say that it even made the men and officers blush on occasions.

Chapter 11

I move up in the world

Our food varied little to begin with being supplemented rarely when we made landfall with fresh greens and strange fruits the like of which most of us had never ever before seen. The eternal pork from barrels that had been loaded earlier and the everlasting dried peas were a constant. We grew to fear the bad weather that meant the fires had to be doused in the galley as this meant that our rations were even more primitive and made my memories of meals in my parents' farm seem like permanent Lucullan feasts.

But if our food was primitive, consisting as it did of hard tack so frequently as soft tack was rarely available, our arrangements regarding hygiene were quite abominable.

There was an arrangement at the front of the ship whereby it was possible to relieve oneself in comparative modesty as long as one held on as one did so. At night as we were locked below we were provided with the usual vessels that one would find in a bed chamber, but having to serve so very many they were larger. The smell on occasions was truly atrocious. If we had the good fortune to be provided with fresh vegetables what usually ensued were cases of the flux increasing to such a marked degree that many found it imprudent to continue to wear any form of underclothes.

Eventually, as we moved further into warmer climes, this became habitual with some women who envied the sailors who were able cast off their upper garments to reveal chests and backs, some of which carried tattoos of striking originality. With such exposure to the hot sunshine after some redness the sailors began to turn brown. Many of us, particularly those that had been more delicately raised, avoided looking at this display of naked male flesh.

However, after some while we all became so habituated to it that we accepted it as being normal. Then, as we moved into even hotter seas the sailors sought the shade, as did we all, praying for some rain to relieve our desiccated state.

When the rain did come it was usually of such magnitude that it was almost a treat to stand out in it; not only to be cool but also to wash ourselves more thoroughly than was generally possible with the small quantities that was given us on a daily basis. Sometimes however the rain did not come and neither did the wind and then all sank into such a torpor where decks burned feet that were placed on them and the sun shrank the wood of which the ship was made so that it leaked even more than usual.

I must tell you now of the attack that was made upon my person led by Jane Candover whose family originated in Ireland where, she was wont to say, that King George's soldiers finished the work of ruining her family that Oliver Cromwell had begun.

Her family were all as a consequence paupers and wherever they travelled they brought trouble with them in thievery, mischief and general depravity.

Now she had taken on the role of being the principal trouble-maker on board. She was the very antithesis of blessed

Saint Francis of Assisi on whom she often called to witness her travails.

We were generally free to move about the ship as long as we kept away from certain parts such as the Quarterdeck which is almost as holy a place on a ship as any shrine with the Ship's Master playing the part of God almighty. Jane, by her troublesome activities, had spent many a dismal day below decks in chains that did nothing to sweeten her temper. In consequence she sometimes allowed it to flower into such rages that it took several crew members to restrain her, and so doing they received many a kick or blow, for she was a well-built sturdy lass, that resulted in bruises described by the men in jest as Jane's love bites!

On this particular occasion we had had several wearisome days of slack sails. hot foetid air below and a disgusting stench around us, for as we discharged our ordure and other noxious effluvium over the side of the ship it stayed there floating around us.

Normally with a breeze however slight we would move and leave it behind us to sink eventually beneath the waves as poor Nell Gower was to later on, as we committed her body to the deep.

Jane ran at me screaming obscenities and clutched at the loose gown that I was wearing that shaded me from the worst of the sun. I tried to pull away without tearing the material. Material was too precious to risk being torn. She let go suddenly and I lost my balance, falling so violently that I lost the bonnet that had been made for me by the pretty little pregnant milliner from straw that came aboard the last time we had entered a port to take on water and victuals.

I tried to rise but Jane pinned me down and put her foot upon my gown. Shocked, I saw that she had something shining in her hand. I held her arm as she tried to strike me and she would have done so had not some crew members leapt on her, bending her arms behind her to take the manacles that they held ready to imprison her.

Apparently this was no sudden whim on Jane's part. She had been heard telling her cronies that she would cut me and disfigure me so that no man would look at me again without a shudder. Now with her hair awry and thrashing like a fresh caught fish, they taunted her. Knowing what she intended, they had let her go free so that she might incriminate herself by her own hand rather than the words of unreliable convicted felons.

They were also unwilling to act on the information immediately as it would endanger the informants, and they wished to keep secret that they had such informants who were ready to peach on their mates.

I was in no real danger. The surgeon helped me stand up and asked if I suffered in any fashion. My reply that I had lost my hat which had rolled across the deck and fell into the muck alongside was treated as the biggest joke and repeated ad nauseam, even the Ship's Master finding it worthy of his attention over dinner later. In our circumstances anything that could be repeated as an amusing event was seized upon. The surgeon bowed to me and went to the quarterdeck where after some words with the Captain and some laughter, he returned to say that I was to go aft and stand upon the quarterdeck.

I climbed up and stood next to the great wheel that steered our ship and was nearly blinded by the brightness of the brass that was everywhere polished to such perfection. One source of bright reflected light was the ship's bell that was placed next to the hourglass that was regularly turned. This bell was struck in an orderly way that signalled the time.

I never mastered the arcane system despite it having been explained to me several times by the surgeon, who proudly showed me at the same time his chronometer with its inscription showing that it was a gift from monies collected from those he had treated on a previous sailing.

I stood there humbly, expecting to be blamed in some way for the disorder having learned that when there was trouble most often all involved, both guilty and guiltless, were held accountable. The sun was hot and I was now bareheaded and becoming faint.

The captain and surgeon continued a conversation of which I only heard snatches. " Useful" and "skilled" and "has a cool head", were some of the surgeon's words.

I could scarce hear the Captain's for his back was to me, but I heard his "Very well," and the surgeon then returned to me smiling and said that I was to move as he had persuaded the Captain as to my usefulness as his aide.

Looking back I think that there had been a plot not only to entrap Jane, but also to get me away from the other convicts. At the time however, as I moved into what I would have regarded as less space than my father would have kept a pig, I was delighted. Some space to myself, some quiet, somewhere to put my few poor belongings and know that they were safe. My small chest was stowed below along with all the others. Not all the women were as well equipped as I was. My father had laid out cash to ensure that at least, whatever my destiny, he would try to ameliorate the worst excesses of its undoubted harshness.

So I made the best use of my new space and some of the women were pleased and some were not. I was by this time developing not exactly an indifference to the others but a way of excluding them from my thoughts that enabled me to maintain some serenity of spirit. I had also kept my belief in the boundless goodness and mercy of God who I knew saw all my sufferings.

My conversations with the surgeon continued. Our having to deal together with so many medical matters and emergencies meant that he increasingly came to rely upon my steady hand and what he termed my abundant good sense. He also said rather vaguely that when we reached our destination he would try to use his influence to assist my future. I was not, however, to rely upon this, he added, thus raising my expectations and casting them down at the same time

Chapter 12

More Births and bad weather

From my new cramped but, to me, luxurious quarters, I was summonsed within a few days to aid in another birth. The heat had given way to rain and the rain to wind and so we sped along in good heart and all felt comfortable and easy save poor Alice Loveday, my pretty milliner whose time had come.

This time matters were not to be so easy. We had a moving ship and an expectant mother whose slight build was going to hinder her bearing her child with any ease. Around us we had some canvas made into a rough shelter and within this on a pallet lay pretty little Alice pale and frightened. As we toiled together with me encouraging and she responding she gradually grew more and more fatigued. I was mortal feared that this time I would lose her and the baby.

She closed her eyes then opened them saying:

"It is not only the pain but the awful thought that my child will be a bastard."

"Many kings have had bastards a'plenty and many have done well in their time."

"Who?"

" Why, William the Conqueror was one such."

"How about Napoleon? I have often heard the seamen say that he was a bastard."

Despite our desperate situation I laughed.

"Oh! Alice, I think that they mean not his paternity but the nature of his personality."

"Well, the man who is responsible for my condition this day is certainly a bastard."

In time, despite her severe exhaustion, Alice produced a lovely boy who she called William Loveday.

We had left Cape Town with more than enough food and water, and, I might add, bottles of spirits to last us the journey, were we to receive God's blessing of a smooth passage. God sends the winds that drive us forward, but sometimes he sends a scrap too much. When I said this to the surgeon he took it that I was complaining and said that we were not put into this world to enjoy ourselves, but to do the will of God, and if this meant that we had to suffer then so be it. I had said this as the wind at that time was screaming like a demented harlot, plucking at our clothing, making us unsteady and throwing waves upon us so that we were permanently drenched, battered and deafened.

Despite this we still stayed on deck preferring the elements to the noisome 'tween deck miasma. I found the fresh air invigorating for even my little quarters were cramped and stank.

This particular wind was reckoned by the seasoned seamen on our little bark of very little account. I was to see later what they considered to be a real blow. Such winds can accompany fierce storms that batter and smash and tear apart what seems to be so solid in port and so puny when we are racing along with mast high waves alongside us.

Let me try to describe the ship's motion and progress at such a time, always remembering that any such description must fall way below the actual experience. Still, we have invented words so let me use them.

At first the ship picks up speed. The canvas sails that are so thick and coarse are strained in the wind so that they resemble a muslin petticoat on a wash line, strained to the utmost and permanently filled.

The multitude of ropes and cordage that keeps everything in place thrum in a constant agony of discordant and tortured noise.

Then the seas mount higher so that we seem sometimes to be sliding down the side of a valley of water into a void that make all think that only God will bring us up out of it.

We have shut all spaces where the sea might penetrate en masse. Instead it is forced under great pressure through such cracks as remain until all things below are wet and all creatures soaked and shivering.

All ships leak so another noise is added to the storm's orchestra, that of the pumps which of necessity must be kept in constant action by teams of men. The pumping can become desperate if we take on board more water than we spew out. Under us, running back and forth is the stinking bilge, running over the sand, shingle or whatever we have as ballast. This is our own personal sea that we carry with us within our wooden walls and is a constant threat to us.

Naturally we have no galley in operation. Fires cannot be lit. Food cannot be prepared, so hunger is added to our other woes as the storm continues. And it seems to have no end. It seems to become a personal, animated, evil entity delighting in catching you and pulling or pushing against some thing hard where you break some part of you or collect fresh bruises.

At the height of the storm the seas sweep across the decks and crash onto the men wrestling to maintain their grip upon the great wheel that controls our rudder. I have heard that rudders can be smashed and this leaves the ship with nothing to guide it so it simply runs before the storm, all praying that the storm plays itself out before the ship is cast upon some rocks or dashed against a wall of ice as great mountains of ice can be seen in some seas.

Once these storms are over the seas can return to such calm that it is difficult to remember the pain and distress that was endured by all.

We were enjoying one such period of calm when one woman, Elizabeth Sothern, who was sitting watching the waves as they parted before us, simply got up and threw herself over the side.
A boat was launched and as the sea was calm we expected to be able to rescue her, but she was gone, dragged down by her clothes that would have impeded her attempt at swimming, even supposing that she had this aquatic skill.

We discussed this distressing incident later and both the captain and the surgeon said that they had seen this happen on a number of occasions There was even a name for it: rapture of the seas.

I asked whether the woman might not simply be a suicide, worn down by her present lot and fearful of the future. Not so, I was told. The other women, shocked at her death described her as level-headed and optimistic. She had talked animatedly of the new life that lay ahead having heard that she could be married and might have land.

Chapter 13

Arrival in Australia

Our arrival at Australia was accompanied by a fierce thunderstorm and as we one hundred and six women and five children were rowed ashore we presented a sorry spectacle. A crowd had gathered to see us arrive. In the main they were silent. There were a few comments made about our appearance, but the general feeling was of disappointment. I think many men had been expecting something better than our bedraggled crew. God alone knows what they had been told about us. I suspect however that they had been told that a shipload of potential wives were being sent to them, and we did not fill that particular bill; looking a forlorn wet parcel of womenkind that would not have attracted a second glance in any town in England.

Eventually though, many of the women were married and some almost immediately, and some became pregnant almost as immediately too and so produced some of the first real Australians, if you discount the original inhabitants, which, of course we did.

Tramping through the ankle deep mud we arrived at some tents where we were split up, each one holding their own pathetic bundle of such clothes and personal belongings as they had managed to cling to during the voyage. Several had nothing at all. Some with nothing nevertheless maintained a pretence of not being afraid, but, I can tell you we were all a'feared despite all we had heard on the ship. What if they had lied to us to keep us docile?

I held onto my books and some undergarments, and having put on as respectable a dress as I could manage I tried to keep up my spirits by holding myself as proudly as possible. But I must tell you that as I surveyed the so-called settlement my heart was in my muddy boots.

I was just about to be taken I know not where, though I did hear someone say something like Pearlmutter, when the ship's surgeon pushed his way through the muddy wet file of soldiers who were herding us as though we were cattle, to grasp my bag and gasp:

"Come with me!"

An officer tried to block his way and almost drew his sword but desisted when the good doctor waved a piece of paper at him saying;

"Governor's orders"

Wet, muddy, dazed but determined , I tried to hold onto that bit of dignity that I still had left as I was led into the presence of an elderly bearded man seated in a chair under a canvas sail rigged up as an awning. Out of the corner of my eye I could see the rain running off the canvas and across a carpet under the seated man. He ignored it and looked at me.

"This her?"

Dr Arnold nodded. Then he said:

"Despite her conviction for felony, a most sober, industrious and moral young woman who, I can most honestly say, will be an ornament to your household."

"Right" said the bearded man, standing up, "I have always been ready to trust your judgement Joseph."

He then turned and walked off into the rain that ran off his hat.

"Amanda", said Dr Arnold, "I have spoken for you and that is Mr Spackford who requires someone that he can trust to run his household. You are now part of that household and I know that you will not disgrace my choosing of you. Go with him, and God go with you."

Dazed as I was by this turning around of my fortunes, I was not so 'mazed as to forget my manners.

"Thank you, and God bless you. I will not betray your trust and faith in me", I said turning to follow my new master's back as he walked away to where some convicts held horses. They looked at me curiously but said nothing as I made ready to enter my new world.

So I entered Mr Elias Spackford's employ. I found all those experiences on my parents' farm and those upon the seas in the Norfolk of such value that I quickly made myself almost indispensable. To be honest most of Mr Spackford's servants were poor creatures, many unlettered and unused to any form of discipline other than that of the lash, so I quickly took control, making enemies on the way. But that is the way the world turns, I have found; and it is better to hold to a decided course once one has set upon it. Here was a chance that rarely comes to redeem oneself. I would grasp it with both hands.

I was determined to use my authority and knowledge and experience to subdue all those over whom I had been set in order to bend them to better ways in which they had hitherto been accustomed.

My main domestic adversary was Margaret Senchal. Transported with her mother for stealing cloth from drapers in Cheapside she was a clever hussy. Both she and her mother would dress as ladies, ask to see such materials as muslin or damask cloths then, while one diverted the young apprentice assistant, the other would stuff cloth under her dress. They were remarkably successful in this and it made them enough to buy clothing in which to perpetuate their larcenies.

When not stealing, both would involve themselves in deceiving men, who one must admit, should have known better than to have consorted with women of this ilk. Modesty forbids my explaining in greater detail what sundry means of indecent and lewd behaviour they used.

Both bawds were able to pass themselves off as ladies, having studied to improve their language and deportment.

Margaret's mother died on the ship which left Maggie, as she was more commonly called, bitter and resentful of authority and claiming that far from being justly convicted as a felonious trollop she was a victim! She had wormed her way into Mr

Spackford's confidence using a simple-minded country lass, pretty Susan Abercrombie, as her cat's paw.

Sue's story was a familiar one. Turned off by an employer by whose son she had become pregnant, she lost her child on the way to London where she hoped to find employment. It was delivered in a ditch by the side of the road and was stillborn. Having heard her tell her story however, I was fairly sure that it might very well have been born alive but being abandoned by a half-witted girl died of exposure. No-one finding such a dead baby would think anything of it. The dunghills were usually where they were found.

In London, after work as a scullery maid, she was turned off again as the family shut up their town house to move to the country as the season was over. In desperation, having joined the ragged ranks of beggars sleeping in the streets or down noisome alleys she was used by the beggars as a diversion, while they attempted to steal from the gentry. Everyone used pretty, silly Sue.

Of course she was caught while the real villains got away. In fact being sentenced to transportation meant that she was saved from the streets, and as Maggie and her mother looked after her first in Newgate then on the ship, she survived as a grateful slave of Maggie. For her, Maggie's word was gospel.

Chapter 14

Running a household

Running a household in Australia was not as easy as it would have been in England. I had no market each week. I had no nearby town where I could get things like hinges, nails, string, shears and other implements. I did what I could with what I had; then like everyone else, I did without. One thing we had in plenty was food as we were growing our own and raising our own stock. Our windows were small to keep out the heat, and we had a wide verandah for shade. I was bothered at first by the insects but after a while having learned from Jonas, our black boy, to use herbs to keep them away they troubled me less.

I was soon able to get the production of milk and cheese underway. Both Maggie and Sue were quick learners, but I really needed another pair of hands.

Someone to help me in the house and pantry, someone to do the laundry and cope with bread making.

Elias Spackford suggested that I ought to select another young woman convict to assist me, and went on to say that I ought to go to the Female Factory where female convicts were sent directly they arrived off the ship. It was where I should have been sent had not Dr Arnold intervened for me. Looking back I think he had an ulterior motive apart from the sense of me selecting someone suitable to work with me. I think that he wanted me to see the degrading conditions from which he had saved me.

The system that existed often meant that as the new women prisoners arrived, the settlers and officers would choose the prettiest young convicts as their servants. The really troublesome and hardened female prisoners were not put into chain gangs like the men; instead they finished up by being sent to the Female Factory in Parramatta, so it was a pretty desperate place.

I was sure to find someone there who had been in domestic service I was told, so I undertook the arduous journey to Parramatta which I thought I had heard as pearlmutter when I first arrived. The trip took several days. It was mainly by boat up the river through swamps which gave way to some cleared land. There in a primitive building I found the women convicts who were not at all pleased to see me, preferring visits by men who had come seeking wives. This was the custom and many successful marriages had been contracted following the selection by throwing down a kerchief in front of the selected woman by a man who wished to be wed. Were she to pick it up she, by this action, accepted what was a proposal of marriage. You may say how primitive this was but can you really tell me that with young women being dragooned into marriage in England to please their parents or maintain estates that is a better system? At least the women here could refuse an offer. They rarely did however preferring marriage to bondage

I was shown the long low room which comprised the factory, where there were several young women at one end who were spinning and dealing with wool in a most skilful fashion. Even young girls were occupied in this way all clustered around the one fireplace that was replenished by the convicts. I was told that this fireplace was the only means of cooking. I was moved to comment that these premises were scarcely conducive to good health and that other more suitable premises ought to be constructed. I was informed that plans were indeed in hand that encompassed barracks and a factory. It was hoped to improve these women by introducing them to regular employment and development of domestic skills including needlework of every description. A sentiment of which I heartily approved.

Amongst the number of women was a quiet young woman with a badly damaged face and smallpox scars. The others shunned her but that did not seem to bother her.

I did not enquire why she was here rather than being employed in town, but asked about her history and skills. As a young woman whose mother had died, she had been in service from a very young age where the constant mocking of her appearance had led eventually to her attacking another servant. The other servants had then given false evidence against her saying that she was a vicious almost demented young woman who had flown at one of their number in a veritable paroxism of rage. As to skill, it seemed, according to her own subdued account, that she had plenty, having had no time for those pursuits that other prettier girls were wont to indulge in.

Her name was Jane Alambard and of course, her nick-name was Plain Jane. I liked her and thought that she would do very well but might have to be protected from coming under the influence of Maggie I determined.

So, as we journeyed back, me having signed the necessary papers on behalf of my benefactor, I instructed her carefully.

I did this ceaselessly as we journeyed along as to her duties and how she was to answer to me in all things and not to listen to any others. She dutifully listened to me and displayed eventually, under that demure appearance that I had found so attractive, an iron resolve not to forsake any of the many instructions that I imparted to her.

With another pair of hands I was able to indulge myself in the collecting and use of herbs and fruits. With these I made cordials and physics to treat the animals and the people who made up our small establishment. Jonas, our black boy, accompanied me as I sought out plants, giving me advice about them and about the creatures the like of which I had never seen before in my life. How strange they were. Another proof of God's infinite ability to fill his world with animals to delight and be subject to man's needs.

Jonas warned me about snakes. He told me that that they would be more frightened of me than I should be of them.

"They hear you coming, they go, but always wear boots in case they are deaf."

He pointed out on several occasions herbs such as: River Mint, Native Thyme and Cut-leaf Mintbush. He stressed that I needed to be sure that I knew them and many others such as Round Lime and Blue-leaved Mallee so as to be clear in my mind that they were not poisonous. He also showed me poisonous plants and said that they would quickly take me to white man's heaven.

And so for some time I built up a contented and useful life, working hard each day and relaxing with my employer on the verandah each evening having enjoyed a good meal cooked by Jane. She turned out to be a jewel of a servant and I must tell you that eventually someone asked Plain Jane to be his wife. This happy conclusion was long after some less congenial events that were to come later in my life.

Chapter 15

I am married

My employment was not onerous. I had previously, on the ship, worked considerably harder, and now that I was in charge of a household I enjoyed the stimulation that it provided. I also enjoyed the company of my employer, and I could tell that he was easy and relaxed in mine. As a previously married man with no children he turned to me for advice and I was pleased to provide it. We spent time together reading and discussing all sorts of things. Elias was of the opinion that Australia could, and would, grow to be a powerful nation in its own right. The Australian magazine was a sign of that, he said.

We were both intrigued when The Australian magazine first appeared. Was the colony growing into the state that it could support such a venture?

Apparently it was. I was dubious about its content but was appeased when Elias pointed out to me that it was actually called: The Australian Magazine Companion of Religion, Literature and Miscellaneous Intelligence.

Yes, by now it was Elias and Amanda. We had grown together despite our difference in ages. Perhaps it was because of the difference. I was wary of men, having been led astray by one in the past, but Elias was different. We had lived as master and servant for about three years now.

It was still a shock however when one evening he said that I must know that he was fond of me. He added that he had come to depend upon just as he had depended upon his late wife. I wondered what he might say next. He was a settler with a position to maintain in such society as we had.

I could hardly expect a proposal of marriage, yet this was what he seemed to be moving towards.

I sat still with my hands shaking a little so I folded them together and he then said:

"You and I are not getting any younger. I may not have many years left to me and I do want to leave what I have built up in safe hands. I know you like me. Do you like me enough to be my wife?"

I know that this was not a very romantic proposal. I also know that in those times and under those conditions in which we led our lives he was right to pitch it as simply as he did.

My reply was:

"My dear Elias I will gladly be your wife. I have respected you, become fond of you, admire you and agree with what you are trying to do. But please do not expect too much from me if we are wed.
    As you know, from me having told you of my previous history, I have been grievously hurt in the past."

And so we were wed.

Our marriage, as so many others at that time, was carried out swiftly and Elias respected my wishes for us to grow even further together before we consummated our union.

I can say this though, that consummated it was, but not blessed with any issue. Dr Arnold later confirmed what I already suspected, that having had a miscarriage I had caused myself such an internal mischief that I could not conceive as a consequence. I did not shed any tears over this. What's done is done. Elias quietly accepted the fact that we were not to have children and to tell the truth I think that he might have been relieved.

Chapter 16

My Husband Dies

My afternoon sleep was interrupted by shouts and cries. I had adopted this as a means of survival in the hot wet season having been introduced by Elias to this siesta, as the Spanish call it

What now? I thought crossly.

Has someone broken another plate? or, more seriously, one of Elias's best glasses? I got up groaning at the constant back pain that inflicted me these days and glanced in the mirror. A pale washed-out young woman looked back at me. Not that young, but young enough for me to stick out my tongue in childish defiance. Was I really only twenty-six?

I adjusted my dress where I had unhooked it to allow myself some ease as I slept, drew myself up and went out through the rattan shades onto the verandah. All three maids confronted me. Maggie, her face contorted with emotion said,

"He's gone."

Susan repeated in her dull voice,

"Yes gone."

The other maid, Jane, said nothing but nervously twisted her soap-chapped hands in the sacking skirt that she wore. Although grateful for having been rescued from the factory, she had been overawed by our establishment, and her looks made her shy and unforthcoming no matter how she was treated by us.

"Gone where?" I demanded.

"Who's gone?"

"What are you talking about?"

Then, goaded by the heat and the stupidity of the maids I said:

"For God's sake one of you, tell me what's happened."

"It's the master", said Maggie, then turning, she walked off sobbing.

Losing what little patience that I had retained until then I pushed past the other two and went to where I knew Elias had his afternoon siesta once he had smoked his after-lunch cheroot. He was to all intents and purposes still asleep; yet this sleep had a certain stillness that I recognised, a stillness that was a sleep of death. As I said it was something that I had experienced a dozen times. Some were men, some were women and some were children, but they all shared that deathly stillness.

The surgeon who rode over when we sent one of the convicts to him confirmed what we already knew. He came, not quickly, as we had sent word that Elias was dead.

"If I told him once, I told him a dozen times" he said after he had inspected the body.

"But your husband Elias was a stubborn man and liked to remove his boots as he took his afternoon nap, which was all very well while he rested. Then, when he arose to relieve himself, begging your pardon for such indelicacy, he usually neglected to replace them and this is the result. I told him. I told him.

"Yes", I said.

"His feet swelled in the heat", I added.

"Just so, Just so. But why is he on the day bed?

He looked thoughtful.

"My guess is that he got up, went outside, got bitten by a snake, see here are the marks, then staggered back to fall upon the bed. I expect it might have been a Taipan. They are the deadliest, but it could also have been a death adder or a brown snake or some other variety. All these are highly venomous.

Usually they keep away from us, but if we disturb them they can, and do, strike with tragic results. You have no idea of the number of dogs that get killed this way, particularly if they are recently come to Australia."

Then seeing my stricken face, he stopped his conjectures and said that he would make the necessary arrangements for the funeral and burial. He added that in this heat it would be wise to do this swiftly.

Following the doctor's advice we had a quick funeral and burial, and that was to tell against me later. Why was he buried so hastily? What was I trying to hide?

Chapter 17

I am tried for murder

Following the funeral I tried in the next few days to get everything back to normal. My peace was shattered however when Maggie announced with a strange look that there was a gentleman to see me. I said that I was seeing no-one but behind her an officer from the court stood waiting.

He was pale, polite but determined. He said that he had to insist on seeing me despite the fact that I had recently been through the turmoil of death and a funeral.

"I am here" he said "to investigate the death of Elias Spackford following a complaint laid against you."

He declined my offer of tea and took the chair that I indicated. I sat on my side of the verandah opposite him and folding my hands I heard him out.

"We are struggling to maintain order here far from the old country in what could be a truly lawless situation, so when someone is accused of murder we have to take it seriously."

"But who has accused me?"

He consulted his papers drawn from a leather satchel.

"One, Maggie Senchal and with her Susan Abercrombie."

Of course, the maids. No wonder Maggie had had such a strange look in her eye as she told me there was someone to see me.

"But Maggie has always resented me because I supplanted her, and as for Susan everyone knows she has little concept of reality and will do more or less, anything that Maggie tells her."

"Nevertheless I have sworn statements made before witnesses that you poisoned your husband.

It is alleged that you did this by using plants that you collected from which you extracted noxious liquids."

He paused.

"You do collect plants?"

"Yes" I replied dully.

I felt a noose being drawn about my neck.

"I collect plants, herbs, simples what you will. I collect them to add to our cooking to make meals more nourishing and palatable. I collect them to treat our animals.

He looked at me sharply.

"You make medicines?"

"Not exactly. I would not call them medicines. Treatments. Does it matter what you call them?"

I rose and went into the main room where I found my copy of Culpeper. I returned and placed it in the officer's hands.

"That is an English translation of the Pharmacopoeia Londonesis of the Royal College of Physicians, which Culpeper called A Physical Directory, or a Translation of the London Dispensary.

"This book, and others in my possession, are the basis of what I have attempted to do here in this wilderness. Of course I have had to add other herbs that are native to this land such as: River Mint, Native Thyme, Strawberry Gum and Gundabluey. I know of considerably more as my blackfellow has shown me them.

The offcer's eyes widened.

"You let an aboriginal show you these? How can you trust him?

I did not answer.

"You are not a doctor?"

"I have never held myself out to be such. We have doctors here upon whom I rely, though they still insist that they do not accept that herbs can be very helpful in many medical situations."

He scribbled some notes. The noose tightened. He rose and bidding me good day he left. I sat for some while after he had gone listening to the screaming of the birds and wondering what would happen now.

I tried to carry on as normal ignoring the looks and whispers of the servants. Mostly they continued as before but Maggie flounced about in such a manner as to indicate quite clearly to all who might see her that she thought that I would not be her mistress for much longer. Every night as I went to my bed I prayed that the following day would resolve my uncertain state. And every day when I arose I realised that I would probably have yet another day of anxiety to add to my problems.

But as the days went by I became more composed. I had done nothing wrong and the doctor who had attended soon after Elias's death had said that it was a snake that had killed him. Surely that would be the end of the matter. Still I wondered what would happen next.

Would someone ride out to me and tell me what decision the authorities had taken? I knew that some convicts had been falsely accused and because they were convicts no notice had been taken of their side of the story. Would that be my fate too?

Chapter 18

Acquitted!

What happened next was a charge of murder. My trial did not last long. Some good friends of Elias spoke to an Arthur Spens who had been a judge in Australia then went back to England. He returned to Australia in 1820 with his wife. She was a frail lady who found Australia a trial. It was said that his close interest in the rights of aboriginals went against him with the people who ran Australia.

He was in private practice and agreed to represent me. I asked him once why he went back to England and then came out to Australia again. He told me that he had been born abroad, where he was educated, returning to England to enter the legal profession.

He first came to Sydney in 1817 hoping to overcome the prejudice that followed from him having been educated abroad.

Here in September of 1818 he was made an acting judge of the Supreme Court. Then in 1819, as his appointment as judge was not confirmed, he resigned and went back to England. He said that he might be a shade touchy about his background and too ready to take offence. But, he could still not overcome the establishment in England so he married, mostly for money, he admitted candidly, and came back.

At the trial both Maggie and Susan gave evidence against me saying that they had observed me on divers occasions prepare poisons from herbs that I had gathered. They also gave evidence about Elias and me, saying that we sat together drinking on the verandah after lunch when I had given him the poison. He had then gone to the day bed where they found him dead.

They both told the court that the previous evening they had heard us arguing.

They even tried to use Jonas, but the court refused to hear anything he said saying that it was inadmissible; they knew that he would refuse to take the oath.

Arthur Spens told me that it would be to my favour were I to take the stand. He said declining to put myself before the prosecuting barrister and the jury would be construed as my attempting to hide something. So I stood in the witness box and recited the oath as firmly as I could. I must say here that my courage almost deserted me as I faced everyone, remembering the time before when the judge had declared that I was a most wicked and degenerate young woman and that I was to be hanged. Were the same words and the same sentence to be repeated?

My barrister had impressed upon me the necessity to appear calm and respectable so my dress and demeanour was that of a Quaker. I was asked whether I gathered herbs and whether I used them to make concoctions.

I replied that I indeed made tisanes and cordials. Did I give these to my husband I was asked. My answer that he preferred rum produced some amusement.

"But you did on several occasions give him some?"

"Yes, when he had the ague."

"You are not a doctor?"

"No, but I have learned much as a farmer's daughter in dealing with animals, and later on in this country."

"But men are not animals are they?"

"We do however share many things with them: lungs, a heart, a liver, kidneys and so on, but the Almighty has in his infinite wisdom given us immortal souls, so, no, men are not animals."

I heard a whisper behind me:

"But they can be brutes."

I looked around at the soldier guarding me who looked at me innocently. I later found that he, along with Arthur Spens, had tried to persuade the senior officers from their punishing by flogging, claiming that it simply brutalised all who were involved in such practices. He had also tried to persuade the authorities that the convict production of Farquhar's "The Recruiting Officer", directed by an officer should be a model for other similar endeavours.

I turned back to hear the next question;

"So you gave your husband cordials and whilst you did so you could easily have slipped into such a drink something more poisonous could you not?"

"Yes, I could. But I did not. My husband died of a snake bite."

The prosecuting barrister looked pained.

" I did not ask you for your opinion about his death."

"Nevertheless it is a fact as you will hear from the doctor who attended him."

"A doctor who is a friend of yours?"

"Yes, and of my dead husband."

We had an adjournment during which I said to Arthur, my barrister:

"Surely I am not to be condemned from evidence from two convicts?"

He replied, drily, "Why not, as you are such?"

I must have looked stricken for he hastened to reassure me that their testimony was valueless. He said that it was no more than a series of assertions based upon no real evidence. He said that in any case we had the evidence of the good doctor who examined my husband.

But when the doctor was called a man stood up and said that he could not be at the trial. He had been called away and was a thousand miles at least from Sydney.

After another adjournment during which I had to remain in custody, I was brought up again.

I was brought before the court to hear that my barrister had put to the court that the doctor's notes made at the time of my husband's death were sufficient testimony to clear me of all wrongdoing. This was accepted and so I was acquitted.

Following the trial and the removal of Maggie, for I was able to argue that by her accusing me without the smallest particle of evidence she had shown such enmity towards my person that I was in danger were she to continue in my employ, I threw myself into the work of improvements.

I had read that in 1812 a certain Macarthur had pioneered the introduction of Saxon Merinos. Elias had also advocated the importing of new stock to improve what we already possessed. He had done this to some extent so I was determined to follow his example.

This became my life for several years. Each day that I arose I was determined to improve what I had been so lucky to inherit. So I consulted widely, read all I could and drove all who worked for me to achieve these ends.

I sent messages to England once I had determined what it was that I needed. Sending word to England for the ordering of stock made me consider that I ought to see whether I could get news of my parents.

Arthur Spens encouraged me in this as he said that surely they would be delighted to hear that their errant daughter had flourished. He directed me to a Mr Henry Savery newly arrived in the colony who had been educated at Oswestry Grammar School. He said that he might know, or be able to find out for you, how things are with your folks.

Savery was a gentleman, a forger who was nearly hanged and only just avoided that extreme penalty by being transported.

Arthur told me that Savery had won many people over since his arrival and it was likely that he had just been unlucky in his business dealings. Anyway Savery's concern to rehabilitate himself and gain respectability had been enabled by being put into the Colonial Secretary's office.

He is just the man, I was told, who would be able to gain any information. So I made it my business to meet him and I found that he was indeed a most pleasant fellow who promised to do what he could for me. When I next met him he told me that he was petitioning for his wife to join him and, indeed, had some success in that he hoped that his wife would join him in the very near future.

"I have requested of my wife that she make diligent enquiries on your behalf as to the present situation of your parents. Do you have brothers or sisters?

"None, I was an only child."

He looked thoughtful.

"So, in the unhappy case of your parents not being of this world, know you who would inherit?"

"I know not."

"Well", he went on briskly, "No matter. Leave all in my hands, I will not let you down."

The next I knew was that Mrs Savery had indeed arrived but in circumstances that were not very respectable, having contracted a liaison on board with a Mr Algernon Montagu, who was on his way to Tasmania to become Attorney General. I sought Arthur Spens out and asked him to tell me all he knew. Arthur, swearing me to silence, told me in the absolute utmost confidence, not in any way to be communicated to another soul, that the Savery's had had the most dramatic quarrel.

Following which Savery had cut his throat in a bid to commit suicide. He had been saved by a doctor who had been called immediately.

This, I told Arthur, was common knowledge, and that I rather doubted that I should have trusted Savery with any of my affairs; so far for example, I had not had a word from him about my parents. I told Arthur that Savery seemed to me to be a most plausible man who had taken in many fools including Arthur and me.

Arthur had the grace to blush at my words so I turned the conversation onto other matters asking him how fared his wife as she had been unwell yet again.

His face reflected the bad news that he was about to impart. Impulsively I took his hand as he told me that she had taken a turn for the worse. In fact, according to the doctor, she was not likely to survive this particular bout of fever. She had always been delicate and Australia with its extremes of heat and damp and trouble with insects that debilitated those that were bitten, was her undoing.

I knew that Arthur had married for money but, as is often the case, they had been drawn together in their struggles in a new land and he now loved her.

"Oh dear", I exclaimed and was shocked to see Arthur's eye brim with tears that rolled down his face.

"Never mind me", he replied.

"I am quite used already to the idea that I shall lose her."

"So what shall you do?"

"Lose myself in work as always."

Poor Arthur's wife succumbed and we had yet another funeral. He then did exactly as he had foretold, throwing himself into his work with such abandon that friends became quite worried as to his state of mind and approached me to assist them. They put it to me that I could divert him, draw him into a more sociable situation where he would be unable to dwell on the past.

So over the months I became the hostess of several evening dinners where the more respectable members of the bar, and their wives, came to enjoy a good dinner and some reasonable conversation. And the conversation, of course, included gossip.

Chapter 19

Freddie reappears

The name of Savery was often mentioned as we dined, and that poor man's progress in the Colony was picked over by all. And, as his friends had intended, Arthur and I became even closer.

Considering the fact that he had represented me and that we shared many interests this was scarcely surprising,

Over the port and cigars one night after dinner I heard the name Captain Paffrey being mentioned in connection with the push to oust the blacks. I had said nothing supposing that there might be more Paffreys in the world than just Freddie. In town the following day to collect some produce however I saw across the street a familiar walk accompanied by what I now recognised as an arrogant bearing. Once upon a time I had seen it as the stride of a man proud to be an officer in a crack regiment. When I saw it was indeed an officer who was pushing people to one side and that he wore the epaulettes of a captain I felt sure that this would be Frederick Charles Paffrey, and as we both reached the end of the street together I recognised him.

I would have passed him by but in our small community that would have occasioned more comment than speaking to him. He bowed to me then startled, he said:

"My God ! Is it really you Amanda?"

I inclined my head, not trusting myself to speak. To be honest, although I was appalled to see him I was also delighted that despite my being thirty-two and no longer a young woman he recognised me. Vanity, vanity, all is vanity.

"You remember me then?"

Of course I remembered him, as indeed I remembered the pain and anguish that he had caused me. But having spent so much time seeking to remove him from my mind I was most reluctant to admit him back into it.

Nevertheless we had shared something in the past and I could not deny that.

"How are you Freddie?"

"I am well, and I see that you are quite raised up in the world to a station in life that I ever thought you deserved."

Saying this he took a step towards me and I retreated fearing an embrace.

"Yes, I am as respectable now as I never was when you deserted me" I said somewhat bitterly.

Oh! Amada, he replied in a low voice, "I had to do it. Do you think I have not regretted my foolish actions every day since then?"

My face betrayed my doubts at his protestation.

"When I heard of your privations I could hardly believe them as I had thought that you would simply return home to your loving parents and would eventually marry some rustic beau who would make you happy. Did you not have some farmer's son with whom you were besotted?"

"That's all in the past now" I replied.

There was a moment's silence between us which I broke.

"So, Captain Frederick Charles Paffrey, I see that you have got the promotion that you so desired. Were you successful in India? We have heard such confused reports of events there."

His brown sun-seared face twisted in the bright sun and became ugly.

"Do not believe all you hear of me Amanda. Such calumnies as are being circulated has meant that I have had eventually to call out some spreaders of lies about me. Only the ban on duelling has saved some from an early demise."

I was confused. I had heard little about him and certainly nothing to his discredit. He saw this and his face smoothed and the usual pleasant smile that I remembered came back.

"As you so rightly observe I am advanced in my Regimental career and I am here to help rid it of the scum that still pollute it and so make it unsafe for such ladies as yourself."

"How so?" I asked, fearing the answer for I had heard similar expressions at the dinner table and knew that Captain Paffrey was talking about the indigent population, not the convicts.

It was true that on several occasions they had attacked we Europeans, but I had observed that many had been so provoked that they could scarcely not have defended themselves or their homeland.

Some of my so-called educated compatriots chose to smile and make little of the blacks' beliefs, and I must own here that I too had initially considered that my Christian beliefs were being insulted. The continued ignoring of our hands held out in friendship, their nakedness and their smell made it difficult to see them as real people.

Latterly however I had begun to try to understand how it must seemed them to have such beings as we come in strange vessels out of nowhere with weapons that spoke death so noisily and quickly. Maybe they saw us as savages. We have certainly acted savagely. And we have mocked their beliefs, such as they were, and trampled over their sacred ground.

I turned to Freddie who stood there in the hot sunshine with his smell of leather and cigars competing with the ever-present smell of cookery, horse manure and humid earth. He tapped his sword to emphasise his points as he made them and I could see, under that bravado, the little boy that was there still who must have tapped his slate in the same way as he repeated his lesson to the dominie.

"In short, I am here to rid you of these disgusting savages", he began, and as he went on his manner became wilder as he explained how he and several others were to accomplish this.

"But that is murder."

"It is killing, yes, but in a war killing is necessary."

"But we are not at war with them", I said pointing to the women and children sitting in the shade of some trees nearby.

He made an impatient gesture.

"Oh! Amanda", he said " I see that you are still the romantic despite all that you have endured since coming to this terrible place."

"It is not that terrible that the likes of you cannot make it more so. I hold onto my true Christian beliefs", I replied, my face getting hot despite my parasol.

"I try to be honest in my dealings with", I hesitated "all God's children."

He laughed. If I, and what I said, was amusing to him I would not stay. I was too incensed to say another word. I turned and walked away.

Speaking to Arthur later that day he confirmed that there was indeed a plan afoot to get rid of the blacks. He told me of the intention to carry out a black war to clear Tasmania of all the aborigines.

"Then you must stop this", I said firmly.

"If only I could, but my position as a lawyer who is not part of the establishment means that I really have no power. Anyway, the Governor thinks that the encroachment of white people on the black hunting grounds has so upset the Tasmanian aborigines that they have retaliated to such an extent that we must do something about it. So he has agreed to this action.

Much later on, when I thought perhaps that everyone had thought better of it, I heard that a Black Line campaign had indeed been started.

Chapter 20

News of my parents, blackmail and marriage proposals

Two months later we heard that the Black Line Campaign had been almost totally unsuccessful. The troops and others who had been involved had been spread out along a front that was so wide that it had been possible to slip through it. The ground was so rugged in some parts that to escape was comparatively easy for a native. Major Douglas of the 63rd Regiment, aided by other officers including Captain Paffrey, along with many settlers, took part in this attempt to corral the aborigines on Eaglehawk Peninsula.

The intention was to capture the natives, and they did capture a man and a boy. It was a costly affair; we lost four or five troops who were killed accidentally. Much later on we heard that the cost in money terms was nearly thirty thousand pounds.

How much could have been done with such a sum had it been spent upon the natives to ease their sufferings brought to them by the white men.

I supposed that Freddie had survived. I was not too concerned about him nor his safety so I did not enquire. In any case I did not wish to draw attention to the fact that I had known him in the past. My concern at that time was to find out how fared my parents and I was persuaded that I might get this intelligence from Mrs Savery.

Despite being ostracised by part of society, Mrs Savery still managed to retain some sort of position so I determined to visit her. She had been involved in a strange affair that was in the The Sydney Herald. There was something about a libel action which I never understood. All I cared for was to hear what she had determined as to the fate of my parents in Shropshire

She received me in some agitation as her husband had been placed in prison for debt.

She told me that she wished that she had never set foot in Australia and intended to take the advice that had been offered her to go back to England. We sat taking tea using our fans in an attempt to remain cool. I was the more successful in this endeavour as I had learned to wear much less clothing. By contrast Mrs Savery, intent as she was in maintaining her slender grasp upon her position, was dressed in what I took to be a most fashionable set of clothes that, no doubt, had been most acceptable in England. I had taken the cane chair as I knew from experience that they were infinitely cooler than the overstuffed chairs with their horsehair stuffing that had been brought from England.

She also told me in an off-hand graceless fashion what I most feared to hear, that is that she had determined that both my parents had died. I received this news calmly.

She, on the other hand then began to rage against her husband, the Governor General, Algernon Montagu and a whole series of other persons whom, she said, had treated her in so vile a fashion that she was nearly unable to continue her life in Australia.

I tried to get from her how she had obtained the news of my parents in Shropshire and she said in the most off-hand way that her father's agent had found out what I had just been told. Her son, Oliver, came in at that moment and I must say that her whole demeanour changed in an instant as she embraced him and asked what she was to do.

Having no answer to give her I took my leave, waiting until I arrived home to give vent to my feelings. Arthur finding me in tears comforted me and I must say that his comforting arms not only provided me with solace but with hope for the future as I now knew that of all men this was the one who really stirred my heart.

Arthur stood up and said:

"When you are more composed I should like to return and speak to you further."

His demeanour was solemn and his look steady. He took up his hat and cane with never another word.

He then left and I sat wondering just what the future now held for me. I would have sat there some time after what had been an exhausting day had not one of the servants come in to tell me that a gentleman had called whilst I had been out and left a note. He left no other message and did not give his name. I felt uneasy. Was I to hear something else to my disadvantage?

I opened the sealed note to read:

Amanda

You will have heard of the debacle that I was involved in where we failed in our honest endeavour to rid Tasmania of those blacks that are a plague there. Now I am to be the scapegoat in this venture so I must perforce turn to you for the means for me to leave this accursed country. I do not need a great sum.
As you were once my wife, I do not suppose that you would care for me to tell all of that time when were so intimate.

I shall be at Hyde Park this evening at eight on the South West side where it is quietest. Be sure that you meet me there.

Freddie

I re-read the note. I felt ill, sick and faint. The note was clearly written and the message equally clear. Freddie intended to tell everyone about our previous liaison if I did not give him money.

And I knew that once I gave him some he would simply carouse with it and return for more until I had no more to give him. Nevertheless I had to meet him.

So it was that later that night I went to Hyde Park as he had instructed me to find him beneath one of the huge native trees festooned with bats. He was smoking a cheroot and its smell swept me back to Portsmouth years ago when we had promenaded the streets and attended gay gatherings.

He decided to go straight to business.

"You have it?"

"No I cannot raise the sort of sum in such a short while that you would need to go back to England."

"Well get it. Meet me here in two days or I shall tell all."

He turned negligently and wandered away the smoke and smell of his cheroot trailing after him. I turned to find my way blocked by a soldier.

"You cannot trust him," he said.

"How dare you spy upon a lady and gentleman's conversation."

"You are no lady and he is certainly no gentleman."

I was shocked.

"I know you as it was I that guarded you at your trial. You are a convict and he is a dog."

I tried to retain some composure but the events of the day were pressing upon me and I felt faint.

"What do you want?"

"To help you. I know more about you than you realise. I have been courting Jane for some while now and she has agreed to marry me once I have finished my time with the Sixty-third."

"So that is where you know of Captain Paffrey?"

"Yes, I was with him at Eaglehawk Neck. He is a dog who treats others as dogs. I am not alone in my opinion of him. Others share my feelings as he has sickened many with his casual brutality. You know that he is suspected of having done away with his wife in India?"

"No, I did not know that."

"Only when his brother officers closed ranks was he saved; but he still had to return to England to avoid the scandal. His coming to Australia was a way of mending his fortunes as he is always in debt."

He paused.

"Well, may I marry Jane?"

"I am simply her employer but would never put obstacles in the way of her getting some happiness in this life. Will you make her happy?"

"Who knows? I shall try. So you are saying yes then?"

"Yes."

"Good. Go home. Do nothing about this. Leave all to me. Above all, tell no one, I mean no one at all, including a certain gentleman who could be compromised, about anything to do with this. DO   YOU   UNDERSTAND ME? He said in a fierce parade ground voice.

"But I am supposed to meet....."

"No. Do nothing. Tell no one." He repeated in a lower tone.

"And, my only connection with you is that I wish to marry Jane. You do not know me. Now go home."

What was I to do? My every instinct was to take some action. I am not the sort of person who sits and does nothing. The days that followed were a torment. I went to see Mrs Savery but she had gone back to England taking her boy with her. I tried to remain calm and when Arthur called upon me I sat with hands folded into my lap as he spoke to me.

"My very dearest Amanda", he began.

I trembled and he saw it.

" I know that you are upset about your parents and it does you great honour to grieve for them in this fashion after so long away from their company and their influence, but what I must say I must say now. Please forgive an impetuous man as I am sure you must have realised by now I am."

His taking of my discomfiture as being caused by the death of my parents both encouraged me and saddened me.

I was encouraged as I could remain silent about Freddie, and whilst saying nothing, seem to be grieving. I was saddened as I guessed what Arthur was leading up to and it meant that we were likely to be starting a fresh part of our lives with me playing false.

Sure enough he did go on to ask me to marry him, but lawyer as he was the preamble to the request setting out the pros and cons of marriage for us both took so long that I nearly missed it! To tell the truth I was hearing "Do nothing. Tell no one." echoing inside my head, and had to ask him to repeat his offer. At the same time I said to him that I had to apologise for being so distrait.

Just at that moment Jane came in to ask if I required anything. I made up my mind.

"Yes, please bring a bottle or two of that French wine that is so esteemed by all, and some glasses, enough for the whole household.

We have something to celebrate. Ask everyone to come in. Get everyone in please, now."

She scuttled off and I heard excited whisperings as she returned with the bottles and glasses. Arthur poured out the wine that he opened with a satisfying plop. The staff crowded in. Arthur waited and I said after a pause:

" I would like you all to drink the health of the future Mr and Mrs Arthur Spens as Mr Spens has done me the great honour of asking me to be his wife."

Arthur clapped his hands together in delight. All the others drank then put down their glasses and applauded too.

"Please don't", I said almost in tears by now.

"You make me feel like an actress."

Arthur kissed me which display of affection did make me cry and provoked more applause.

I learned later that not one of my employees was surprised at my announcement; all had been expecting it for days. But the next bit of domestic theatre had a different actress, Jane, who moving centre stage said:

"I too have something that cannot be concealed any longer. Mr James O'Brian, who shall shortly be a soldier no more, and I are to be wed too. Please wish us well."

This last request was said with such poignancy that everyone murmured or said:

"Good luck", or, " Of course", or simply "yes."

I hugged Jane and whispered to her that both Mr Spens and I would be giving her a dowry. Arthur topped this by asking whether he might give her away. Now it was Jane's turn to cry.

Chapter 21

A mysterious death, and I meet Abel Magwitch

Our weddings were duly celebrated each in its own fashion; mine was a quiet affair as we had both been wed before and wished not for any great ceremony. Jane and James however had numerous people who knew them and wished them well and all these enjoyed the show and subsequent feast. Arthur kept his word and gave Jane away and there were many tears shed as her delight transfigured her face. Only the true love and devotion showed to her by James outdid her. I moved to Arthur's house eventually but stayed in the farm homestead for a while.

Some days later Jane came in and laid upon the table a copy of The Sydney Herald.

She opened it to a page where written elegantly in ink were the words:

Do nothing .   Tell no one.

Under this reminder was an item that I read, feeling progressively fainter as I read each word.

MYSTERIOUS DEATH OF OFFICER

On Wednesday night the body of Captain Paffrey of the 53rd (Shropshire) Regiment of Foot was discovered near one of the large trees that remain in Hyde Park. His throat had been cut and nothing remained in his pockets thus giving credence to the theory that he had been the victim of a foul robbery.

His body had apparently lain there most of the night. A half smoked cheroot lay nearby. The brand was a popular one with military gentlemen.

Captain Paffrey had recently taken part in the largely abortive sweep in Tasmania where his conduct as an officer gave cause for concern. An undisclosed source of information indicated that he was not the most popular of officers, and having completed some time in Australia, where he was attached to the 63rd Regiment, was due to return to England.

We can reveal that he had made enquiries about travelling on the Sarah, but had not finalised his arrangements.

We have repeatedly warned the Governor General that the city is still a dangerous place. Since the Hyde Park Barracks were built more ruffians have been placed in them and we urge the authorities to maintain their vigilance in respect of containing them to the safety of the public.

Jane picked up the sheet containing this item, screwed it into a spill and lighting it from a candle she lit the others that stood upon the mantelpiece that had ever been the joy of Elias when he was alive. She then regarded me steadily as she dropped the spill into the fireplace. As it burned to nothing but ash she said:

"It's all over now."

I wanted to say something, but she shook her head and told me that the ship carrying the stock that I had ordered to be sent had arrived. She told me that I should go to the harbour where I might see the stock being unloaded if I hurried.

Riding to the harbour brought me to a mad scene of animals and men, the animals calling out each in its own way and the men in a variety of dialects.

Everything was confusion. People shouted, animals swam ashore or were ferried in the ship's boat.

That ship now swam serenely off shore as if it had not survived a dozen storms and adventures as it brought yet more convicts to us. But I was looking to see whether the rams I had asked to be sent were safe. They were and being cared for by a big-boned rough convict who, having seen them safely ashore, approached me along with a small spry man who I recognised but couldn't name. He was the ship's carpenter.

"Begging your pardon ma'am," he said, "Alfred Trimble, who you might recall repaired your verandah the last time I was here."

He doffed his hat most graciously and I rewarded such gallant behaviour with a nod. His large convict stared at me and said:

"Excuse me for asking, but did we never meet before somewheres?"

I looked hard at him and said that to the best of my recollection we had never in this life met before today.

He went on to say:

"But, perhaps you might recall a certain time when in England a certain young woman needed a farrier, and a couple of shepherds, one old and the other younger, did tell that young woman where to get one."

I looked at him. I certainly recalled the incident when I was on my way to meet Freddie in Petersfield. I looked at him carefully. There was something about him. I asked about my mare and he described her to me. A countryman will often retain such details in his mind that a city dweller would scarcely be capable of.

Before I could say another word he took me aside and told me what he knew about a certain Amanda Jane. How she as a young lass had been deserted by an officer who had gone to foreign parts. How she had later been taken up and transported to a penal colony. I looked at him trying to remember.

I still could not be sure that this was the very same man so we went to a lean-to where I bought him and Alfred Trimble a dram and told them some of my history after reaching Australia. As I did so he listened carefully. At the end he said how glad things had turned out so well for me and told me how he was hoping to help a young man in England better himself. I said that as I was so pleased that he had taken such good care of my stock I would gladly have given him some money as a reward but I feared that it would be stolen from him.

I said that as a convicted man he would be at risk from all; not only the other convicts but many others who would like to take advantage of him.

At this, Alfred stepped forward and said that he was taking Abel, as by then I knew him, under his wing and they were to be working for a spell out at Vaucluse for Mr Wentworth.

"He is to be my assistant. But when I go home, as I must, for I am signed on as carpenter for the Sarah I could take any money that Abel might earn and also any that you might see fit to give him. I shall pass it on to Jaggers, the lawyer, on his behalf."

So we arranged that Alfred would come to me and I would give him some money to take back to England. Later on Alfred told me that Compeyson, who had been sentenced with Abel, had come on another ship and that getting Abel to work with him was also a ruse to avoid Compeyson.

He said:

"Each one is poison for each other. Abel would gladly swing on a gibbet if he could murder Compeyson. While Compeyson would do Abel any kind of mischief if he could."

Chapter 22

Magwitch seeks my help

I heard subsequently that, as Abel was experienced and was fully recommended by Alfred, a sheep farmer had readily taken him inland with him. This was all part of Alfred's plans to try to keep Abel and Compeyson apart. I was unsure where Abel had finished up but I knew that it would be on some land where they had ring-barked the trees to make them die, thus allowing the grass beneath them to flourish and to feed the sheep.

Then for a while I heard no more until one day he came, twisting his hands around his hat, the bearer of good and bad news along with a request.

When Abel came to see me bearing the sad news of the death of his master I expected that he would have to tell how and when this had happened so I duly settled down to hear the full story.

They were all out looking for stray sheep and had stopped to drink tea. John, who I believe was a half wit, wouldn't stop scratching at some pictures that the natives had drawn on the rocks where they had sought shade. He was told to desist, but he did not, it was hot and no one made him obey.

Then some local natives approached them. They were daubed all over with white clay and carried spears. John, who had been told not to, still carried on scraping at the funny figures that were on the rocks muttering under his breath.

He was muttering something about bloody savages. Abel knew that something was wrong. He told the others to stand up and get back.

They all turned and tried to scramble over the broken rocks to a safer spot but they were too late. The natives rushed at them, spearing John and killing him; they also speared Abel's master but he drew a pistol and shot one of the natives before falling over.

He gave his other gun to Abel telling him to shoot. Abel did so hitting another black man and the natives fled.

Despite his master being wounded, Abel was able to get him over a horse and get him back to the farmhouse. Abel said that it was the longest twelve miles that he had ever endured. At the homestead Ada tried to treat him using local herbs. Abel then went back out to see whether he could find John's body in order to give him a Christian burial. Before he did so he was called in by his master who thanked him and said that he would not forget what Abel had done.

But almost immediately Ada sent for Abel out in the bush and he came riding back. He was asking for me, Ada told Abel, insistent that he had to be brought home. It was obvious that he was very ill. They all prayed for him to survive, sitting with him trying to keep away the flies and wringing out cloths to wipe him to try to keep him cool. It was not to be.

Before he died he told Abel to look in the old sea chest where he kept his papers. Abel found them and found that they included a will. He told Abel that he had made this earlier when he saw how reliable and loyal he was. Abel said that he knew that he had done something of the kind on one of his infrequent visits into Sydney. He had hinted as much to Abel who thought that he would be leaving everything to a relative. It turned out that he had no-one, and that was why he had come to Australia. He told Abel that apart from a bequest to Ada he was to have the bulk of his estate.

He died that night as Abel sat with him. Later on when Abel asked the others where Ada was they said that she had gathered some things together and walked off into the bush. Being a black she knew how to survive where others would have died, and they all assumed that she had simply gone back to her Abo family.

Abel showed me the will and I could see that it was all in order. I told him how to proceed now so as to be the new owner of the homestead. He was worried about what he should do about Ada's share. I gave him such advice as I knew he would need. He then asked me for some help as he wanted to improve his estate, and so together we devised some plans that entailed me using some of my monies to assist him. His knowledge and experience served him well. He was a good master to his crew of workers, who developed a loyalty to him that was to serve him well later on. I, of course, had the advantage of a lawyer husband who sat as a judge so I was able to draw on his experience to underpin my advice to Abel.

It was about this time that Arthur became friendly with the Macleays and often met Alexander over business matters. They, the Macleays, were rather a proud set I thought, particularly when they set about building an extremely expensive house at Elizabeth Bay. Of course they had to have John Verge to supervise the building.

I rather think that he persuaded Alexander to overreach himself. I never set foot in it because by the time that it finished the Macleays were in difficulties to do with money. In the end the son, William, took over the house. Arthur was never so friendly with William, something to do with politics I think. It was a lesson to us. We kept our old house, or rather, I should say, Arthur's old house that was so small but comfortable. With no children it suited us.

I used my money instead to help Abel and in time Abel repaid the money that I had advanced. And as he had used it wisely we all prospered.

Abel, despite his rise, did not change very much. He amused Arthur who called him an Australian rough diamond. We met occasionally on business and when his carpenter friend came with news of his protégé Pip we all sat and drank in the news about the Queen and other similar matters as well as news of Pip.

I knew of Compeyson. I did not tell Abel as I did not wish to unsettle him. I also did not wish to stop him in his progressive work on the homestead but I knew how Compeyson was faring.

Like many others who came as convicts he plotted to take advantage of any situation that presented itself. An accomplished liar who had supported himself by false pretences, he was skilled at putting himself in the right when he was manifestly wrong. As soon as he could he wormed his way into a situation where he developed some power from being able to handle records and documents. He overreached himself because that was his nature. Having found a soft billet he could not resist falsifying the records to someone's advantage for which he was paid.

He was caught by a simple slip of the pen. He changed some records in 1835 and put 1834 on them instead. This was as the year 1834 had just ended. A simple mistake made by many.

This was noticed by another convict who, having corrected this simple error, looked for others and was astonished to uncover a whole pattern of deceit. He could have kept quiet but as he did not like Compeyson he informed on him. This led to Compeyson being sent back to do hard labour, but the authorities knew their man and secretly recruited him as an informer.

They wanted to know when something had been planned: an uprising, an execution of a convict, or an assassination of an officer who was too harsh.

Sometimes the information was acted upon and sometimes not. Arthur knew about him, saying that he was a necessary evil. He also knew of the part that Compeyson played in the plot where he informed on his comrades. He never told me all the details but I knew that Arthur was not complicit in Compeyson's return to England. It was others who decided that his treachery should be rewarded and that, as he was now too well known, he had outlived his usefulness as a secret informer.

Arthur explained that by rewarding him a message was sent to other informers that their role was valued.

As I said, I kept my knowledge from Abel hoping that his path would not cross that of Compeyson. And I secretly hoped that he might meet a really bloody end. It would have given me much pleasure to have heard that someone had wreaked vengeance upon him. Do not be too surprised at my attitude. You must remember that although we had the semblance of order and we had the law, as in so many so-called civilised countries there was an underbelly where another form of justice existed. The established authorities sometimes maintained a precarious hold on their power by turning Nelson's patched eye towards what they did not wish to see or know about.

In time the need for this kind of secret control was to give way to a more civilised way of maintaining public order.

It came about as more and more settlers arrived and more ex convicts took up grants of land and became less willing to lead savage and unrestrained lives. It also arrived as food became more plentiful.

Chapter 23

Politics and a watch

I have frequently observed that wherever and whenever men are gathered together, and have a full sufficiency of those things to meet their needs, that their minds turn to other matters. Some waste their talents and their money while others seek to use them in the service of others. Others, despite having sufficient for their needs are unable to resist corruption. But what ever path they choose many use politics to achieve their ends. Politics is to men as play is to children. Women will never dabble in such childishness, they have the more serious things of life to consider, although many are complicit in the actions of men but this is because their natural good sense has been suborned.

Arthur was no exception to the rule. His entry into politics was because of his belief that he could thereby do good. Of course, it also advanced his career but as he used to say:

"One hand washes the other."

I never knew if this was cynicism or realism.

He also said that he was interested in getting convicts as voters. I never really knew whether he was like Macquarie, who in his time really seemed to believe in general suffrage, except women of course, or whether he would use them to support only himself. He was certainly a member of the Australian Patriotic Association and I was forever hearing what

Mr Wentwoth said about this or that. Actually, I had a secret positive feeling for Mr Wentworth who seemed to have come from nowhere, as it were, to a position of prominence where he seemed not to have forgotten his early beginnings. There were others whom I did not admire. I shall not name them here.

"But Arthur", I would say, on hearing that he was consorting with Mr A or Mr B, "They are villains of the deepest die whose interest is only in lining their pockets."

"Of course", he would reply patiently, "but the world may have been made by a perfect God, but the devil is in that world and he tempts these men and they have fallen. The plain truth of the matter is that I have to work with them or they would work against me. I need them as they can easily undo much of what we have achieved."

One evening, when Arthur was at one of innumerable meetings to do with politics, Jane came in with a packet in her hand which she laid upon the table. It lay there on the chenille cloth and we both looked at it before Jane began to speak.

"'Do nothing. Say nothing', was what my husband used to say, but today he died. He left me these," she said indicating the two bonny children that accompanied her.

"Go and play."

They ran out, glad to be released. We heard their voices as they went off to see the animals.

I started to say something, but she held up her hand to forestall me.

"He also left me this."

She unwrapped the cloth that was stained and ragged and revealed a beautiful gold watch.

I picked it up and looked at the inscription on the back.

" I know this watch."

"I'm sure that you do; let me tell you something about it that you do not know. On a night that a certain officer died, James was in the park ready to do whatever was necessary to protect you. He told me that he heard a cry and saw the smouldering tip of a lit cheroot fly through the air like a firework. He ran and saw that it had been knocked out of that officer's mouth as he was brought low.

Crouching over him was a black man taking things from his pockets. Blood was still coming from a gash in his throat but he was dead for his main artery had been severed. The black man did not try to run away but simply said that this was a bad man who had to die for the sake of the members of the tribe. James picked up the watch and said that he wanted it. The black man shrugged and said that James might have it. He said:

"Keep it. It is useless. You cannot eat it or make things with it."

"I will tell you the time."

The man laughed.

"What use is that to me?"

James asked what the native would do with the other possessions that were laid out on the bare earth. The native said that they must be destroyed for they were tabu. He wrapped them in some bark and slipped away with them into the night.

"Now we must go back to the times when James was a soldier and took part in a sweep in Tasmania. One night while he was on guard in the dark, an officer who had drunk too much boasted to him that he had not only managed to rid himself of an inconvenient wife but had also ill-used several young women in the past, and that one in particular had finished up as a convict. He went on to add that he had not only persuaded her to run away with him but had also stolen her father's watch, presuming that the father would assume that his daughter had stolen it to maintain herself. Later, no doubt when he became sober, he realised that he had confessed to someone who was now a danger to him."

I stirred, I was disturbed by this account. I went to say something but Jane again forestalled me with a look.

"I'm sure that you have heard that some soldiers were shot by accident and died during this shocking affair.

What this officer did not know was that on the night that he spoke to the soldier James had taken the place of another who was sick.

So when the officer examined the muster records as part of his regimental duties James was not on duty that night. A Private Percival Flight was marked down as being on picket When they had departed I again gave way to tears until Arthur came in. I told him of Jane's loss but said nothing of the watch.

I felt no unease at so doing for I reasoned that silence about the past was the way for me to steer in all my future. The past is always done. The present we live; the future is nothing yet. And it will be nothing for all of us at some time.

duty that night instead. It was this soldier that James stood in for when Percival had a bout of the flux."

"So later the following day, following some confusion by a erroneous sighting of a native, Private Flight was shot, apparently in error. Of course the officer was exonerated, it was a terrible mistake, but mistakes do happen."

I picked up the watch and held it. It was warm. Everything that you touched in Australia in the heat of December was warm, but I imagined that some warmth from my father's fingers lingered within it. I bowed my head and the tears flowed, tears that I had not been able to shed before.

And with those tears came a release, a letting go of my family, my country and the remembrance of the past. I felt sorrow too as I had imagined that a good man had done a dreadful thing to protect me. Now, at last, I knew the truth.

I put the watch away and said:

"We can now put these things behind us. We must look to the future. What shall you do now that James is gone?"

"Why, keep on with the shop. What else? Alfred still brings enough from England for us to sell, and so we thrive. He says that Jamie has all the makings of a carpenter so I shall have him indentured as such when the time is right. As to Olivia, despite her dreaminess, she is a good girl who helps me in the business and already can read and write and cipher sufficiently to be an asset to me. She will take the business over when I am gone so she will be provided for, and if she finds a good man to marry I shall be even more contented.

Both Jamie and Olivia ran in at that moment calling for their mother to see the new calf. She held them both proudly and I felt such pain then at my loss of not having children that I would have cried some more.

But Jane seeing this said:

"Come, we must go now. We must go home. Say goodbye and thank' ee as your father taught you." Her voice, so steady until that moment, broke and she suddenly let go her children and put her arms around me and wept while Olivia said:

"Don't cry Mama."

Jamie just stood silent at this show of emotion. He frowned and said nothing but his look spoke more than words. I thought about his father and hoped that Jamie would turn out to be as good a man as he was. He showed every sign of being a steady lad, just the sort that Australia needed if it was to rise above its bloody past.

Chapter 24

I help Magwitch yet again

Alfred Trimble's accounts of Pip's progress as a gentleman were recounted to Abel as we sat around a table together. Alfred had already handed over to me a copy of Mr Dicken's book 'Oliver Twist' that I had requested he purchase for me. I laid it aside promising myself future enjoyment as I read it, before passing it on to others who were as interested in this work as I was.

"He is as proper a gentleman as you would wish to see, travels in coaches, dresses in the very latest styles, spends money (your money) lavishly and is often seen at balls and the opera".

"The opera", repeated Abel.

"Yes, and can frequently be see in the company of such attractive young women as would be suitable company for the queen should she so desire such company."

"The queen", repeated Abel, transfixed.

"Yes, the queen, and the hours that he keeps are those of a true gentleman who has no need to earn a crust, but lives for pleasure. He rises late and keeps it up to the small hours.

I could see that Abel was about to say "The small hours" so I broke in and said briskly:

"Well, I'm sure that we are all delighted to hear about the progress of your protégé, Abel".

He shook his head, not in negation but rather in wonderment that he had apparently managed to have achieved his aim.

"I must see him. I must go to see him. I must......"
"NO" we all chimed in at once, sitting forward in alarm.

"Dear Abel, I know how strongly you feel about Pip but you will mar all that you have done if you pursue this mad idea of going to England."

He shook his head.

" I shall go in disguise. I am altered now. No one will know that it is me."

"You are a damned fool, and this is a damn fool idea."

This from Alfred only made Abel roar with anger. He stood up; he hit the table; the glasses jumped spilling their contents. The smell of rum filled the air. His veins stood out in his head as if he was about to have a fit like the one that carried off poor Amelia Fosdick.

"Who are you to tell me what I may and may not do? Who are you to deny an old man something that is most dear to him?"

He fell back suddenly looking much older. He picked up his glass, and finding it empty, gestured at Albert to fill it.

We all said nothing but looked at each other. Perhaps if we said naught he might come to his senses.

He didn't.

He put on his hat, drained his glass, picked up his stick and left without another civil word. I stood up too clutching my novel. I had asked for something and had received it. Maybe we were wrong to deny him the one pleasure that he sought. What right had we to make that decision?

I stood up. I was about to go after him when he came back still visibly agitated. I sat down again. He was still determined to see 'his' gentleman and as he sat down with us he persuaded us that, were we not to assist him in his mad plan, he would do it by himself.

So we devised a plan that would lessen the chances of him being taken up both here and in England. A ship was due to sail soon back to England; and could carry a gentleman who having been a settler and made enough to pay for such a journey was returning to see his relatives.

All it required was money and that was no problem. It was essential that the master of the vessel should believe that he really had a returning settler, so I was to be the go-between, with the fiction that Mr Provis would be joining the ship at practically the last moment of sailing as he had to come in from the very interior of the country.

On a warm January evening, following a heavy shower that cooled the decks, and with the lightest of breezes that made being on board a vessel in the harbour a delight, we assembled for a dinner to say fare thee well to Mr Provis. He had successfully ridden in from the outback and been rowed out to the ship where we would all enjoy a hearty dinner, with the exception of one who would be taken ill and have to be rowed ashore and helped to his horse.

This would be a certain Abel Magwitch who on reaching home would be so ill that he would be bedridden for weeks.

Despite, or maybe because of the danger, we were noisily boisterous, exhibiting behaviour that under normal circumstances I would have deplored.

My husband was not there as he was dispensing justice on a circuit that meant much travelling. You do not need to know who else was at that dinner. We ate roast mutton, roast potatoes and greens, washed down with so much wine that the master said in mock alarm:

"Desist, I pray you, for we shall have naught for our voyage."

At the meal's end we went ashore, including a gentleman who, having been helped from the skiff, said in a muffled voice as he had his cloak close wrapped around him:

"I am not well. Was that mutton not off?"

The two men ashore, standing knee-deep in the surf holding the boat steady, exchanged amused glances, as they knew that such illnesses could often result from an excess of spirits unwisely indulged in. Despite his moans however, the gentleman, who to all intents seemed to resemble Abel Magwitch, mounted his horse and rode off, several people bidding him: "Goodnight Abel."

Two days later we heard from Abel's homestead that he had taken to his bed with extreme ague, the flux and vomiting. However the doctor who managed to visit him several days later found that he had recovered sufficiently to ride out on an extended tour of the farthest reaches of his lands. So we attempted to fool the authorities, not realising that others knew of his departure; others who would profit from informing the authorities of his arrival in England.

We simply believed that having got him onto a ship in disguise he was safe. We knew that he planned to change ships and by so doing would not appear to have come to England from Australia.

I thought that he ought to have gone beyond England and so make it seem that he had come from America or somewhere equally foreign. But Abel had made up his mind as to how he would do it, and he was a stubborn man. Besides, he said to me, I cannot wait too long to see my boy as I have made a gentleman. My years upon this earth are not infinite.

What if I should die before I acquaint him with the truth about who his real benefactor is? He seemed to think that this would be a real tragedy. We know now that a real tragedy could have been avoided had Abel not been so pig-headed. We also know now that Compeyson, the constant devil in Abel's life, was yet to make the final appearance in the tragedy that was not only to bring down Abel but would also destroy Pip as a gentleman.

Chapter 25

Knighted !

It was Christmas 1844 and we celebrated it with roast beef, thinking that, although it was still strange to be eating our Christmas dinner in the heat, we felt at ease about it in a way that we had not felt before. Up to now I suppose that life in the colony was still strange and a struggle and it was because we still felt that we were Britons that we clung to our previous ways and thoughts. This year however it seemed less important. We had made a new life for ourselves in this new country. I for one would never now go back to the old one.

Why return to London or Portsmouth when Sydney had churches, a museum and streets, where the streets were busy with all kinds of horse drawn traffic including hackney carriages. And the country!

The country, when you had a chance to see it, overwhelmed you with its sheer size, grandeur and richness.

We had everything except gold. But God help us if someone discovers that commodity, said Arthur. My feelings were also influenced by the news that there were plans to build a proper Government House. My word! We were becoming respectable!

More and more people were paying to come as settlers. Australia had changed, without our realising it, from a penal colony to a land of opportunity. I wanted to know how this had happened. Arthur gave it as his opinion that hard work, money and politics had done it.

He said:

"When you consider that there was nothing here in 1789; and that by the time you came in 1815, we had only been here twenty-five years, but had already established ourselves, it's truly amazing.

Then over the next thirty years, look at all the things we have done. We even have a distillery where the finest gin is produced!"

"Yes, that must count as a most civilised step forward", I replied.

Arthur ignored my ironic tone and continued:

"I tell you that we cannot remain a separate group of states, nor can we just remain a colony of England. Look at what happened in America."

I closed my eyes and Arthur's voice droned on. I fell asleep. Arthur did not mind. He knew that his efforts in politics were producing results and they were more than a gin distillery!

Looking back I suppose that it was something that I should have expected. Arthur was a respected man, a clever barrister, a judge and an adviser to the government.

Nevertheless it still made me gasp and look for a chair to sink down into when he told me that in the honours list he would be appearing as a knight.

Naturally I shall not have to go to England for the ceremony, he told me. And in due course at a ceremony in Sydney he was invested into the most Noble Order of the Bath, or some such order. All I remember is the extremely pompous and self-important behaviour of some people who I remember in the past were glad to scramble with the rest of for a living!

You do know that this now means that you are officially a lady, Arthur told me. I examined my hands and got up and looked in the mirror. He looked surprised at my so doing.

"You know", I said, "despite what you have just told me, I cannot for the life of me detect any difference in my appearance. Maybe it will come out in my behaviour, which, I must say, will remain pretty well the same."

I went back to the mirror. I remembered looking into one the day that Elias died. I know that it is vanity, but I think that I still look much as I did then.

I still have most of my teeth, thanks to having avoided sugar, so my smile remains as it was. I also have the hair that I felt so proud of when I was a girl. To be sure I also still have the constant back-ache that Doctor Roseberry says is common in ladies of my age!

Chapter 26

I meet Pip

In all the time that I helped Abel in his endeavours to make Pip a gentleman, it never crossed my mind that one day I might meet him, so it was a complete surprise when this sad looking gentleman appeared at my husband's chambers asking for me. At that time I both managed our farming interests that had grown considerably, and my husband's legal affairs, in that I assisted his clerk. My surprise grew into delight as he introduced himself. Of course I was wary because of the nature of Abel's return to England, but when I heard how Abel had been betrayed and was now dead my wariness turned to sorrow and not a little anger.

I was able to take Mr Pirrip into a private chamber where he told me that he had travelled to Port Adelaide on the Symmetry arriving on the 7th November.

He had then made his way to Sydney. He had come around the coast preferring the sea to our indifferent roads and was staying at the Aarons Hotel. I insisted that he came to stay with us and he thanked me and said that he would indeed like to stay with us if that was not putting us to any great trouble.

We went home and on the way he remarked upon the buildings that we passed, saying that parts of London were undoubtedly grand, but other parts such as Whitechapel and Shoreditch were slums that ought to be pulled down and rebuilt. He thought that Sydney deserved status as a city. I asked him whether he might stay in Australia and he said that he had no plans at the present time.

Once at home, he told me the details of how Abel had been betrayed, how Compeyson had perished during the abortive attempt to get Abel away to safety at Hamburg, and how he and Herbert Pocket had avoided being arrested themselves.

He said that Compeyson must have used his network of disaffected men in England to keep himself informed so, despite Pip and Herbert's best efforts, he was always hard upon their heels.

Pip said that he knew that two men had been seen whilst he and Herbert were with Abel at the Ship Inn. He did not know whether they were Compeyson's men or part of the London Police. I asked whether he could not have ignored the police. After all I said, surely they cannot command much respect in England. He told me that despite the initial anger against the idea of a police force that was seen as something foreign, they were now accepted, as crime had diminished since they started. In the eighteen thirties, he said, things in London were desperate. There are still problems now but they are lessened.

I asked why he and Herbert had not been arrested for assisting a returned convict?

Pip explained that Wemmick, Jagger's clerk, had spoken to the authorities and persuaded them that both Pip and

Herbert had been taken in by a notorious crook, Abel Magwitch. Magwitch, he said, had lied to them that he was a rich Australian seeking to settle somewhere in Europe, who so convinced them that they were totally taken in by the rogue.

Jaggers, as a good lawyer, had nodded at this fiction, having carefully kept himself free from any involvement that might be to his disadvantage. I recognised the actions of a discreet man of law.

At ease as we were, I asked why he had decided to come to Australia. His visit was prompted initially by the fact that he was still estranged from Estella; but he also desired to meet me having heard so much about me from Abel. He thought that I must be a truly remarkable woman to have risen above my earlier trials and wanted to meet me, so I offered to tell him my whole story.

This I duly did when Arthur, having made Pip welcome, departed upon one of his circuits. Pip was in no danger, but I and several others in Australia were. He saw immediately the need to keep the story secret, at least until Arthur and I and several other good people had departed this world. It might, in future, make a story worth relating, but not yet.

In the meantime, as we had no children and Pip was in no hurry to return to England, we took him into our family and found him employment. As time passed he became almost like a son to us. So much so that we decided to ensure that in our wills he would inherit substantially. In other words he would have great expectations.

Part three

Made an Australian

Pip's Story

Prologue

I stood up and looked around me. As far as the eye could see there were tents or small shacks and a constant grinding level of noise made by a wave of workers that made it difficult to hear anyone or anything else. The air was laced with the smell of food being cooked and smoke from the fires doing the cooking. I hunkered down feeling nauseous. My companion was still asleep wrapped in his grubby blanket. I envied his ability to sleep in this turmoil.

I faced another day of unrelenting effort that would leave my body aching even more than it did now. It was already hot and the sun had scarcely risen. Later on the heat would intensify. I would become even dirtier than I was now. As it became hotter I would sweat and stink even more than I did now. The flies would cluster about me, disgusting me.

How had my life come to this? Why was I labouring like a convict in a penal colony? Just two weeks ago I was living in a civilised household in Sydney, waited on by servants and going to work in an office where little was required of me save regular attendance. In short, I had a sinecure.

This is how Pip's account begins of what happened to him once he arrived in Australia. You will have read in "Amanda Jane's Story" how she assisted Abel Magwitch to make a gentleman of Pip. Both she and Arthur Spens welcomed Pip and treated him as the son they never had. His future looked serene. This account, which was found in a drawer of a desk when an old house was being remodelled, tells another story.

Pip embarked in London on The Symmetry on 24th June 1845 and arrived at Port Adelaide on 7th November, before going on to Sydney. He must have travelled incognito, not wishing to travel under his real name after all the problems that he had had in London.

Chapter 1

Goldrush

I stood up and looked around me. As far as the eye could see there were tents or small shacks and a constant grinding level of noise made by a wave of workers that made it difficult to hear anyone or anything else. The air was laced with the smell of food being cooked and smoke from the fires doing the cooking. I hunkered down feeling nauseous. My companion was still asleep wrapped in his grubby blanket. I envied his ability to sleep in this turmoil.

I faced another day of unrelenting effort that would leave my body aching even more than it did now. It was already hot and the sun had scarcely risen. Later on the heat would intensify. I would become even dirtier than I was now. As it became hotter I would sweat and stink even more than I did now. The flies would cluster about me, disgusting me.

How had my life come to this? Why was I labouring like a convict in a penal colony? Just two weeks ago I was living in a civilised household in Sydney, waited on by servants and going to work in an office where little was required of me save regular attendance. In short, I had a sinecure.

My clothes were laundered regularly, and clean hot water was available when I shaved using the finest steel razors imported from Europe. When I went to work I rode in a carriage drawn by a well-groomed horse. And yet I felt every day that my life lacked direction and meaning. I still missed Estella and had no-one else to fill the empty space that she had left when we parted in England.

I had even contemplated becoming a soldier, going into battle to wrest a standard from the enemy, then returning in glorious triumph. But the officers that I come into contact with persuaded me that buying a commission would simply allow me to enter a world where hard drinking and hard riding, hunting dingoes instead of foxes, would be my life. The days of glory where one led one's men to victory were over.

Amanda Jane and Arthur were sympathetic. They knew what had driven me to Australia and also knew that I still had to find my own way there. In the meantime they treated me as the son that they never had. Arthur had found me employment and I lived with them. But they had other real relatives, and they were much less sympathetic to me when the blow fell.

Chapter 2

I lose my Benefactors

I had known that both Arthur and Amanda Jane, or as I should properly call them, Sir Arthur Spens and Lady Amanda Jane Spens, had had health troubles that were exacerbated as a result of living in Australia. Lady Amanda had been transported to Australia as a convict and had suffered extreme privations, and Sir Arthur's health had always been frail. But it still came as a tremendous shock when both succumbed to a fever and died within weeks of each other. I am convinced that as Lady Amanda died first, Sir Arthur quickly followed her into his grave for his heart was broken. I knew from what Amanda Jane had told me, when I first sought her out, that he had lost his first wife because of the Australian climate.

I had come to Australia in 1845 to find out how Magwitch had been assisted by Amanda when he was transported here as a convict. I wanted to know more about the circumstances that made it possible for him to send money back to England to Jaggers. Jaggers was the lawyer who took me away from my life as a blacksmith on the instructions of Abel Magwitch and so ensured that I became a gentleman. Both Sir Arthur and Lady Amanda Jane took me into their household and treated me as the son that they never had. Lady Amanda told me her story but swore me to secrecy as it concerned others who had assisted Magwitch to return to England.

Then came the news of a gold strike in Australia. We read about it in the papers, and tales of men picking up gold nuggets out of the earth and making a fortune began to make me wonder if I too should go and do likewise. Both Amanda and Arthur were appalled at the very idea. They knew from their earlier experiences what sort of men would be in the rush. I was not to be dissuaded however. I had some money that I had put aside during the time that I had been in Australia and I determined to use it to equip myself. I had heard that it was necessary to have more than just a spade and a tent. I would be prepared so that no matter how hard the work was I would overcome all difficulties and so return with a fortune!

But now added to the blow of their death came yet another. Despite all that they had done to make sure that following their deaths I should be cared for, I was informed that Sir Arthur's relatives were disputing the will. And, as if that were not enough, they were insisting that I leave Althrop House immediately, a house where I had been so well-received when I had first come to Australia. Lady Amanda Jane's money was, of course, assumed to be that of her husband.

To add to my misery of losing benefactors, money and a place to live, I was informed, quite brusquely, that I was no longer required in my post. It seemed that the fact that I had it depended upon Sir Arthur. With him gone someone else could be given it. Someone, I was told, who was Sterling.

I had told Estella, when I had returned briefly to England to see Joe and Biddy, that I worked pretty hard for a living that I considered sufficient. I meant of course that I laboured in an office. We had met by accident when I visited Satis House, where I learned that she had let it decay as she only owned the ground now. I did not ask how she maintained her station as a lady, deciding that it would have been impertinent of me to do so. We parted as friends but I wished that I might have been more. I returned to Sydney and my life of office work and dinners. It was at one of these dinners that I first met Edward Hammond Hargreaves.

I sat for some time remembering the last conversation that I had had with Edward where he had tried to persuade me to go to California with him to dig for gold. I had laughed then. Digging in the dirt was not something that gentlemen did. Edward, despite being quite an odd sort of a chap, was always welcome at Althrop House.
We had been discussing farming as the way in which the country could be enriched, when Edward said that the true wealth in any colony was in the soil, and was gold, silver and other precious metals. Even tin, he said, was valuable if found in sufficient quantities.

"I am shortly leaving for California to seek gold," he added. "What about coming along with me Pip?"

I was astounded. Such a thought had never occurred to me. In any case would it be altogether proper for a gentleman to dig in the dirt? This invitation came back to me later when I met Edward on his return from America. I had thought that he would have been depressed at returning with nothing to show for all his efforts. But, not a bit of it. He was rather even more ebullient than before and I soon learned the reason why.

He explained that as he had worked his claims in California he had noticed that the gold occurred more frequently where there were certain outcrops of clay or rock. These outcrops, were to his way of thinking, similar to those that he had seen in Australia. By Australia, he explained, he meant New South Wales. He told me about it in the most matter of fact way, and to tell you the truth I simply thought that he was rattling on as he so often did, so I gave it little heed. Instead I poured him another drink and we returned to inconsequential gossip. Later on rumours circulated that the government were paying him to look for gold for them. Then I heard that they were not paying him but that he had claimed a government reward for having found a goldfield. He had recruited others to look on his behalf having taught them how to prospect. I thought that if I had maintained my friendship with Edward it might have been me that he had recruited. "There is a tide in the affairs of men....."

I later learned that he had indeed found gold, and in such quantities that he was saying all sorts of extravagant things. He named the district where he found the gold Ophir and said that he would go down in history and that he would be made a lord. I cannot now remember what else he said but it inflamed me to action as it did many others. So, having lost my benefactors, my home and my employment, I determined to do what so many others were doing. I collected my little store of money that I had saved and went down to the harbour seeking a boat to go to the goldfields to pick up nuggets and make my fortune. There I found the Speyside, and upon a payment of what I considered to be a vast sum of money I was allowed to embark, having been warned that I would need to provide food and drink for myself as none would be provided on board.

Chapter 3

On the Speyside

It was on the Speyside, a ship that sailed from Sydney to Melbourne, that I met Tony Magrello, who was one of a party of prospectors that had been in America. The Speyside had been taking prospectors from Australia to the Californian goldfields and was now taking them to the ones in Australia He spoke to me and soon knew that I had money with which I planned to buy equipment. He offered to help me choose the right stuff, saying that as a new chum I would be swindled if I had no-one looking after my interests. Tony was a short, bandy-legged man whose legs served him well enough in mining operations but were a distinct hindrance when he needed to walk any great distance. His upper body was muscular and his forearms, that were tattooed with faded indistinct pictures, ended in large brown hands with stubby fingers and broken nails. He had a broad brow above surprisingly light blue eyes, a wide jaw with several missing teeth and a thick neck around which he constantly sported a red neckerchief. In repose his face fell into a frown. He often frowned in concentration when tackling a difficult task. His frowns quickly went however when he was amused or diverted.

A few men on the boat were really tough characters who had previous experience of the goldfields in California, but the main body of seekers was a mixture of young hopefuls and old - *last throw of the dice* –timers. All had been dazzled by the tales of wealth that could simply be picked up. And this was true, as the canvas bags of gold that steadily came to the ships in the harbour to be banked testified. Some were labourers with work-hardened hands. Others, like me, were soft specimens, all dreams and no muscles.

The Speyside was very crowded. Indeed, I only sailed with her by taking a place on deck where, with many others, I prayed that we might avoid truly bad weather. Luckily we made good time and, with some exceptions where some office boys overindulged in spirituous liquor, we avoided sea sickness. You cannot imagine what a mixture we were. I was nowhere near the eldest. We had grizzled old miners, cardsharps, shop hands, sailors. Persons from every trade and calling seemed to believe that they only had to dig in the dirt and they would be fabulously rich in a few days. None seemed to consider that they might not be so. All spoke constantly about what they intended to do once they had made their pile.

The Chinese huddled together and were regarded with suspicion by the others. Their clothing, almost universally blue cotton blouses and trousers that was loose and baggy, were eminently more sensible than what most us wore. I resolved that I would trade in my respectable garb for something more workmanlike as soon as I was able to.

As I walked around the deck I saw that only a few were really tough types such as I had seen in Deptford near the London Docks. I could see that they had well developed bodies and one, whose hand I had clasped, as I was introduced to him by Tony, made me wince at his grip. He laughed at my expression.

"You are surely not going to dig with those soft hands? I can see that you are a stranger to real work. A gentleman like you don't belong here. How did you come to this country? "

I tried to assume an attitude of indifference to his comments but to be honest I was worried that I had taken this bold step, and it was only having Tony at my side that encouraged me to persevere.

When we landed at the port, amongst a forest of masts of abandoned ships, we stampeded to the small government shack where we paid our first thirty shillings for a month's permission to hack out of the soil what technically belonged to the Queen. According to the law, everything belonged to her, and the authorities in Victoria made sure that if someone wished to dig in her dirt they had to pay for the privilege.

It took me some while to get my licence as I had to wait patiently as others got theirs first. Then, with that important piece of paper firmly stowed away, Tony and I moved on to buy gear. Many had brought their own. Some were bent almost double under their loads. They still needed provisions however, and top of the list was canned meat. I smiled weakly as Tony bought several tins of 'tinned dog'. My how the prices had increased! Even I, who had had someone else to supply my food in the past, recognised that we were being gouged. Still, we reasoned we could easily get all this outlay back once we had gathered our share of the golden dust that we heard littered the country inland.

Getting there was no problem. You walked. Very few had horses. Just another mouth to feed, and something else to look after when you might be gathering gold nuggets and putting them into your pockets. And where to go was no problem. A steady stream of men snaked out from the port and we just joined them. I asked Tony whether we shouldn't be trying some new fields. He looked at me in disgust. Where would that be? he wanted to know. Did I have some intelligence of a place where the gold was waiting for us?

I kept quiet after that and hefted my pack onto my back and blessed Tony for his advice in packing it so that it sat snugly on my back. My shovel was strapped safely on the very back. He had advised me to pick a solid one that would not disintegrate, saying that I might need it to defend my claim as well as work it. My tent was the smallest that I could buy as Tony told me that I would not be spending much time in it. Sleeping when I could be digging did not make much sense when I had paid good money for a licence that would run out in a month.

As we marched along I calculated out loud how many days we had in which to make our fortune, for I assumed that we would scarcely be working on Sundays. This made Tony snort with laughter. So I again kept quiet. Obviously I had much to learn. In effect many diggers did keep the Sabbath, but as the Celestials did not there was an immediate source of friction between them and Christians. The Europeans who kept the Sabbath saw the Celestials gathering gold while they did not. It was made worse as the miners were able, on Sundays, to see what was happening in contrast to the weekdays when they were so busy that they had no time to be envious of the Celestials.

We staked a claim and began digging. Near us were others including several women, a fact that surprised me as I had supposed that all the diggers would be men. Some were helping their men folk, but a few seemed to be working on their own despite the fact that no licences to dig were taken up by women. I ascertained this at a later stage when I had more time for observations of this sort. They tucked up their skirts and fastened them out of the way then set to at the rockers at such a pace that I would have been pleased to have reached. I often started well but as the day wore on and it got hotter and my hands hurt and my back ached I slowed down. Even the women seemed to find me a joke. Certainly most of the men did.

By contrast, Tony worked steadily and easily, singing Italian love songs that amused me initially then irritated me, as he did not have a very large repertoire. At least it was a change from the hymns that a particularly red-faced digger working nearby chose to accompany his labour. At times he would stand up and ask us belligerently whether we were not all on a duffer rush. He was a hatter who had dropped on it previously, made a small fortune then drank it all away, or so Tony said, who seemed to have an unfailing source of information about everything and everybody. He also spoke in an argot that was as strange to me as any that I had heard in London. Constant repetition soon made the argot and the strange phrases more familiar to my ear.

It was this same man that got into difficulties one day, for he had neglected to shore up the sides of his hole sufficiently, and as a result it began to slide in onto him. I heard his wail of terror as he scrabbled madly to extricate himself. Calling to Tony I slid through the sticky mud that was everywhere, occasioned by the floods that we had had in previous days. Together we used planks and other materials to hold back the edges, and then, as others arrived, we managed to fashion a sling from an old canvas hammock. This we got round him, and having some ex sailors in the now large crowd of helpers, they showed us how to set up some sheer legs. With so many hauling on the rope attached to the sling we were soon able to suck him out of the mud and lay him on the side of his hole.

If we were expecting thanks then we were disappointed. This hymn-singing Christian abused us all roundly for knocking in the side of his hole and swore that we were all trying to frighten him away from his legitimate claim. Several of the miners were all for stuffing him back into his hole but cooler heads prevailed and we left him to make what he could of the mess.

I was utterly drained and readily took a drop of, what a women who was selling it swore was, best port wine. It was nothing of the sort; it was the crudest grog but it bucked me up no end and I bought Tony a pannekin of it for us to share later. I'm afraid that this then became a habit with us. Our food was so awful, as neither of us could really cook, that we needed something, first to wash down what we produced, and last, to take the taste away and cheer us up. We needed cheering up for so far, apart from the smallest amount of gold- dust, we had not dropped on it at all. The problem was that we did find some gold. Had we found none I think we might have abandoned the whole enterprise. We saw others doing this. They sold their gear and made their way back to where they had started.

My stomach constantly reminded me that it needed decent food. I several times had dysentery, and having fallen and cut my face I was constantly bothered by flies that seemed to find my bloody cuts irresistible. My hands were swollen, despite the rags that I had wrapped around them in a vain attempt to protect them, as I laboured like an English navvy. The latest pain that I had to endure was an inflammation that turned into a carbuncle that I had lanced but still gave me much pain. Delicacy dictates that I cannot indicate that part of my body where it erupted. I can say though that I had much difficulty in sitting with any sort of comfort or ease. Unlike Tony, who had lice, I at least avoided that indignity as I scrupulously washed myself, using water that was so precious that it cost us gold dust to buy it. Tony affected to be scandalized at my waste of clean water.

Had I neglected to wear a hat I should also have suffered from the sun. It did not seem to bother Tony, whose shock of frizzy hair, that he refused to have cut, defended his head from sunburn. A small man, with short thick legs and a thickset tors, he said that in fact he was Sardinian and that some of his ancestors came from Africa. Despite his lice and the fact that he smelled atrocious, he seemed a favourite with the various women who sold grog or other things. He told me that his secret was that he treated them all as ladies. He spent a great deal of time on occasions talking to them and when I reproached him he would produce a slice of mutton or half a loaf of only slightly stale bread as evidence that he had not been wasting his time.

Chapter 4

You are stupid

As I stood there in the dirt, noise, stench and heat, a young man approached me. He eyed me and told me that he had been watching my progress, or rather lack of progress, for some time. He was very young and well dressed and had an air about him of someone who knew what he was about. His first words to me as he squatted beside me were a shock.

"You are stupid to grub in the dirt like these others, like an animal, instead of behaving like an educated gentleman which you so obviously are. Why don't you copy me?"

"What should I do?"

"Ask the diggers to give you what they have been collecting with their labour."

I stood there incredulous.

"Ask them to give me their gold! Why should they do that?"

" Because you will give them what they must have."

"And what is that?"

"Food, clothes, anything to enable them to continue in their stupidity. Have you seen how they behave when they do strike it rich?"

I had indeed and I had marvelled at the way in which hard earned gold was squandered on the most trivial of things. Champagne, absurd clothing, personal ornamentation of every kind and meals that were often fed to the dogs as they were far too big to be consumed.

"And where will I get such things?"

He rose, took hold of my dirty jacket, and led me to a small shack where several celestials were gathered.

"I am John Adam and these are my associates, for what that is worth. I came here, as you did, to seek my fortune as I did not wish to follow the example of my parents who have slaved hard all their lives, for starvation rates. They are tailors, or rather my father is, and my mother is a seamstress. They have a small business in Melbourne. I quickly realised that my fortune would not be made as a tailor, but would be made here, but not by fossicking in the ground."

He stopped.

"Have you read the Wealth of Nations?"

I was taken aback by this sudden change of topic.

"No. Is it by Charles Dickens?"

He gave a short barking laugh that owed little to his being amused.

"My God, but you sterlings are all the same. You come out here and lord it over us currencies. Then when we scratch at your shiny paint it comes off and what do we find?"

He paused with eyebrows raised in question.

I gestured my inability to give a sensible answer.

"We find", he began deliberately, "We find that you have not begun to take advantage of the education and money that you have had poured out on you, but instead you rely upon nepotism and favouritism. Then, when you do strike out on your own, you descend to the levels where you try to emulate the workers instead of using your brains. That is if you have any", he finished bitterly.

He sighed heavily and somewhat theatrically.

"But I need you."

As he said this he was interrupted by a cry.

"There he is, don't let him get away the dirty blodger."

Other men, also calling out, ran at me. I was grasped so that I could not use my arms. I was pushed into the side of the shack. I felt the rough cut timbers against my cheek. My arms were twisted. I was forced onto my knees and I felt the muck suck at them.

"Hold on," said John.

"Never mind 'Hold on' ", said a big man with a leather hat. "He's killed his mate."

I was dragged by a group of men back to my dig where Tony lay with the blanket now pulled back, revealing bloody gashes and crusted blood. John followed and stood looking.

"There", said leather hat, releasing me, "Your mate, dead."

My head ached. The noise went on and the flies swarmed about Tony Magrello and the sweating men. They landed on my neck. I dabbed at them ineffectually.

"Well?" said my leather-hatted tormentor pushing me against the rocker.

All the hate engendered by my situation rose in my chest and would have emerged as words, had we not been interrupted by the cry of:

"Blues!"

At the shout of "blues" the crowd around me moved away, except my captor. He held me tightly as the two constables clumped clumsily through the muck. The younger one looked as if he was going to be sick.

The older one said, "What's this?"

My captor, still holding my arms, pointed at the body with his chin.

"He killed him, his mate, took his gold, tried to make a run for it but I stopped him. Go on search him. I caught him for you."

I stood mute as the blues searched me.

"No gold here."

I coughed. I felt ill. They all looked at me. John pushed towards me. I put my jacket on again as John stood beside me.

"I know nothing of this. We drank too much last night. I fell asleep and when I awoke I thought Tony was asleep still. I certainly did not run off."

"No, I took him to meet my business colleagues", said John.

He indicated his shack where there was no sign now of any C(elestials. I was to learn that one of their skills was to disappear when there was any trouble.

Chapter 5

I enter trade

The big man with the leather hat said "Sorry mate. That other bastard told us that you had done it."

I shook his hand and told him that I accepted his apology. He later became one of our best customers. And so I learned a basic tenet: be sweet to everyone, as you never know when they will come to you asking for something that you might be able to provide.

Later on I was told that thefts of gold were common. Sometimes a tent would be slit open to make it easier to get at the dust. Maybe Tony woke to find that we were being robbed, tried to stop it and paid the dearest price. I later found that many such murders were also commonplace.

Left on our own, John repeated:

"I need you."

I wanted to know why.

He said:

"I want you to be one of us because you are educated and a gentleman. Normally I deal with all sorts of scum, but occasionally I have to meet more sophisticated people. As you see I am young, but do not be fooled, I do know how to make money. Sometimes though I need an older front man and I think that you will do nicely."

I looked at him. He was certainly younger than I was and held himself well, as if he knew exactly what to do in any situation. His swarthy face was topped with a full head of hair that obviously needed, and received, the attention of a barber on a regular basis. His dark eyes glistened. They darted about as if to seek out any and all opportunities, whatever they might be. When they lighted upon me I felt that he saw through my hesitation and weaknesses. A man to please the ladies in terms of looks, though his nose was bigger than is conventionally accepted as increasing the good looks of a gentleman. But whereas a lady with a large nose is a lady with a large nose, a gentleman with a large nose is said to have character.

I was tired, hungry and thirsty and I had just lost my partner and, it turned out, all the meagre amount of gold that we had scraped from the clay. So I did not take umbrage at what I would normally have considered an overweening attitude. I let myself be led to the shack where, wonderful sight, were bacon and eggs frying in a pan. I would have fallen to immediately had John not offered me, more wonderfully, warm water and soap to wash myself, and a passably clean towel.

After I had eaten John said:

"Now come with me."

I was loath to leave my tent and all my possessions. Tony had already been taken away and his pitifully few chattels were not worth worrying about, but I had a few things that I thought I should like to keep. Amongst them was my copy of

Shakespeare and a good steel razor. But when I collected these the remainder of my gear hardly seemed worthy of any effort on my part. And I was increasingly feeling that I could no longer go on. The flies on my face and the swollen place on my leg where something had bitten me aggravated me and lowered my mood.

I stumbled after John who strode on to where his horse was being minded by a young Celestial. Roughly pushing him to one side he beckoned to me to get on the horse, that he led to a tavern. And so I left the scene where during both day and night there had been disturbances of all kinds. I had experienced stabbings, shootings, stealing and every sort of mayhem imaginable to man, or woman, for there were quite a few women there too. Some were poor creatures drawn there to be with their men. They frequently sat outside what passed as their dwellings, poor assemblies of logs, bushes, canvas and every mismatch of all sorts of materials that would serve to keep off the sun and keep out the rain when it came.

I had avoided them and their offers to me of grog that many sold as a means of living. However, one could not but gaze at them as in their awfulness of dishevelled hair and loose clothing they had a fatal attraction. For as much as real ladies were clean, comely, tidy and fragrant, with sweetly combed hair, these were the complete opposite. And their language was nothing at all like a lady's. I had seen many men blanche at hearing these harridans haranguing all who came anywhere near them, especially when they were drunk; and some seemed to be in a constant state of intoxication.

In the taver, I enjoyed again the utter bliss and absolute balm of hot water. My razor, aided by soap that one of John's Celestials provided, removed most of my stubble, leaving a less wild-eyed face gazing back at me from a shard of a mirror. Clean clothes and some ointments for my face and leg assisted the process of returning me to what I had hitherto regarded as normality.

I began to thank the Celestial who had assisted me, only to be stopped by John who said irritably:

" Don't bother. He can't understand you, and anyway he's a bloody heathen, not worth bothering with."

"But they work for you."

"That doesn't mean to say that I have to like them. In fact I dislike them very much. They are Godless sinners who adore heathen idols. If they were to embrace Christianity that would be different. In any case they stick together and try to cut out the white men. They will work for far less than a white man and for that I despise them. They will even work on the Lord's Day.

I could only say again:

"But they work for you."

John threw up his hands in a gesture of despair.

"Oh, whenever will you learn. You will never get on in this world if you keep thinking about others. It's number one that you have to keep in mind."

I was silent. I waited. Eventually, as I ate some bread and drank some halfway decent coffee, John stopped pacing about and began:

"I have been keeping my eye on you. I have decided that I ought to help you."

"That doesn't sound like looking out for number one."

"Well, it is as you could be a help to me. I am expanding my business. I need someone that I can trust. Someone who has experience of the situation here but also understands how things get arranged. I have achieved a great deal but every now and again I seem to run up against petty officialdom. Sometimes it's merely stupidity, but at other times it's more; it's an arrant attempt to keep me in my place."

"Which is?"

"All right, I admit it. I'm a jumped-up son of a tailor whose background is probably that of a government man."·

"Government man?"

"All right, a convict. You, on the other hand are a gentleman. You know how to approach people, how to soft-soap them, how to be at ease with them so that contracts can be discussed and bargains struck. After all, if you, as a gentleman, strike a bargain, you will keep it. Your word will be accepted, unlike mine", he concluded bitterly.

" I may not be the gentleman you think I am."

"You look and sound and behave like one."

"All that glisters is not gold", I said sadly, holding out my battered and grimy copy of Shakespeare's plays.

"There you are then", he said excitedly. "That's exactly my point. Who but an educated swell would quote from a book? I don't know what you mean but it sounds perfect to me."

So I entered another world; a world where gold was king and money was queen. And what did I become? Well, I became a most successful merchant. I salved my conscience somewhat by schooling John so that he too took on the outward trappings of an educated gentleman. I persuaded myself that I was doing this so that John might have the educational advantages that came with my tuition. I enjoyed the process. It gave me much satisfaction to introduce John to sonnets, to plays that explored the human condition, to books that stretched his mind and made him think.

But all the time, within me something gnawed at that idea, something that said that not only was I not a gentleman, but I was assisting John to pass himself off as one. And, was I not doing for John what Magwitch had done for me? I pondered this idea in the long hot nights when the temperature seem not to go down but to stay as hot as if the sun still shone. Was Magwitch right in assisting me to be something that I was not? Was I right to help John to pass in society as a gentleman? Did it matter? If so, to whom?

Chapter 6

Escape from hell

I continued to work in the goldfields, but now I was engaged in a wholly different sort of enterprise. As I went about my business, I marvelled at the ease with which the country was despoiled. John said, and I agreed with him, that no matter what heaven on earth men discovered they soon turned it into hell on earth. He bore some of the blame for the changes that were wrought in the name of individual prosperity. I too can scarcely plead ignorance of the way we attacked the land. I wondered whether it would ever recover. I was comforted somewhat when I saw places where men had torn out whole sides of ravines which, now they had yielded their golden treasure, began to be reclaimed by nature. Then I turned to where before me hundreds of tents, or things that passed as tents, covered the ground as far as I could see. Everywhere in between them there were holes in the ground. The ground was clay in the main. It was yellow. Not yellow like gold, but a dirty yellow. The holes were of all shapes and sizes depending upon the whim of the miner who had dug them. They also followed where gold had been discovered. I was always careful to watch my step as I walked around these holes, as it was easy to fall into them, and some contained water that stank, either because it was simply stagnant or because some rubbish or animal parts had been discarded in them.

The noise was continuous and didn't stop even at night, although it did take on a different quality, reflecting the brawling and carousing and occasional gunfire, in place of the unceasing rumble of digging and rocking of cradles that went on all day.

Many men and women were ravaged by diseases which got no treatment as we had so few doctors. The way in which we lived, the diet we most of us existed upon and the fashion of our shelter from the elements, all contributed to a collective state of misery. As I moved amongst the miners, I remarked upon this to John. I wanted to know if anything could be worse. In answer he took me to hear how several miners had lost their way, once they had struck out on their own, and had later been found dead. One account told of a digger who had been found curled up as if asleep. He was surrounded by his belongings, and looked as if he could have been awakened. The only problem was that he had been reduced to a skeleton. Wild animals had torn at him leaving him only his gun and other items that served to identify him. At least it was determined who he was.

Another man was found dying lying under a fallen tree where he had crawled for shelter. They gave him food and water but he was too far gone to save. Unfortunately he was a foreigner and no-one could understand his pathetic last words. He constantly repeated them and became increasingly agitated as no-one responded. He died still repeating them, and once he had done so, his belongings were searched for clues as to his identity. There were none. Was he really worse off than the still alive miners?

I remarked that it was all a lottery as was most things in life. John angrily disagreed. He thought that if you worked hard and used the correct technique, then you could increase your chances of becoming rich. You had to learn how to puddle and use a cradle and develop skills such as tin washing to get a fortune. You had to learn from others and to do so quickly. I asked him how he had started, and he told me that it was by gathering up the discarded items that would-be miners had set out with. Apparently many of them had equipped themselves so thoroughly, that well before they reached the diggings, they came to realise that they had overburdened themselves. Consequently they simply abandoned thoroughly good equipment or clothes that John collected and sold. This gave him capital that he used to buy more supplies, which he then sold. I remembered how Tony had cautioned me against buying too much clobber that we would only regret having to haul all the way to the fields.

Thinking of Tony made me ask John whether we should do something about him. He looked at me astonished.

"He's dead, what more is there to be done?

" We might seek out his murderer. Perhaps we should offer to bury him."

"Not our business. The blues will look for someone they can accuse. Anyway, I expect he is buried by now. In this heat it is necessary to get the bodies underground as soon as possible. He might have been a chum of yours, but I'm sure you won't miss him now he's gone."

John was right. I did not miss Tony. I was so taken up with all that I was learning that it left little time for anything else. One day John said that he thought that we might put our association on a more regular footing. He proposed that we should be partners. He said that I had learned enough for us to set up together in business. He added that I was not to think that he was doing this for my sake. I waited and he explained that he feared that if he did not take me on as a full blown partner that I would leave him and set up on my own in competition!

Chapter 7

Adam and Pirrip

And so was born:

Adam and Pirrip
Purveyors of Excellent Supplies.

I met people and dealt with them as suppliers whilst John organised what we should buy and the prices that we should charge. He also organised the premises, as we quickly moved from tents, that were hung about with red flags to indicate that we were emporiums, to more sophisticated premises. As we did so, so did others. Banks appeared along with saloons, hotels, shops and theatres. The latter were particularly popular as the miners were starved of entertainment and now many of them had the wherewithal to purchase it. All sorts of singers, dancers and entertainers, whose acts defied description until one had seen them, arrived drawn by gold.

As we moved from our original ramshackle half tent store to more permanent buildings our reputation grew. Unfortunately it was a reputation that had several parts to it. First, our suppliers knew that they could totally rely upon us to pay in full and in time. John insisted upon that. When occasionally we received goods that were not up to scratch, he simply paid up and we never did business with that supplier again. He said that he was not in business to argue with people but to buy and sell at a profit. Of course it was left to me to meet the somewhat aggrieved vendors with whom I was perfectly civil but equally adamantine in our refusal to buy their goods. Naturally word got around and eventually no-one supplied us with anything other than what had been precisely specified.

Next, our tools that we supplied were good ones. We often bought a whole toolkit from a disillusioned digger, cleaning it up and selling it on. These usually had crowbars, pickaxes, spades, buckets and cradles in them. Some also had wheelbarrows to move the soil. I think there really were a few who thought that they would drop on it and would need the wheelbarrow to carry away the gold! Many more, however simply came across hungry quartz that yielded very little reward.

On the other hand we charged so much that many grumbled that we were bloodsuckers, battening upon the hopes of poor men who were desperate to make something of their lives. John brushed all such criticisms aside, saying that as we had to take the risk of buying in the goods we had the right to set the price. He added that they did not have to buy our supplies. They could go elsewhere as we had many competitors.

I protested that they charged as much as we did. He said that this proved his point. We all took the risk of bringing in these things and therefore should be recompensed sufficiently for our trouble and risk. When I found out later in my work for Adam and Pirrip that John regularly drank with our competitors and had verbal agreements with them to maintain high prices, I tackled him about this.

"Pip, you have to understand that if I do not charge these prices there are ways in which Adam and Pirrip can receive the attention of some of the least law abiding fellows who will not scruple to burn our premises and destroy our stock. Do remember that we have here in the fields many Vandemonians who have been flogged in the past. And, once the gold runs out, we shall not be able to make such profits. We need them, for what will Adam and Pirrip do then?"

"Why do you hate the Celestials and the Vandemonians so much?"

" I do not hate them. I despise them all. They are life's failures. The Celestials cannot make a successful life in China so they come here to rob us of what is ours."

"It's only ours because we took it from the black people who were here before us."

"And what were they doing with the land? I will tell you. Nothing. We came to find that they were neglecting everything. You remember the parable of the talents and the stewards. Well, the blackfellows in Australia did nothing with their talents so we had to take it from them to improve it. And look what they have become. Instead of following our good examples they follow the worst. Look at the way they drink and sit around although, God knows, there's plenty they could be doing. They are scum, just like the scum that were transported here. Do not try to tell me that there is no such thing as a criminal class as I can show you plenty of them here."

"And as for the Vandemonians, they are brutes, criminals who have had to be subdued and kept down by the lash. They are a challenge to honest men like you and me. We now have

247

a duty to hold them down. It's our turn. Just look at the bushrangers, and the way in which they terrorise honest settlers to provide them with provisions."

He ran out of breath so I was able to bring him back to what he had been saying before.

"So we need the Celestials and the others?"

"Yes. We need them, for what will Adam and Pirrip do when the gold runs out as it most surely must in time?"

I waited, as I knew from past experience that John might not know that he was posing a rhetorical question but in essence that was exactly what he was doing. I was not disappointed. He stood up to begin his lecture and as he did so I noted that the slim, elegantly dressed, young man that I had first encountered had become slightly corpulent. He was now bearded, and, where those parts of his face were not shrouded by the beard, they showed distinct signs of over indulgence on alcoholic beverages. I had remonstrated with him on several occasions but to no avail, despite the fact that I believed that his health was beginning to suffer.

"Railways!, he began dramatically.

"Have you not heard how railways in England and railroads in America are the way in which everyone travels?"

"Surely you are not suggesting that we build railways?"

He made an impatient gesture of denial and for the next half an hour set out his vision for the future. A vision that was closely attached to steam. He said that railways would need coal, steel, tools and men. We would provide what was needed. Just as in the goldfields we did not do the digging ourselves, but provided the wherewithal to do so, others would build the railways in Australia and we would supply the means to do so. We have the cash, the experience and the contacts so we will be able to make ourselves a fortune.

Chapter 8

Shakespeare

In time I found that John's education was fairly rudimentary. He was intelligent and eager to learn as long as he saw that it had some profit in it for him. His eagerness to learn was also held back by his holding very positive views on several subjects, which included, amongst other things, the idea that Europeans were superior to all other races. Using my complete works of Shakespeare I tried to introduce him to the Bard. He soon gave up, saying that the plays were too difficult. I pointed out that they were plays, and as such were meant to be seen on a stage as entertainment. His reaction was to challenge me to find a theatre that was putting on one of these plays, where they were being played as Shakespeare meant them to be played. He said he knew that such plays were being performed, but with such ribaldry! Did I want him to see those?

I remembered how Tony on the Speyside had declaimed speeches from "Othello" and "Hamlet", and when I asked how he knew these had told me how the miners in California had been mad about Shakespeare. I must have looked doubtful so he had pulled me over to one of the forty-niners who confirmed his story. In fact I sat on the deck and he enlivened my journey as he told me that when the forty-niners arrived they not only sought gold but also entertainment. Any show was welcomed.

Many of Shakespeare's plays were performed in California, usually, he added, with the utmost vulgarity. He offered to show me how this was done, but I declined. Practically every one of the plays was performed. Why was

Shakespeare so popular? The answer was that the miners recognised the plots as something that they could relate to. Hamlet and Othello and Romeo were recognisable characters. They might utter high-flown speeches but their problems were down to earth. And many a miner with nothing else to occupy his mind memorised some of the well-known speeches. Just because they were engaged in manual labour didn't mean that they were idiots with no minds. The plays also gave them something that was lacking in their lives. They craved entertainment and the plays suitably, or unsuitably, changed to include vulgar amusement, met that craving. They also reminded them, as they grubbed away, that there was a finer life to be had.

So it was scarcely surprising that the tradition of rather rough versions being offered had come to Australia. I understood now some of the comments that I had heard about the performances, how some miners were not allowed in and how the comments of those who had gained entry frequently had disrupted the playing. What was happening was the miners expected the plays to include topical references and up to date jokes and if there were none, they supplied them themselves. Then I saw a playbill where it was stated that Othello was to be performed with Gustavus Brooke and the delightful actress Fanny Cathcart. It was also said, when I enquired, that there was to be an attempt at a real performance, so I booked seats at the Queen's Theatre for the following week.

Both John and I were delighted with what we saw. It's true that I thought Brooke was not up to what I had seen in London, but this was in Melbourne. And Melbourne was in the process of changing from a rough, tough, muddy, stinking, dirty little town to a much more sophisticated and grander town altogether. And I have to say that it was miners who brought it about. There was one, who having made a fortune, promptly spent most of it on building a theatre. Of course it was not all Shakespeare, although I now found that John became quite keen on the Bard. There were all sorts of other performances, some of which John enjoyed as much, but I held back from. They were more robust and caught the imagination of the miners and frequently had women dancers whose rather revealing dresses and immodest gestures drew sharp comments from some of the more respectable townspeople. I think to be honest that those who were most scandalised were women; their men folk often agreed with them but still attended the performances.

Chapter 9

Estella comes to find me

Ignoring the curious looks and ribald comments she walked up to me. Her hair was disarranged and her dress whipped about by the sandy wind that was blowing that day. She stopped, and looking at me said:

" You are a hard man to find."

I led her into the lee of the cabin and sat her down on some old boxes. The celestials watched impassively. I was not interested in what they thought of me. I was not interested in what John would say. I was only interested in why she was here. I waited for her to speak. Despite being in the shelter of the cabin her dress and hair was still being whipped about. But they were not so disarranged as my feelings were at that moment.

Eventually she said, " We were friends and, when I heard the facts of my mother and how I was cared for by Miss Havisham and the fact that I am not the lady that I thought I was, I knew that there was only one person who would understand what had happened to me and could help me. Will you help me Pip?"

I bowed my head, both to indicate that I would help her but also to hide my emotions. Then I asked:

"How did you find out?"

"Jaggers is dead. His papers were taken over and someone, I know not who, saw fit to acquaint me with some of what they found in them."

"Which is?"

"That my mother was a murderess who was saved from the gallows and the madhouse by giving me up. And, that a transported convict was my father. I still do not know who he is. Do you know Pip?"

I hesitated but a moment.

"He was Abel Magwitch, my principal benefactor. I am sorry but I have to tell you that he is dead."

She looked at me impassively. I could not tell whether her stillness was stoicism or relief. I was about to tell her more when John came around the corner and said:

"It's true then what they are saying. A real lady has joined us at the diggings. Won't you introduce me Pip? Or am I too crude a fellow for you to be acquainted with now that you are being visited by a lady?"

"Estella", I said, this is John Adam, a gentleman in whose employ I am presently engaged. John, this is Estella..."

I stopped as I realised that I did not know what name Estella was using. John ignored my pause, raised his hat and said that he was pleased to make her acquaintance. He went on to say that although I had introduced him as a gentleman, he was not one. He was, he said, in trade and that precluded him from claiming that rank. Eying me carefully he added spitefully that I too was now in trade, and doing very well at it.

We all fell silent. John, in a rare fit of good behaviour, sensing that we wished to be alone said:

" I will see you back in the hotel where we need to go through those figures again."

He emphasised *figures* as if to say this man is employed to work on figures as if he was a clerk.

He turned around casually and left us. Estella said:

"I am now known as Estella Brown and I have put it about that I am here to write about what is happening in this part of the world. Things are changing; I will be writing for newspapers and magazines so maybe I am really no longer the lady that I was, if I ever was, that is."

"You are right, things are changing. I am changed. I too am no longer the gentleman that I thought I was."

I was about to say more when we were interrupted by a despairing wail.

"Please, do not, I pray you. Think of my children. I must support them somehow."

An obese, ugly woman, with greasy hair flying in the wind, shouted abuse at two men who struggled with her. People stood around watching as another man, by throwing a lighted torch, set fire to her tent. As they held her back she screamed:

"My babies are in there. Oh God won't someone help me, for Jesus Christ's sake get them out."

Estella ran to her, and entering the tent with some others, dragged out two small children who seemed to be dressed in flour sacks. The woman was released and ran to them scooping them up and crying piteously. They began to wail too. As the tent and its contents burned, everyone turned away and the men who had seized the woman turned their backs and walked away.

Estella returned to me saying:

"You must do something about those ruffians."

"No, we cannot interfere. Those "ruffians" are the law here. What they are doing is quite legal. She is breaking the law by selling grog. As a grog seller they are entitled to destroy her tent. That man, the big one with the hat, is Hermsprong in charge of the police, and those men are the police."

A large lady with a pleasant smile picked her way towards us through the muck.

"So you found him?"

"Yes."

Then turning to me Estella said:

"I should like you to meet Miss Caroline Chisholm who was instrumental in my coming to Australia."

I bowed, and Miss Chisholm, unloosening her bonnet strings but retaining her less than fashionable bonnet, said:

"I am most pleased to make your acquaintance at last. Miss Brown had enlivened our journey with such accounts of you that I was most intrigued to ascertain your progress in this fairest of colonies."

She turned to Estella.

"You will not take it amiss if I take it upon myself to point out that a bonnet would not only add to your propriety, but would also offer some relief from this fierce sunshine."

Here she undid a parasol that was battered but still serviceable and holding it above Estella's head gently led her away, Estella smiling all the while looked back at me mouthing the words:

"We shall meet later."

I called after her:

"Yes, later."

And as I did so I returned her smile, realising that I had not smiled so readily for some while.

Soon after Estella found me I was able to meet her and she immediately asked me how much I knew about her mother and father. She said that as I had often said in the past that I loved her I would surely not deny telling her what I knew. I said that I did indeed have some considerable knowledge but I hesitated to impart it as I did not wish her to be hurt in any way. Seeing her here in Australia after having parted from her as friends in England awaked in me thoughts that we might move to more than mere amity. I felt though that I should have to tread with the utmost delicacy.

We arranged to meet again. She said that as Caroline had been of the utmost assistance to her she now felt that she ought to render such services as she could to repay all the help that Caroline had given her. This meant that she was less free to meet me than she would have wished. Nevertheless, she was able to spend an afternoon with me when I set out in some detail all that I knew. I must say here that I found Estella much changed. She still showed the sort of spirit that enabled her to help that poor woman who lost her meagre dwelling, and her actions in rescuing the children were those of a woman who could be moved by pity. And yet, something had gone from her character. She was not now the proud and pretty young Estella who I remembered had said that I might kiss her. Nor was she the haughty young woman who manifested such a lack of concern for my feelings about her that I despaired.

Before I met Estella again I cast my mind back to the time that I took dinner at Jagger's house, that strange house in Gerrard Street, in Soho. That was where I saw Estella's mother, Molly, employed as his housekeeper. I realise now that somehow a bargain had been struck, whereby he employed her and by so doing ensured that she was constantly under his control. The other part of the bargain was that Jaggers would find someone to look after the little girl that the housekeeper had threatened to do away with. To accomplish this, Jaggers first used his lawyer's skills and got the woman acquitted. That little girl was Estella and the person who was chosen to care for her was Miss Havisham.

I began by telling Estella what I had learned from Abel's own mouth. He had told me his life story as Herbert and I were engaged in assisting him to escape from England and the hangman's noose. I set it all down later on, and when he was dead I wrote it out.

I told her that Abel never knew his father and was abandoned by his mother. He was brought up in fair grounds, looked after by gypsies and eventually managed to find his way in life as a shepherd. He met Estella's mother who was called Mary then, married her and they lived happily with their young daughter who at that time was called Emily. He was betrayed by a gypsy who so ordered things that Mary thought that Abel was seeing another woman. It was this woman that Mary murdered. She came back and threatened Abel that she would do away with Emily if he pursued her.

So he stayed away and did not know what happened to Mary and Emily. He took up with a bad lot, Compeyson, and together they were transported, but not before Abel had met me on Romney Marshes. In Australia he prospered to such an extent that he was able to pay for me to become a gentleman. Then, unable to resist seeing me, he came back to England where, despite all our efforts, he was arrested. He died in prison. I do not know what became of Molly.

Of course this is a paraphrase of what I actually said, for I knew the story in such detail that it took me all afternoon and the best part of an evening to relate it. When I finished Estella said quietly that she knew what had happened to Molly. A retired clerk had sought her out to say that he had some intelligence for her. He told her that Jagger's housekeeper had died, but before she did so had asked him to pass on to Estella a locket with the name of Emily on it. It was wrapped in a scrap of newspaper. Estella thought at the time that that Molly must have seen her, and taken a fancy to her and so left something to someone as she had no-one else to give it to. Estella took the locket and the scrap of paper because Wemmick, the clerk in question, asked her earnestly to do this. She had put them away and had not looked at them again, never imagining that they were anything to do with her.

The following day Estella brought the locket and the newspaper to me. When we opened the locket we found that it contained three small curls of hair. All were of different colours. The newspaper, very creased and brittle, was an account of a trial, a murder trial where the accused woman had been brilliantly defended by a barrister of law called Jaggers.

Chapter 10

Run, save yourself

I looked up astonished at the noise. We had been so concerned with our discussion and getting the price right that we had ignored all that was going on around us. We had met at the request of a small group of miners who had sat in the open air with us where it was cooler. We stood up looking at the scene. Dozens of men, with a leavening of women, were streaming towards us, calling out together something about rights and licences. Most of the men were bearded and, judging by their garb, obviously miners. Many had guns in their hands which some threw away as they ran past us. One called out to us:

"The stockade's gone. They've broken through"

John said:

"I do not like the look of this. Come let's go."

Without waiting for me he turned rapidly, leaving me with the other, and I turned too, meaning to follow him. John ran so quickly that I soon lost sight of him. It was then that I saw the banner being fought over and the soldiers and troopers following the retreating men and women. As they pushed past me, several were knocked over, and because they were so close to me I reached out to help them, only to lose my balance and fall heavily amongst them. Shots were being fired as I did so.

Others fell on me, and all around me I heard swearing from both men and women. I lay on top of someone whose clothes were rough against my face. My leg was caught against a wooden rocker. In pulling it free I tore the material in my trousers and I remember thinking stupidly that these were a good, possibly my best pair of trousers. Some blood ran down my leg and the mud seeped into my boots. I noted that the mud was yellow, stained with the muck from horses that had been there. Dogs barked and the man below me bellowed angrily as he pushed me roughly off him. He stood up. I heard more shooting and this galvanised him into running away, leaving me with a younger man who lay sobbing, holding a bloody arm. Suddenly two soldiers came upon us, which made the young man stand up and run off too, pausing to shout at me:

"Run, save yourself."

I thought that the soldiers would assist me so I stayed, but instead they pushed me down into the mud and dust, then, while one went on, the other knelt on me. I heard cries of:

"On, on, keep the line. Keep the line."

An officer on a horse cantered past. The soldier holding me down said:

"Keep still, damn you."

I stopped struggling. I felt a great weariness come over me. I relaxed and closed my eyes. My captor on my back shuddered and groaned. He moved sideways. I opened my eyes dazzled at first with the brightness of the day. Then a dark shape came blotting out the sun. It was a miner holding a spade. He held out a calloused hand to me. I took his hand and he pulled me upright, my head swimming.

"Better get out of here mate."

He gestured at the sprawled figure of the soldier whose hat had fallen off revealing a bloody mass of dark hair above a white neck. I stood there shaking. Stupidly I tried to hold my torn trousers together as my rescuer regarded me grimly.

"They will come back," he warned.

"Here, have a pull of this."

"This" was the strongest grog that I have ever taken. Handing back the bottle I thanked him and walked away shakily. As I walked, others walked beside me, some as battered as I was, others less so but all in a state of shock. No-one took any notice of me for I was simply one of many bearing the marks of what had obviously been some sort of riot. Most of my bruises and scrapes were the result of what had happened at the beginning, when I had been discussing a delivery of calico. Others were much more injured. One man being carried in a piece of canvas like a hammock at sea was so inert that I judged him to be dead.

I stumbled on, my boots catching at every obstruction as I was so desperately tired. I realised that the grog had been so powerful that I was half drunk which did not make it any easier to get along. My trousers flapped. I stopped and catching up a piece of twine I fastened it round my torn trouser leg at the calf. This rather feeble act of trying to return to normality encouraged me to straighten up and press on to where I saw in the distance John and Estella. Estella looked the more concerned of the two and when she led me into some shade I saw that this was where others were getting some attention.

Looking at the others, I felt ashamed of my inability to rise above this mishap when I saw their cuts, their blood and their bruises. A woman, in a brown stuff dress and plain bonnet that reminded me of the Quakers, was crying over the body of a man that was laid out in the dirt.

"Her husband", whispered Estella to me, as she used water and some of the samples of calico that we had been carrying to wash my face and leg.

"Caught in the charge and took a ball straight through his chest. He bled to death before any one could do anything for his hurt."

John insisted that we should all remove ourselves as quickly as possible. So, supported by them both, I was taken from the shambles. John looked as well turned out as ever, having escaped all by his swift actions to remove himself from danger. I delicately refrained from saying what I thought about his flight. In my mind however I was firmly of the opinion that he had run away and abandoned me. Once we were safely away Estella went back to help with the wounded.

I asked John what she was doing here in the goldfields. He told me that she had given up her writing and had been assisting Caroline Chisholm who had persuaded the government to erect a series of shelters for miners. These were sheds along the routes to the diggings to help make travelling conditions more comfortable for gold seekers. John's opinion of Caroline Chisholm, howeve, was that she was a meddlesome women.
"She's so self-opinionated, so always right," he complained.

"Do you know that she claims to be a water diviner?"

The following day we began to realise the extent of deaths and injuries as Estella brought word of them to John and me. Over a dinner of roast lamb we discussed our experiences.

"After John found you I organised such care as I could. Most had injuries that merely needed cleaning and binding up. Supplying fresh water was essential."

"How many were killed?"

"I do not know. There is still a great deal of confusion. You were lucky Pip that John was able to organise your rescue."

I looked at her in astonishment.

"My rescue?"

"Yes. He risked his life in going back to find you."

I looked at John who modestly dropped his eyes to his dinner. He pushed some potatoes around.

He murmured:

"Please, let's say no more about it."

There was a silence. I experienced such a rage that built up in my chest that I almost choked; and then as I felt my face redden I put down my fork deliberately and decided to speak. I had to tell the truth. John had run off with no thought as to my danger. He had abandoned me in order to save himself. It was what I would have expected of him, but to try to pass himself off as my saviour! I hesitated. I decided that I could not say exactly what had happened. I could not in Estella's presence call him a liar. Instead I said:

"Right. Let's say no more."

I drained my glass. John smiled at Estella who smiled back saying:

"I know that you will excuse me. I am so desperately tired."

We rose as she left us. I remained standing, so did John who looked at me with a mocking smile.

"You did not rescue me."

"I came back."

"After you had run away."

" I went to get help."

"You ran off. Then you met Estella and realised how it would look if you didn't do something. So you turned back and met me as I extricated myself."

"Pip. Estella believes that I am a hero. Others do too. No matter what you say now will change their minds. Everyone loves a hero. Even Caroline. She is married to one. At least I think he was a hero in India. You don't hear much about him nowadays."

"Why are you so opposed to what Caroline and Estella are doing?"

"Oh! I suppose that she and Caroline think that they are acting for the best, but all this assisting miners and concentrating upon getting women married in Australia is so much cant. They are not thinking about the well-being of the poor souls at all. It's just a scheme to get more Christians into Australia."

"But you must admit that she is helping women who would otherwise languish in England."

"No, I admit no such thing. Caroline Chisholm organises the import of women who otherwise would be servants or employees in England, which is their true place in life. By her actions she is encouraging them to aspire to a level of society that is not theirs by right."

He threw back his head and declaimed:

'The rich man in his castle, the poor man at his gate,
God made them, high or lowly, and ordered their estate.'

"Surely we have grown beyond that now? That was written when things were a great deal different."

"I would remind you as a Christian, who supposedly believes in God Almighty, Everlasting, that some things are meant to stay the same."

The following day, seeking to make some sense of the riot that I had been caught up in, I heard that a Henry

Seekamp had been arrested and charged with sedition. He was charged as the editor of the Ballarat Times where there had been a series of articles, not written by him, that were considered seditious. He was later charged with seditious libel. I wondered whether they would go on with this charge or whether it would be dropped once the Eureka Stockade incident had been allowed to fade with time. It did seem to me that the authorities were looking for a scapegoat. As an editor he would be just the right sort of person that they could make an example of.

Strangely this same man was later to be involved with Lola Montez who, when she performed her erotic Spider Dance at the Theatre Royal, raised her skirts so high that the she scandalised the general public. She was much better received by the diggers at Castlemaine who loved her eroticism and applauded her saucy efforts to entertain them. She had come from America where it was rumoured that she had had several amours and was now, not only entertaining the miners, but also capturing hearts. There was also talk of her involvement with nobility in Germany, where her scandalous behaviour sold many newspapers and ensured her continued employment as a dancer.

Chapter 11

A ladies' man

"Why John", I said in mock amazement, "You astonish me, you really do. I never took you for a ladies' man. Yet here you are pomaded and shaved and perfumed and dressed in your utmost absolute best. Who is she?"

He had on his best brown coat that was cutaway to reveal a snow-white waistcoat that topped his skin-tight buckskin breeches. Beneath them were his top boots polished to a state that compared with looking glasses. His red neck bulged and rose above a cravat that I had never seen before. Nor had I ever seen the gold stick-pin that secured it. His hair was most carefully arranged to make the best of his curls that owed less to nature and more to the art of the hairdresser.

Now I really was astonished for John blushed even redder and muttered "Lola".

"Lola who?"

"Lola Montez, damn you."

Saying this he straightened his cravat, that didn't need straightening, and left me abruptly. I sat with the business books before me contemplating a lonely evening, as I had to struggle with them and the buckets of receipts and other papers that made up our accounts. It was one of John's eccentricities that he insisted that we kept our papers in galvanised buckets. He reasoned that we had several times witnessed fires that had destroyed such papers. Galvanised buckets do not burn and their handles make it easy to pick them up to carry them out of harms way.

Lola Montez. I knew the name. She was a notorious dancer of whom little was said to her benefit unless you asked a miner about her performance. I resolved to see a performance myself. I resolved to do it straightaway. The books could wait. I pushed everything to one side and went upstairs to make myself ready. The man that stared back at me in the mirror was much less well turned out than the one that I had chaffed earlier but just as determined to see Lola. Then, going out of the hotel, I went along through the usual frenzy of the main road, picking my way through all the garbage and detritus that seemed necessary to a town that was in a state of rapid growth. I turned down to a theatre where I had heard that she was appearing.

There a gaudy poster showed a most indecorous picture of what seemed to be a Spanish Gypsy entangled in a spider's web. I looked around at the crowd who were elbowing themselves past me. No-one that I recognised watched me as I bought a ticket from a harridan whose bad teeth and worse breath hurried me into the rudimentary theatre. If the air outside was malodorous, inside it stank even more of unwashed bodies, perfume and alcohol. It wanted but a quarter of an hour to the appearance of Miss Lola Montez the celebrated and talented danseuse who, I had read outside, was making another visit to this theatre following her successful tour in Sydney.

Two dogs provided entertainment of a sort as their respective owners failed to keep them apart. They fell upon each other to shouts from the men and screams from the women who declared that they were never in so much fear of their life as at this moment. The fight was a short one as their owners also fell to fighting each other until they were ejected, despite having paid to enter.

Chapter 12

Theatre and a supper

    I gazed around. To my left sat a sad looking man who chewed slowly and thoughtfully at a damper that I hoped afforded him some nourishment, as it did not seem to be providing him with much pleasure. He drank noisily from a tin cup what I imagine was tea but could have been grog of some sort. I say of some sort as there were many recipes for something described as grog. He then finished his repast with a greasy slice of mutton. This took longer than the damper and during this time my stomach growled at me in despair at my having neglected to have my tea before coming out.

    To my right spread a biddy who was admiring her rings. Her hair was ornately coiffured, her dress elaborate. It comprised layers of all kinds of materials of which French lace seemed the greater part. Everything that she wore or sported spoke, or rather shouted, that she had struck it rich. Her gold strike sat beside her, tastefully clad in cotton trousers streaked with clay tucked into thick leather boots. His rather greasy flannel shirt was open so that all might enjoy the sight of his thick gold chain against his hairy chest. His thick sunburned arms were folded across his chest. No-one I had ever seen previously had such huge rings in their ears as he.

    Further away sat a group of celestials that I noted were shunned by all. Dressed in their habitual blue smocks and baggy trousers they stopped their chatting in that hypnotic singy-songy style of language cadence and looked down when they saw that I was looking at them. I knew from my previous experience that any attempt on my part at conversation with them would be abortive. And I was coward enough anyway to eschew contact with them so as to avoid attracting the miner's wrath that I was siding with those heathens. As my gaze wandered from them the biddy caught my eye and said as she held out a hand:

"Like my rings?"

I nodded.

"Cost a packet, but he don't care , do you darlin'."

'Darlin'' stirred, unfolded his arms revealing several tattoos and spoke in a breathy rumble:

"No. Only the best for you sweetheart."

'Sweetheart' glowed. She held out the other hand revealing in her smile some less than savoury looking teeth. Gold shone, diamonds sparkled and her eyes twinkled.

"Come here to see Lola Montez, have you?"

I assented. How could I not do so? I was seated with a rag bag of spectators in a theatre where behind vivid red curtains was Lola, John's object of devotion and admiration.

"She's wonderful", rumbled 'Darlin'.

"More than wonderful", said 'Sweetheart'.

"Just wait till you see her".

We sat swatting away the flies until the curtains were dragged back and 'Sweetheart's' claims were vindicated. Although many had told me about Lola's abilities nothing that had been said to me prepared me for her in the flesh, a phrase that I do not use lightly. I suppose that separated as we all were from most female company and entertainment, any smidgeon of talent exhibited to us by any half-way attractive woman would have enchanted us. And we were enchanted, entertained, and eventually, totally enslaved, every man jack of us.

How did she do it? How can I do justice to her and her performance in mere words? To begin with she was exotic, mysterious, alluring and seductive, and that was before she had even begun to dance.

Her collective audience, myself included, drew in a collective breath, almost seeking to draw into themselves the very essence of her femininity. Across the smoking lamps that served as footlights came an aroma from her that promised secret delights of unimaginable delightfulness. You think I am exaggerating? I was there. I saw, heard, smelled Lola; and would have tasted and felt her had I but half a chance to do so. She inflamed our senses with her lusty spider dance and we loved her! Who would not love someone who wove a spell around us all, drawing us into her intimate world of forbidden desires.

My God! I was not surprised that John was enchanted by her. My only surprise was that the whole audience was not similarly caught in her toils. Perhaps they all were? For as she danced, a shower of small golden objects fell upon the stage bouncing and rolling around her as she performed. Not missing a step nor a beat in the music she collected them all up. I was alarmed for I could see that the objects were small gold nuggets that the miners had spent such time and effort in wresting from the soil. I was amazed at the way that they carelessly parted with this largesse so easily. Easy come, easy go, indeed.

Her performance ended with such a crescendo of cheers that you would have supposed that a more exalted personage, such as Her Majesty the Queen was receiving homage. I left with my head hot and my throat dry. Others jostled me towards a ruffian who demanded that I held still the glass that he had thrust into my hand so that he could the more easily fill it. And fill it he did, so that it slopped over onto my trousers.

"Drink! Drink!" He urged.

"Drink a toast to Lola."

I cautiously sipped and found that it seemed to be champagne, a discovery that was verified by the sight of the bottle that the ruffian was raising to his lips.

"Lola! Lola!" Was the cry.

All around me more bottles were being opened. More champagne was being drunk and, as I found later, this was a normal occurrence when Lola Montez performed. One man lay slumped on the floor and I too felt on the verge of insensibility. Too late I remembered that I had missed eating in order to see the daring dancer. It was at that precise moment that she appeared to a storm of applause with John at her side. He nodded coolly at me as if it was the most natural thing in the world for him to be squiring such a notorious and licentious dancer, and led her to the hotel across the way.

She turned, I supposed to wave to her admirers, but surprised me by speaking to John then dropping his arm and coming over to me.

"Pip"?

I nodded.

"When John nodded to you I wanted to know who you were. John told me that you were his partner. I think that you might join us. That is if it pleases you to do so, for I see that you have already begun to enjoy the evening, and a supper would round it off splendidly, don't you think?"

As she spoke I could see John's face getting darker but I ignored that and said that I would be delighted to join them. She took my arm, took away my glass that she gave to a bystander who gazed at her with undiluted lust, and led me over to John.

"John, you didn't say that Pip was so handsome."

"Handsome is as handsome does", he responded.

She laughed, enjoying having two strings to her bow, or should I say two beaus to play off against each other. And that was when it began. That was the exact moment that we began to work against each other instead of combining against the world.

We went in and our supper was served to us in a private room. No word was spoken. The innkeeper just led us into a hot little room where curtains were pulled across despite the heat, I supposed to keep us from the vulgar gaze. This was necessary as everyone knew that the infamous Lola Montez was in the hotel. I sat feeing uneasy as the innkeeper set another place for me, all with no words being spoken. He bowed and left. We ate a magnificent meal, the centre piece of which was a sturgeon. Lola wrinkled her nose at it and complained that she was tired of sturgeon.

Once the table was cleared John lit up one of his foul smelling cheroots, offering me one that I declined. I took a small glass of port wine instead. Lola accepted a cheroot and leaning back and smiling through the smoke at me, shook her ash upon the less than immaculate floor. As she did so she asked whether I was truly from England or was that a story that I had put about in order to hide my real antecedents? I sketched my background briefly as she seemed genuinely to be interested. Then, emboldened by the atmosphere and the wine that I had taken, I asked Lola about her early life.

"I'm Irish, of course. Don't look so surprised. I can, however, trace my family back to a Spanish grandee who was on the Spanish Armada. He was an Hildago in charge of a troop of soldiers who all perished as the Santa Cristobel was driven onto the rocks on the shore of Ireland. As a Roman Catholic, he was accepted by the local population once they had looted what remained of his ship. He was unable to return to Spain immediately and lost his life later in an abortive effort to sail back. Before he did so he left several reminders of his stay and I am one of numerous descendents. I've inherited his looks and temperament, but to be honest I have had to juggle a little with my name. My audiences like to have a mysterious and sultry woman doing the famous spider dance. Olivia Gilbert doesn't have the cachet that an exotic dancer needs which is why I dropped it.

She laughed at my expression and coughed as she drew on her cheroot. She stubbed it out in a plate and left it smouldering.

"Really John, you ought to buy better ones than these. So you really are a gentleman, and not the son of convict, or a tailor?"

This question was flung out at me with a slight emphasis upon the last word. John stirred at this. Up to now he had remained silent. Red in the face and sweating now, and stung at the reference to his parentage, he said:

"Oh Pip is a gentleman all right. No-one can fault him. His connections might be a little strange but he out-classes me. And now perhaps he ought be going. I am sure you have bills to add up or manifests to examine Pip."

I stood up a little unsteadily. I bowed. I felt slightly sick and I knew that if I did not soon get some air I should indeed be so.

Chapter 13

Betrayal

I determined to talk to John about his friendship with Lola. It was most unsuitable and unbecoming of someone who aspired to become a gentleman, and if I were to do my duty as his friend and mentor, I would have to point this out to him. Of course, I was under no illusions that my advice would be welcomed let alone accepted. John was obviously ensnared by this woman who was exercising a most unhealthy influence upon him. She had ensnared him like a fly in a web where she was the spider.

I liked that mental picture and held onto it as I shaved. It gave me the courage to rehearse in my mind my words that I would use when talking to John. If I was to have any effect I had to pick them carefully. Then I paused, razor half way to my chin. I thought of John and Lola sitting together in the tavern last night. Maybe I should seek out and speak to Lola instead. Perhaps I could appeal to her natural instincts as a woman. Surely she would respond to such an approach? I pictured us together, two civilised human beings, having a civilised conversation in order to assist a mutual friend. I liked that picture.

Finishing my shave I washed away the soap and with it any intention to speak to John. As I put on my white linen that had been laid out for me I dwelt on John's response when Lola, suitably briefed by me, gently rejected him. The linen was a metaphor for his clean start, and I would be responsible for it. By the time that I was fully dressed I glowed with pride. Both Estella and Caroline would be proud of me.

From outside came a shout:

"Here they come!"

It was followed by an increase in the general noise that was always in evidence out side the hotel. I stepped outside into the dry heat and into the overpowering smells that horse dung and dog shit provided. That smell and more heat was soon increased as a crowd of excited noisy people pressed against me, caught hold of me, then swept me along towards a veritable cavalcade of carriages and horses that were entering the town. Soldiers were everywhere, sweat running down from their caps across their bright red or deep brown faces, depending on how long they had been in the colony. Some looked nervous, and all had black backs to their badly cut and fraying tunics where they were stained with their sweat. Some even had a white rime of dried salt to the edge of their blackness showing how long they had been marching in the heat of the sun.

An officer on horseback trotted by returning the salutes of the soldiers with a languid wave of his riding crop. I heard nothing in the crowd except comments on how much gold had been brought in this time. I was about to stop and ask someone the total amount when I suddenly espied Lola riding in an open top carriage as if she was a lady. She had a parasol to shade her but was using more as a way of getting even greater attention than usual and I could see her clearly. For a moment I thought that the man next to her was John, then she moved her parasol once again coquettishly and revealed another man's face!

As she drew level with me she looked directly into my face and laughed out loud at my disapproving expression. She said something to her companion who laughed too. I felt my face, already flushed from the heat, get hotter. I felt a strong wave of emotion rise up in me. It was so strong that I felt faint. But what made me feel really ill was the fact that I had to admit to myself that the strong emotion that gripped me was that of jealousy! I should have felt anger on John's behalf at his betrayal, or relief that Lola had shown her self to be no more than the hussy that many thought her to be.

Instead I felt that it was I who had been betrayed; and I had to admit that all my fine feelings about turning John from this woman were a distortion of the real facts which that it was I who was obsessed with her. I was the one who needed protection.

"Who was that woman?" asked Estella, who unknown to me had also been watching the arrival of the gold in the crowd.

"You seem to know her."

As I made no answer she looked puzzled.

"How exciting to see all this," she went on.

I still made no answer so she walked away. I was torn. Should I go after her? What would I say?

I decided that I ought to see John. It seemed to me that the most important thing was to help John and I could best do this by telling him exactly what I had seen. I would put aside my thoughts about Lola. The difficulty was that he had absented himself and no-one seemed to know where he had gone. Days went by and still he was not at home nor was he at the offices of Adam and Pirrip. I had a shrewd suspicion that he might be with Lola who had gone to Ballarat for further performances there.

On an impulse I went to Ballarat where, just as I had suspected, John was attending the theatre where Lola was performing. I found him outside, unable to gain attendance to her dressing room, looking ill and half drunk.   I tried to persuade him to leave Ballarat but he insisted on staying. I was sure that he knew about the other men. He showed me a copy of the Ballarat Times where there was a most unpleasant review of Lola's performance the previous night. As we stood there Lola came out, and with a retinue of admirers and hangers-on she marched off down the street. We followed. A crowd gathered as she swept along and we all stood outside the offices of the Ballarat Times as she went in.   What happened next I only found out when, after some time, she came out and threw down a riding crop. She marched back and the word went round that she had attacked the editor, Henry Seekamp with a whip.

I could see that I was unable to influence John so I returned to our offices and waited for him to come to his senses. He returned a bitter man and attacked me saying that I had turned Lola against him. He maintained that had I not been spying on him at the theatre Lola would not have seen me.   Apparently after I had left them in the tavern she had taunted him with tales of her previous conquests and said that she preferred me! It was all lies. Her whole life was one vast edifice of falsehoods. All that business of her early life and her Spanish forbears were the result of her imagination. By May she had left Australia and gone back to San Francisco to break more hearts in America.

Chapter 14

Roll Up

In time we patched up our relationship, and over the next three years, as railways expanded and were extended, we carried on expanding and extending the firm. During this time I saw Estella fairly regularly whenever she was less engaged in her work with new immigrants. I kept meaning to broach the subject of marriage with her but somehow the time never seemed right or suitable. She seemed contented to leave matters as they stood. I was thirty-something so considered that there was still time before taking on the responsibilities of marriage. I have to say that my intimations that married women's place was in the home were not well received by Estella, who seemed to imagine that married ladies should enjoy the same freedom as single members of her sex.

However by 1861 I determined that I ought to ask Estella to be my wife, despite her strange ideas. I was sure that once I had proposed she would see sense and come round to my more acceptable views. Before I did so I thought that I should acquaint John with my intentions. I had no wish to upset the smooth running of "ADAM & PIRRIP".

John and I had a meeting arranged to discuss the provision of tools to a group of miners who had formed a syndicate, and it seemed an ideal time to speak to him once we had finished our business. In the intense heat we sat around a table where most of those talking to us were rough types but reasonably honest. I had just begun to summarise what we had agreed when......"Roll up!" came a call, and immediately all the men stood up and pushed back their chairs, scraping their boots on the rough floor as they left the room.

Again I heard:

"Roll up!"

I looked at the men as they passed me wondering what was happening. John merely looked resigned.

"Where are you going?"

"Roll up!" came the reply as if that was a sufficient explanation in itself to warrant a complete exodus. In the next few minutes the building emptied. In the silence I asked John:

"Do you know what is going on?"

"They are going to listen to James Stewart calling for action on those blasted celestials."

"What sort of action?"

"Come on, let's go and hear him ourselves."

We left our building and I turned to admire it. It was a symbol of our progress and it made me quite proud to see it.

"Don't get too attached to it."

"Why not?"

"Buildings that belong to Chinese sympathisers can mysteriously catch fire."

Outside we joined a steady stream of men with a sprinkling of tough looking women who were moving to where we could hear shouting. I clutched the arm of one man who I remembered we had done business with in the past. I asked again:

"What's going on?"

He shook off my hand impatiently.

"Roll up. Come and listen."

I turned to John who raised his eyebrows expressively and we both fell into step beside the man. And as we marched along I felt an excitement that grew in me as large as the dust cloud that we were kicking up. Around me I could hear snatches of remarks and laughing comments from which I gathered that the crowd were going to see off the Chinese for the thieving bastards that they were. The man that I had clutched explained that if we did not do something about these scum they would continue to take what was rightfully ours.

We were so far back behind the crowd that I could only hear snatches of what James Stewart actually said. We left before the violence began. Later on I read about the speech in the newspaper, along with the accounts of how the Chinese were hounded and attacked as a result. When I asked how things had so got out of hand, John reminded me that in the crowd were quite a few hardened criminals. If England sends its criminal classes here it's hardly surprising that they continue to follow their natural criminal tendencies, he told me. I tried to argue that this was a myth and that many decent people had been transported.

On our way back we continued to argue and I tried to persuade John that not only were many so-called criminals simply badly used individuals, but that many of the Chinese were innocent as well. He turned on me, telling me to be silent as we might share the fate of these 'innocents'. He went on to tell me how they had taken over honest miners claims when they were absent and that they wasted the water in their greed to get at more gold. He added that they were all gamblers and that they wasted their money on Fan Tan and similar games.

I knew that John was a hard-hearted man who despised the Chinese, but his antagonism to them on this occasion went further than I had ever experienced before. I wondered how long I could continue to work with this man. On the outside he had the air of a gentleman but deep down there was an obduracy, a rock hard objection to any sense of decency. He alleged that he was a Christian, and certainly went to church and openly prayed and behaved as many Christians do, but in truth he was a whitened sepulchre. I sensed that it was certainly not a suitable time to discuss more personal matters.

We did not pursue our discussions with the syndicate and so avoided getting involved in a nasty business where many Chinese were brutalised. I did manage in time to tell John my intentions regarding Estella. Then something happened that stopped any further thoughts of action on my part in that direction. Gold was discovered in New Zealand.

Chapter 15

New Zealand

When the news came that gold had been discovered in New Zealand John immediately said that Adam and Pirrip should get involved. Reports showed that the finds were substantial ones. John, for all his faults, was a Christian and had a theory that God had placed the gold in inaccessible places to draw mankind to them. Then, once the gold had been collected and used to fuel the trading engine, the residue of diggers would become the settled population producing crops and livestock. He reminded me again of the parable of the talents and said that we should certainly expand our efforts in New Zealand as we would be doing God's work.

He thought that we would be going forth and being fruitful and multiplying. In fact it would, in essence, be me who would be doing the going forth, as John was now firmly ensconced in Sydney, controlling gangs of different peoples, who now began to make up the population of that city. He seemed to be involved in as many aspects as there were commercial activities, for his business acumen was that of always being able to see how to turn a profit in anything that came along. And so, as the railways were expanded even more, so even more opportunities for profit appeared.

I asked him once whether he thought that Darwin's ideas were contrary to his bible-rooted ones. He scarcely hesitated, saying that they were complementary. He thought that Darwin had merely uncovered more of God's mysterious workings. He added that he was sure that, despite all the scientist's efforts, we should never uncover all of God's secrets.

I recalled seeing the return of The Beagle in 1836, having travelled to Portsmouth to see its arrival. All London was agog as we had heard of the steady stream of his specimens that had arrived before him. I was disappointed as he had already slipped ashore and made off for London before I arrived. I do not know quite what I expected; the Beagle was quite other than I thought it might be. It was small, almost insignificant, against many of the other craft that were there in the harbour. I did see a naval officer in a very worn coat who someone said was Captain Fitzroy. He appeared briefly on the deck and seemed angry about something.

John had booked me a berth on a ship that still had one available and I pushed my way through the crowds that always seemed to gather around a ship as it departed, desperate to get aboard before she sailed. I was nearly pushed over the side as I carried my bag up the gangway by others trying to get on board. A burly deckhand swore as he caught me. He apologised at his language. It's always the foreigners that cause trouble he said kicking out at the men who were imploring him to let them on.

"No ticket, no come on", he roared at the men as he inspected mine.

Then his manner became even more deferential.

"You the gentleman what John Adam said was coming", he asked.

I said that I was. At this he called for another equally solid seaman to take his place and led me below, where the heat increased with every set of ladders that we went down. At least he had taken my bag so I could keep up with him. Despite that, I was sweating copiously by the time we had reached a ridiculously small cabin. As I sat in my allotted space I thought how travel had changed. It was so much safer now. Was I tempting fate in such indulgence?

We reached New Zealand safely and there, as I stood on the deck, and saw the mad buying and selling of supplie, I felt a certain nostalgia. I looked up at the mountains that stood between us and where I presumed the gold was to be found, and blessed John for not having to be part of that rush of mortals whose activities were more swine-like than I remembered. In effect I did not have to go anywhere near the gold fields, staying in Dunedin, where I flatter myself that my efforts ensured that "ADAM & PIRRIP" quickly became established as a major trading house. Do I also presume too much if I say that the growth of Dunedin also owed much to our efforts? Probably. For had it not been me with my letters of credit and introductions to certain dignitaries, I'm sure some other commercial establishment would have filled the trading vacuum.

Even so, it was hard work each day, meeting this person or that, inspecting cargoes and perusing bills of lading and other similar documents that were now a natural part of my life. In fact I could scarcely conceive of a time when I had not filled my day with such activities. This meant that at the end of each day I went to my room in a local hotel, thankful to have a decent bed in which to spend my nights. I eschewed any entertainments and drank moderately.

So for some months I laboured diligently, sending reports back to record my progress and letters to ask for more of substances that I had ascertained would turn a profit for us. In all this time I scarcely thought of anything other than the business, in which I was totally immersed. The beauties of the countryside I ignored. I stayed in Dunedin mostly, except for one or two occasions when I had to go to a nearby farm for provisions.

The letters from John kept encouraging me to do more. Apparently I was so successful he wished me to stay as long as possible for the firm to capitalise upon the good beginning that I had made. He told me that, as he trusted me completely to represent our interests, the longer I stayed the better it would be for the firm.

Most of the diggers had come initially from Australia, as the word had spread of the strike, and the claims in Bendigo etc had petered out. In fact they still had gold there but it was taking much greater efforts to extract it. I looked amongst them for someone to whom I could safely hand over my work for I wished to return to my friends, and in particular, I looked forward to seeing Estella. In my haste to get to New Zealand I had not been able to speak to her as she had been engaged in assisting Caroline with yet another shipload of young women from England. Several times I had taken up a pen to write to her but I had always been diverted by some minor crisis. I comforted myself with the thought that when I saw her I would be able to tell her all.

Eventually, I secured the services of a bright young man who had emigrated many years before from England to New Zealand with his father, to take up farming. He wished to get away from that activity as his relationship with his stepmother, his father having married again when his first wife died, was not all that he could have desired. He was employed in the hotel where I was staying, and in several conversations with him I had heard about his family situation and established that he had a quick lively mind, could write a decent hand and could deal with figures with accuracy. He also gave me no pause as to his honesty.

Despite having found my substitute, I still needed some time to acquaint him fully with what I expected of him. Added to that was the fact that I had set in train the building of various stores and warehouses that I wished him to oversee, until I or John could come again. He quickly took on this responsibility for, as I have already said, he was an able young man. But I got away finally and sailed back with only the journey round the South Island, and the passage between the South and North Island giving us any trouble, because the weather during that time was atrocious. Once we were well away from the coast our journey was smooth and pleasant.

At Sydney, I hurried to where I normally lodged with keen anticipation of seeing my friends. As I went in my landlady came out looking anxious.

"Oh! Mr Pip. You have company. Miss Brown said that it would be in order for him to stay so I put him in the rooms at the back. I hope that I have done the right thing."

"If Estella, Miss Brown that is to say, said that you should do it I'm sure that you have done exactly what is correct."

As I said this a brawny young man with a battered face came out and saluted me with a bone-crushing hand clasp. He seemed familiar but I was sure that I did not know him. Something about the way he held his head nagged at me.

"You have the advantage of me."

"We have not met for many a year, and I was quite tiny when you last saw me in England."

He was joined by Estella, who inclined her head to me in a rather cool fashion before saying:

"This is Mr Gargery. Pip Gargery."

"Good God! You're Joe and Biddy's boy."

Chapter 16

Pip, old Chap.

We sat, all three at ease, looking at each other.

"Well, Pip old chap", said my namesake.

I laughed, delighted.

"Joe, your father, used to say that."

"Yes, I know. He and my mother often talked about you. They were very proud of you, you know."

I thought about those days. How we used to compare bites in our slices of home-made bread. I said:

"But was their pride in me not somewhat diminished when they learned that it was not the great Miss Havisham but a mere transported convict who had raised me up?"

"Not a bit. Abel Magwitch may have been the instrument of your rise, but he could not have foreseen what you have done with your life."

Estella, taking up her sewing, said:

"So what should we call you?"

"Call me Young Pip, I'm a Pip and I'm younger, so it's obviously the right name. I'm so glad I found you. When they died and I had completed my apprenticeship, I determined to seek you out. I think that you must be the only person to whom I am related now, no matter how tenuously."

"Well, I'm glad you did so. No, we are glad you did so. Aren't we Estella?

She gravely inclined her head. Her eyes were suffused with tears.

"Yes, you are most welcome here. Particularly as I have few friends here apart from Pip, so that makes you especially welcome."

I could see that Young Pip was puzzled, as he knew nothing of Estella's history.

"But how did you manage to get here? And how did you find me?"

"I came as an assisted settler. As a fully trained blacksmith I could do that. I had the address of Lady Spens and when I found out that she was dead I was at first quite lost. Then someone said that I should speak to Caroline Chisholm who told me about Miss Brown and Jane."

"Jane?"

"Jane O'Brian. She has a shop in town. Olivia serves there and her brother, Jamie, is apprenticed as a carpenter."

"Oh yes, I remember. Jane used to be employed by Lady Amanda. She must be quite old now. She was transported here in... do you know when?"

" No, no, she is not really old. And in any case she is quite spry. That's what comes of keeping active. She asked me if Lady Spens gave you anything before she died?"

I shook my head.

"No watch?"

Again I shook my head and as I did so a maidservant came in and said that Mr John Adam was at the door. I told her to tell him to come in, but Estella sprang up dropping her sewing and said he was there to take her to dinner. I stood up and Estella, eyes shining, brushed passed me.

"You did not know?" said Young Pip, seeing my puzzlement.

"What?"

"Estella and John are......"

"What?"

"Perhaps it's best if she tells you herself. While you were in New Zealand she had no-one else to turn to. You did leave her alone. Some might say that you abandoned her."

The next day, following a very disturbed nigh, I went to our head office in Victoria Street, and finding John in his private office I asked him whether he had anything to tell me about Estella. He looked at me coolly and said nothing. I felt my anger boiling up inside me. I went outside in the heat, hoping that by doing so I would be more able to face him. I ignored the look that I got from workers who now numbered so many that I scarcely knew most of them. Some murmured together, breaking off when I looked in their direction.

Returning in a somewhat more composed frame of mind I found that John had absented himself and no-one knew where he might have gone. As I stood there, a somewhat timid female assistant drew my attention to some matters that needed my attention. I dealt with them and some others and within a space of hours I was drawn into my old work habits. I might feel that that Estella was slipping away from me but I had to retain a grip upon the management of "ADAM & PIRRIP." In time I found many of the letters that I had sent to John, some of them unopened.

I gathered them together and, ignoring the increasingly openly rude stares of the staff, I retreated to my own office where I sat for some while. I sat there until tea was brought to me by the same young female assistant who had alerted me initially to the need for action. She also brought several other pieces of correspondence that required an answer. She was more sympathetic than the other members of the staff, but just as unhelpful when I enquired as to John's whereabouts. She told me artlessly that he had not been coming in so regularly now that he was seeing Miss Brown.

I could not bring myself to ask what she meant by this. I sent her away and sat letting my tea grow cold as I began to realise that John had deliberately used the discovery of gold in New Zealand to get me out of the way so that he could ingratiate himself with Estella. Just as I had sent away the assistant so he had sent me off. In his case however he had calculated that my absence would increase his opportunity to do I know not what.

I knew that he had mixed feelings about Estella. He despised her for working with Caroline Chisholm, as he claimed that people should help themselves and not rely upon others. On the other hand, he was fascinated by her early life history and her present demeanour as a lady, which she was unable to alter, even had she wished to do so. She attracted him more than Lola, he told me once when he had been drinking, and used such a low crude reference to the sort of excitement she engendered in him, that I warned him that were he to continue in such a fashion I would be forced to strike him. This threat seemed to amaze him, as he appeared to believe that I shared his sordid view of Estella.

Chapter 17

I lose Estella

Despite my persistence I still did not manage to see John at work, and a trip round his regular haunts was no more fruitful. I knew that he was seeing Estella, so I tried to catch sight of her. So I took to watching and waiting in the busy streets each evening once I had completed my tasks for the day at "ADAM & PIRRIP". As I did so, I worried that I might simply not see her, for she had also kept out of my sight.

What concerned me most was what I would say to her, before I had ascertained from John what their relationship was now. I knew that Estella was fully aware of John's former indiscretions. I also knew that this had not seemed to concern her in the past when she saw him merely as my business partner. Would it concern her now?

Eventuall, my patrolling the streets was rewarded by seeing Estella with Olivia. Relieved that she was not with John, I overcame my apprehensions, and tried to join them, as they went down towards one of Mrs Chisholm's shelters. Hurrying after them, and shouldering people aside in my eagerness, I called:

"Estella!"

She turned and regarded me gravely. Olivia was equally subdued.

"Where is John? Why are you avoiding me?"

She gestured to Olivia to go on without her. Olivia whispered something to her. I caught the word 'safe'. Estella shook her head and Olivia, looking troubled, nodded and picking up her skirts to avoid the dust, went on, leaving us as the crowds forced their way past us.

"This is scarcely the place for such a conversation Pip. I'm also late. We were on our way to assist Mrs Chisholm. I promised her that Olivia and I would be with her by seven. It lacks but ten minutes to the hour so I have little time for you."

She turned to leave me. I grasped her hand. She made no effort to release it. It lay cold and lifeless in mine. She said nothing. Eventually I let it go.

"You had time for me once as I recollect."

She turned back. Her voice was low and controlled but perfectly audible above the sound of the traffic.

"Come with me then. We can talk when I have fulfilled my obligation at the shelter."

Our arrival at the shelter sparked an interest that was due to the fact that Estella was accompanied by a man. I had heard the criticism that Caroline kept the women that she was instrumental in bringing from England in such poor conditions, with poor food, cramped rooms etc, that many considered they were almost slave-like. Consequently, when a man came to visit the shelter, the women were so desperate to escape they would accept almost any proposal of marriage to achieve this. Some said that Caroline dealt with women in this way as she was desperate to flood Australia with married couples who would produce offspring that espoused her way of life.

The shelter was certainly Spartan but clean and tidy and, as Estella was quick to remind me, was infinitely better than what most, if not all, the women had left behind in England. She also reminded me that it was the future that Caroline was concerned with, not the present. I was impressed by the calm way that Estella carried out her duties. Having dealt with all the outstanding matter, she led me to a small side room, leaving Olivia to deal with the arrangements for receiving yet another shipload of women.

"Well Pip?"

I was about to speak when the formidable Mrs Caroline Chisholm entered the room. I say 'entered' because she had so much presence that simply to come in would have been impossible for her.

" I am so sorry to interrupt but I hear we have problems with the Mary Gray."

"Olivia is dealing with them."

"Good, then I shall withdraw."

She did so and I made another beginning.

"I hardly know where to start. I am returned from New Zealand to find nothing at all as I left it. John has disappeared. You are avoiding me and I cannot for the life of me conceive why this should be so. I am beginning to suspect that John arranged for me to be sent to New Zealand so he might the more easily turn you from me."

I paused, my heart beating strongly. I waited, intent upon giving Estella ample opportunity to explain herself to me. I was determined to let her do this, despite the fact that I considered her behaviour almost beyond forgiveness. As we sat there in silence Olivia came in with tea. In Australia it seems they have taken on the English habit of providing tea at any and every opportunity. With the sweat running down my back, caused as much by my emotions as the heat, I seized the cup that was poured for me and drained it. Olivia, smiling at my haste, left the room.

At last Estella spoke.

"Caroline always says that hot tea is best even when the weather is also hot. She learned this in India, where her husband served a long while ago, but I expect you know that."

I stared at her in amazement. This was not at all what I considered a proper explanation for her behaviour. She sipped her tea, folded her arms and went on:

"John warned me that when you came back from New Zealand that you would probably prove to be unreasonable. He also said that you would try to turn me away from him. You see, he has been quite honest with me. He has told me all about his previous life which he has now abandoned."

I tried to speak, but realised that were I to do so I would be doing exactly what John had warned Estella I would do.

"I came to Australia to find you Pip, when I discovered my true identity. I was so pleased to find you that, once I had got over the shock of finding that you were in trade, I was able to forgive you. I forgave you for that lapse as I could see that you had to make your way in the world somehow. I was contented to be with you, but as time went on it seemed that you cared more for your occupation than you did for me. When we were together, I had to endure such tedium as long descriptions of how difficult it was to purchase railway sleepers, or how everyone was out to make more profit than you did. During this time I found that John, by contrast, took a delight in listening to me and not once was he boring. He amused me Pip. Women, even ladies, like to be diverted and made to feel wanted, and dare I say it, loved."

I wanted to tell Estella that John had contrived this; that while he had enchanted her he had seen to it that I was kept at the firm's grindstone. I knew that were I to protest she would know that what he had told her about me was true.

"So Pip, I intend to spend the remainder of my life with John."

I heard this final sentence as a sentence on my own life. I could not now tell Estella the whole truth about John, for she would, if she believed me, despise me as being no gentleman for having told her. If she did not believe me then I was a liar. So I took the only step that a gentleman could. I held my tongue, bowed in farewell and left. I told myself that I owed it to Abel. By his efforts I had aspired to be a gentleman. I was now in trade, but that should not stop me acting as if I were such a creature. Besides, Estella was his daughter and I should respect the wishes of a lady who was the daughter of my first benefactor.

I had to accept that Estella was now lost to me, by my own stupidity. I heard in due course that she had gone to live with John, much to Caroline's disgust. I did not share that disgust. I had always been wary of Caroline's feelings as I knew from what I had seen of her activities that she was ever ready herself to sail near the wind in order to further her ends. She was certainly no saint.

John and I still worked together in "ADAM & PIRRIP" as we had done formerly. We saw no reason to do any other, especially as we had our own areas of responsibility within the firm that meant that we rarely met. Occasionally, the situation dictated that we did meet and we then kept up the pretence that we were partners who shared each other's interests and concerns. Now and then Estella would come to some fete or ball on John's arm along with Mrs O'Brian, her daughter Olivia and young Pip. We were all formally correct and hurt no-one with our past quarrels, yet I sensed that other people knew from our polite behaviour that all was not as it was made to seem.

I could not, of course, simply pretend to have no interest in them all. I saw how gradually Estella lost her early good looks as they were replaced by a serene plainness. In Olivia, I thought that I saw what Estella had been as a child when I knew her as a youth. I may have been deluding myself to draw some comfort from the situation but she seemed to move lightly, almost as if she had been trained to be a dancer. Her fair hair, when she let it down, reached well below her waist, a waist that I felt I could have spanned with my two hand; an endeavour that remained a fancy as I never put it to the test. Outdoors she was never without a hat, so her complexion remained pale and creamy, not pallid. Some women begin small and grow large with age, into copies of their mothers. Not so Olivia, who could almost have passed as a lady, except to those who knew her.

Olivia's mother, however, had expanded somewhat from the time when I first came to Australia, and saw her as she gossiped with Amanda Jane. She persistently refused to hide her face, so as a consequence had a darker, rougher, redder complexion that announced to all that she was no lady. A lifetime's toil had not reduced her step that remained as lively as ever. She adored a ball, and only stopped dancing when a certain breathlessness overcame her. Young Pip treated me with caution and I could only guess at what notions about me had been put into his head by John. He had grown into a stalwart young man with a growing reputation based upon his iron work. I took no interest in his pugilism. No-one could doubt his interest in Olivia. She seemed oblivious of his interest. Was she to do to him what Estella had done to me?

Chapter 18

Disaster at sea

Our business continued to prosper. John was right; any new mercantile endeavour would always require supplies and who better to supply them than an old established firm such as ours? We now added to our growing list of employees, men whose qualities were matched by qualifications regarding knowledge of metals and all kinds of other substances. We could no longer employ amateurs such as we had been. We now had to take on engineers and other similar worthies and my time was often spent in interviewing them.

But as our business prospered our relationships grew worse. Occasionally, either in the office or socially, we quarrelled. It was usually about the stupidest things. On more than one occasion either John or I stalked out of a meeting leaving business acquaintances or friends appalled at our conduct.

In October of 1876 I escaped the growing heat of Sydney to take a series of voyages along the coast, ostensibly to visit several of our agents and other employees. I have to admit that any of our capable managers could have accomplished what I set out to do. I tried however to persuade myself that it was necessary for me to do this and that as Mr Pip Pirrip of "ADAM & PIRRIP" I would have a greater effect. Inside myself, I admitted to that I was simply running away from a situation that had got out of hand

All proceeded satisfactorily until I embarked at Freemantle to go to Adelaide. I joined the steam ship as it sat in the harbour, loading the last of its timber cargo, some of it lashed to the deck. I had a cabin to myself, which I counted as being lucky for we had half a hundred passengers, many of whom were below in much less salubrious quarters than mine. I walked about enjoying the breeze that came off the sea. It was a pleasure after the heat of the day. The sun began to set and it became slightly cooler.

In the evening we cast off. We had caught the tide, and a freshening wind quickly took us out to sea well beyond the harbour. We bowled along steadily with packs of birds crying in our wake. They rose and fell, climbing to allow them to dive down to collect the bucket of fish guts that a deckhand threw out in a wide silvery circle into the sea.

"Supper ready soon."

I nodded, not looking forward to a meal of greasy fried fish that was portended by the throwing overboard of their innards.   But at least my status had earned me a place alongside the captain.   He kept us all amused until the increased rolling of the boat made him excuse himself from our company.

I followed him soon after and was amazed at how it had blown up since I had gone into supper. I had intended to run through the notes that I had collected so far but I didn't fancy my airless cabin. The sea was much livelier and soon, as the wind increased, it became unpleasant to try to stand upright. Pride and the thought of what it would be like below kept me on deck. I knew that in a really fierce blow a sailing ship would stand out to sea, reduce sail and run before the storm.   Our steamer, however continued to butt it's way through the increasing large lumps of water that the wind was whipping up. I still kept to the deck and was comforted by the steady beat of the engines and the thump, thump, thump of the pumps. Eventually I did retire from the upper deck.

I turned in and awoke to the sound of running feet and confused shouting. Dressing hastily, I went up the companionway pushing past several passengers who had come up from the depths of the ship. To their queries about what was happening I had no answers. I was as ignorant as they were as what was going on. On deck I could hear a roaring sound. My God! I thought, that's the sound of breakers. Surely we are not that close to the shore. With all the waves being blown at us it was impossible to see very much. Eventually I determined that it was only the sound of the waves.

I caught hold of a sailor who was making his way along the deck and asked him what was happening. Were we in danger? For an answer he rolled his eyes and as he did so the rhythmic sound of the pumps stopped. We both stood still waiting for them to begin again. They didn't. My sailor gave a great cry and ran off. Around me other passengers began to gather on deck. Some of them were clearly frightened. The older ones were trying to reassure the younger ones, but were not very successful at that enterprise. At this moment a sailor came amongst us and said that we were to assist in keeping the ship afloat.

We wondered what this meant and were answered when buckets were brought up and we were all instructed to assist the crew in bailing. Some men declined to do what the crew were paid to do on their behalf and were pushed to one side. One nearly went over the side. After that he thought better of his refusal. The others joined in, reluctantly at first, but as our situation became ever more dangerous, they lost their reluctance and bailed steadily with the rest. This seemed to go on forever. I heard one of the crew say that the captain was simply steering for the shore as there was little else that he could safely do.

Dawn came with no real change in the light or the weather. With so much wind buffeting us, and so much water being thrown against us, our position stayed as perilous as it had been.   Only the combined efforts of the crew and passengers kept us afloat, as all attempts to get the pumps started again failed. I was beginning to feel extremely weary and would have sunk down onto the deck and given up when the ship's engine slowed and stopped.

Now the ship wallowed in the wave. with no movement forward to keep us heading into them. We began to turn sideways and I knew from what I had heard described many time that we were in danger of broaching. Everyone stopped bailing. Some prayed. Others cursed, and most, I amongst them, just stood dog-tired, wet, hungry, and totally dispirited, waiting for whatever our destiny was to be.

A monstrous wave hit us just as the captain ordered us into the lifeboats. One boat was filled with passengers, swung out and launched. I assisted in pushing it from the side of our ship, noting the rust and rubbish that was left where the lifeboat had been lashed to the deck. Then another monstrous wave came, catching the lifeboat, raising it and dashing it down upon the edge of the ship, so that it capsized and broke into a mass of broken pieces of wood and struggling bodies. The whole scene was of utter confusion, with most of us too shattered in spirits to do anything more.

All the rust and rubbish was gone. An enormous deck hand threw ropes into the sea and shouted at us to help him rescue the drowning passengers. Only the quick swinging out of the second boat and its lowering saved some, whilst other poor souls were drowned before our eyes. Another sailor shouted something about clinker built and carvel built, before running nimbly along the deck forward, maintaining a precarious balance by grasping hold of some of the rigging. By now there was precious little left of most of the fittings on the deck and the remaining passengers clung to whatever they could to save themselves.

We drifted on, with the waves and wind lessening slightly, and we could see that we were in a bay of some sort. From the bottom of the ship came a groaning, scraping sound that outdid any screaming of the women. I suddenly realised that I had been hearing them all along, but had not taken any notice because of the sound of the storm. To be fair it was only a few who screamed so constantly. Others with set visages and exemplary courage, simply carried on doing what they were told, as if they knew that this would be their only salvation.

The running sailor was back and told us that we were aground. We had stopped drifting and moved sideways heeling over, making cargo and passengers slide down the deck. Several people began to divest themselves of their upper and outer garments. It was not a time for modesty. We knew that were we to go into the sea in a bid to strike out for the shor, that our clothing would drag us down.

Another lifeboat was swung out and dropped down into the still boiling mass of water. It was immediately swamped. Then, to my utter amazemen, I saw a woman on a horse alongside the swamped lifeboat. She turned round and urged the horse, with several people attached to it, to swim to the shore. I thought that I had gone mad, that I was the victim of some illusion, some hallucination, but others saw her too and we waited hoping that as she had come to rescue some, that she might come again.

She did, and she had an assistant, a man, who with her riding constantly into and out of the surf managed to rescue most of us. I stayed on deck with the captain; then with him, and other members of the crew, I helped to launch as many of the lifeboats as we were able. All were either swamped or capsized due to the monstrous surf and the inability of the passengers to be expert enough to keep them afloat.

Chapter 19

Saved!

It was now that I realised that it was time to save myself. Somehow I had battled alongside the crew to save the others, as if a guardian angel had been guiding me. I drew strength from I know not where, and I did things that afterwards made me wonder where the knowledge came from to do them. My knowledge of ships was limited yet I seem to do what was necessary, before any one told me to do it.

In the surf that crashed against the ship, I saw the young woman who had yet again ridden out to us on a horse. She was waving to those of who remained. I understood that if I were to be rescued I would have to throw myself into the sea and chance that I would be near enough to her to grasp something, as I seen others do before me. I might then stand a chance of being pulled to shore. I poised myself to jump, but waited long enough for the swell to recede so that I would be drawn back with it as I did not want to be dashed against the side of the ship, as I had seen happen to others. I knew without thinking about it that my best chance was to use all my energy at once to strike away towards the woman on the horse.

She saw me and waved encouragingly. I jumped. I fell into what seemed to be a malevolent creature that wrapped itself about me dragging at me. I kicked off my shoes. Luckily I had already discarded my coat. Frantically I moved my arms to propel myself forward. I kicked. I swore. I struggled and then I reached her.

"Hold on."

I held on to what I suppose was part of her saddle. Someone else was holding on the other side. Drumming her heels against the sides of the horse she turned it towards the shore and towed us both in. As soon as I felt the sands beneath me, I let go, and half crawling, half walking, I scrabbled my way to safety. I stood, but immediately the surf knocked me over and I might even at this late stage have drowned had I not crawled up well beyond the seas that still rolled in endlessly. My feet were cut and my arms lacerated and the salt water stung so that I wept in pain. Then I stood again and made my way to where I could see a farmhouse with barns at the back. Beyond that I could not see. I had no need to, for hands were around me and I was led into paradise. It was warm, dry and comforting. After a meal and a drink I was led to a bed where I sank down into a deep sleep.

Chapter 20

A theatre ticket

With the sunrise came a most welcome calm that made everything look normal. I awoke after a sleep that felt more like unconsciousness. My whole body ached, which was scarcely surprising, as I had pushed it to limits that it had not experienced for some considerable time.

Sitting in the kitchen of the farm, I shared a breakfast with several other survivors. Some others were still asleep on the floor. I should have felt guilty that I had had a bed in which to sleep overnight, but when I saw how some still slept through the noise of the breakfasters in the kitchen I forgave myself. Ham and eggs and tea had never tasted so good even though I knew that round the back in a barn lay several who had been less fortunate than I; they would never eat breakfast again. I forbore from asking how many were saved. I just ate and drank the strong tea, refusing the rum that many added to strengthen it further.

I had lost everything on the ship as it had finally foundered, taking all with it as it broke up. So all my past work with our agents was lost along with my trunk; only my pocket book was saved as I had put it inside my safety pocket in my trousers. I looked at the bank notes that gave me a freedom from care that very few of the other survivors had. With this came an acceptance that made me ready simply to sit and do nothing but listen to the others' accounts of what had happened.

It was curious how this event had affected us. I sat drained of any desire to do anything. Others seemed to be driven to relive every moment in words. One woman exhibited an almost uncanny ability to act out for us several episodes that had impressed her. I later found that she was an amateur actress and it was no surprise to find her in Sydney the following year giving a thespian performance based upon this sad incident. After some time I tired of this and went down to the sea-shore where the breakers were tossing bits of broken lifeboats onto the sands. From a rock where I sat I could see a gentleman approach me. From his garb I guessed that he was a clergyman.

"My dear sir, my name is Donaldson of St Mary's. May I offer you some assistance?"

I stood up.

"No, I thank you most sincerely but there are others who will require your help more than I."

He bowed and turned from me to go on to the farmstead.

"A moment. I do need to get to Sydney. How might I achieve this? I have the means."

I took out my pocket book and using its contents, I not only paid to get to Sydney, but also left some money to aid those less fortunate than I. I was desperate to get back there to try to salvage something from my trips to oversee our employees. I had been spared. I had, at least, to try to redeem myself.

Safely back in Sydney I set to rewriting all my reports from memory, and as I was engaged in this activity, a clerk brought me a sealed envelope addressed to:

P. Pirrip Esq.

I opened it and found inside a ticket for a box at the Theatre Royal. It was for a performance the following Friday. I had long thought that I would go to this theatre ever since it opened in 1875. Reports about its decoration in white and gold and the red plush seats had spread all over Sydney. It was said to have the largest crystal chandelier in any theatre in the world. I doubted that. I thought that it was a story put about by Samuel who was the manager. Perhaps he had sent the ticket hoping to influence some dealings with us. We often had free tickets to such occasions.

Friday was wet and windy but still warm. Pushing my way through the crowds, and stepping carefully over sodden leaves and trash, I went into the theatre showing my ticket to the attendant who showed me the stairs that led up to the boxes. I opened the door of my box and came face to face with Estella! I stared at her confused. I looked at my ticket and the number of the box. Had I entered the wrong one? To cover my confusion I took off my hat.

She reached past me and shut the door. I saw that the curtains were shut so that we were in shadow. No-one could see or hear us.

"You. You sent the ticket."

"Yes. Please sit down."

We both sat. I put my hat on the floor.

" I wanted to see you in private and this was the only way that I could think of how to arrange such a meeting."

I waited, sitting on the edge of my plush velvet seat.

"Pip, don't be angry."

"I'm not."

"Your face tells me otherwise."

I sat back and took a breath.

"Pip. You and John."

"Yes."

"You must stop this war between you. You are tearing people apart including me. And it's bad for "ADAM & PIRRIP" too."

"He sent you?"

"No. Please believe me. I know that I am rejected by polite society for ignoring conventions. Caroline has never spoken to me since I left you for John. We were cut by the Harcourts in this very theatre. Just imagine, the Harcourts whose grandparents were transported convicts. Despite that I still care about the people I love."

"You left me. Hardly the action of that many would regard as an indication of your concern for me."

"I did what I thought was best at the time. I believed that you had abandoned me. I turned to a stronger, helpful man."

"Who is a liar, a cheat, a bigot and an advocate of........"

Her reproachful look stopped me. I picked up my hat. I stood up. I meant to leave, but her outstretched hand and pale drawn face held me back. Slowly I sat down. Beyond the curtain I could hear the murmurings of the assembling audience, accompanied by the unmistakeable sounds of an orchestra tuning up.

"I know all about John. He is unlikely to change. I have burned my bridges and mean to stay with him. I just wanted to see you to determine whether I could appeal to your better nature, to any feelings that you might still have for me, in order to beg you to make peace with him. I must go."

She rose and gestured for me to remain seated as she pulled her veil over her face. She opened the door of the box, made sure that no-one was there and slipped out. I sat and thought about what she had said. She was right. Our behaviour was childish. We ought to stop it. But then I thought of how we had come to this situation. How time after time John had showed himself to be a nasty, cynical bigot. How he had despised his workers who were the source of his great wealth. How he had worked to steal Estella from me by lies and every sort of deceit.

I pulled aside the curtain and looked down, literally upon many who were no better than John. In their scramble for riches and honour, they too had forfeited all rights to my respect. I had not cast them off, so why should I not make some form of peace with John. God knows we were not getting any younger. Perhaps if I continued in our present fashion I would not get the chance to mend our shattered friendship.

The following day I sent word to John that I would be grateful to see him about a delicate matter. To my intense surprise he came at once to see me. As we stood in my office I felt suddenly that this was a mistake, a going back when we should be going forward. Then, telling myself that I was going forward by seeking reconciliation, I began.

"John. We have had our differences and we have taken extreme positions as a result. I think that the time has come now for us to put away these petty thoughts and to return to how we used to be. Well, not quite how we were."

"How did you know Pip? Who told you? Was it Estella, or Olivia perhaps. Yes, it must have been Olivia. I know that you have not seen Estella for some considerable time."

I kept my face a blank. In truth, not knowing in the least part what he was going on about, enabled me to do exactly that.

" It came as a complete shock to me I can tell you. You go on thinking that you will live for ever, then something like this happens."

He leaned forward and put his face in his hands. He sobbed! I sat amazed. I had never ever seen John moved to tears. What could it be that was so affecting him?

"Dr Fordyce says that I have to take life much easier. My heart will no longer stand for any further racketing around. I have to accept that my body is no longer as strong and fit as it once was. Oh! Pip, of course I am ready to be friends once again."

He rose and gave me his hand.

Chapter 21

Train smash

The news of the train crash reached me as I sat as usual, wrestling with figures on jute and bricks. I took little notice of what the clerks were saying until John came into the office almost shouting:

"It's Estella. She's in hospital. They may have to operate."

I looked at him, my mind still upon my figures.

"What operation? Why? What are you talking about?"

"Her legs."

"Legs?"

I was appalled at his indelicacy of his mentioning such a part of Estella's anatomy. John sat down and it was only then that I saw the state that he was in. An assistant clerk brought us tea which he drank in one draught, as I took in his dishevelled state. He was dirty and his clothes were torn. His trembling hands were grimed with black grease and there were smudges of it on his face.

"I have come straight from the hospital. She is asking for you. Will you come?"

I stood up, pushing my papers to one side. I drank my tea, put on my panama hat and went out, followed by John, who began to tell me how he had been travelling with Estella beyond Paramatta on the train. The name brought something to mind. I stopped outside in the heat and felt the difference immediately. I turned back. People pushed against us trying to get past me, as I stood close to John.

"Is this the line where we got the contract for the iron work?"

He hesitated, looked around.

"Does it matter?"

"It might, but let's get on."

In the carriage he urged the driver to drive quickly then told me what had happened. They had been on their way to see both Olivia and her mother Mrs O'Brian. Olivia had started a business, a shop, and employed some of the women that Estella and Mrs Chisholm had been assisting. They had been enjoying the ride. The breeze through the open windows was particularly pleasant as it blew away the heat.

I interrupted to ask whether that was only reason for taking this carriage. John said that he was also desirous of avoiding Harcourt and his wife. After the business in the theatre last month he wanted to spare Estella from any more unpleasantness. I think everyone had heard about that episode so I didn't blame John for his actions.

They were just at Emu Plain, on the slight curve that is at the highest part of the embankment there, when they all felt a juddering. The train began to rock, not badly but enough to make John think that they should slow down. They didn't. If anything they picked up speed and as a result they came completely off the rails, plunging down the side of the embankment, gouging out a large part of it, exposing the inner core that had only been completed recently. The scene when the train came finally to rest was truly awful. Many were thrown out of the train and two were dead for sure. It seemed that Harcourt was one of them. Many suffered appalling injuries that went beyond broken bones and contusions. Several men said that it reminded them of their experiences in India during the uprising. It was the blood that was so horrifying. Estella came off very badly, as some part of the train fell upon her pinning her against another part. It took a mighty effort on the part of several men to release her and was only accomplished by using a shunting pole as a lever.

"Now that she has been conveyed to Sydney Hospital the doctors there are talking of amputations. Thank God for Lucy Osburn. At least we have trained Nightingale nurses now in the hospital. With them there she stands a much better chance of survival. By the way, in case you are worried, there was talk of the way in which the carriages were joined. I heard several rail employees say that the couplings were all wrong, not correctly assembled. No-one mentioned the rails.

At first they would not let us in to see Estella as neither of us was a relative and the Sister seemed more concerned with the proprieties than our anxieties. She also looked askance at John in his filthy state, saying that she did not want her wards to be contaminated. A doctor, bloody but cheerful, told her to stand aside saying that we might go in. I shall not easily forget the sister's pursed lips expressing extreme disapproval and her stiff manner as she stood aside. Nor shall I ever forget the sight of a grey-faced woman who, despite looking suddenly much older, was recognisably Estella. I hung back to let John go to her but she waved him away impatiently and beckoned to me.

"Dear Pip, I had to see you before they operate."

"Must you?" I asked turning to the doctor.

"Yes, if we are to save the foot. We cannot delay any further."

He called for orderlies to wheel her away immediately. As they did so she called out:

"I'm sorry, so sorry Pip."

We waited for several hours before the doctor returned, much less cheerful now.

"You may go in now but she is not to be excited. Please leave when the nurse decides that you should go. She needs calm and rest, and good nursing," he added, smiling at the probationer nurse, who looked too young to be taking on these responsibilities.

Beside her bed we found chairs and we sat in them. I was beginning to realise that our role was reduced to waiting. After some while she opened her eyes and said:

"Thirsty."

I called the probationer nurse who gave her some water from what looked like a child's teapot set. She sighed, smiled, then grimaced as she moved her foot. The probationer nurse beckoned to me so I stood and followed her into the corridor where she handed me a linen bag and a paper.

"Here is a list of things that she will need."

I took the bag and list and went back, meeting John just as he was coming away. I handed him the bag and list.

"She's resting and not to be disturbed. What's this? Oh! I see, yes."

We left together and went our separate ways. I never saw Estella again for in the night she died quietly. John avoided me and it was left to me to find in the newspaper that a qualified medical practitioner and house surgeon employed in Sydney Hospital had said that she had died after the operation. The cause of death was shock to the system, caused by a fracture of her right thigh and the crushing of the left foot, leaving her in such a poor state that amputation was necessary.

So, once again John had behaved badly in not telling me about Estella death, leaving me to find out about it through a newspaper. I vowed never to see him again, but within weeks I changed my mind, as he sent me word that we ought to meet. I remembered Estella's plea to me to end our war so I reluctantly agreed to see him and we met in his office

Chapter 22

Dusty old documents

"Let's not quarrel Pip."

I glowered at John. He was asking me not to quarrel when he had behaved so atrociously? He sat at his desk that was covered as usual with papers. He tapped a file saying:

"These will interest you. I went to the Law Registry today after speaking to Olivia and her brother. They said something to me that their mother had told them. She had heard it from Amanda Jane, and I remembered what you had told me about Compeyson and Abel's last days. It set me to thinking, so I talked to our lawyers and asked them about the list that Magwitch had given Jaggers of the possessions that he was leaving you. I further remember that Jaggers had said that he wanted to memorialise in due course. His intention was to try to get something for you, but it looked hopeless.

"Yes I remember the situation very well. Because Abel had never put his hand to anything, nor made a will or settlement in my favour, I gave up any hope of retrieving anything. It left me in a bad situation I can tell you. Still there it is. The law is quite clear as to what happens to returned transported convicts."

"That might well be so. Abel certainly never put his hand to anything in England, but I have discovered things here in Australia that might considerably alter the whole situation."

"What have you found?"

"What you yourself might have found had you not been so idle!"

I was stung by his words and felt my ire rise in me, as he turned from me and scrabbled amongst the papers, eventually finding one that he passed to me.

"What's this?"

"That is a letter about a copy of the will that left Abel Magwitch the farm that he successfully ran before going back to England. He brought the will to Amanda Jane, who not only ascertained that it was a legally drawn up document, but also helped Abel to get the estate probated correctly. This means that it is still valid."

"But you are forgetting that as Magwitch went back to England everything that he had was forfeit to the crown."

"No. I am not forgetting that. That is exactly the case, but as Abel died before the sentence of the court could be carried out, it could be argued that, it was never finally established that he had in fact returned to England. His death on the gallows would have been the final proof."

"It all seems rather tenuous. It is making bricks without straw to my way of thinking, and that seldom leads anywhere."

"But that is what our lawyers are so very good at! Don't you remember that case at Bendigo that they successfully concluded for "ADAM & PIRRIP"? We thought all along that we would never convince the court that the land was ours. We did though, thanks to Beckridge and Blownding.   Worth their weight in gold those lawyers to us.   You used to call them 'Puffing and Blowing' but you have to admit they do produce results."

"And cost us a small fortune in the process."

"That's as maybe. Now take a look at this."

'This' was another legal document. I took it and began to read it. It was a document that took me some little while to get through , but when I had done so it seemed to say that I was the main beneficiary in a will; and that as a consequence certain land was mine. In addition I had also been left a strong box that was deposited in the Sydney and General Central Bank.

"Does this bank still exist?" I almost whispered.

"No, it went out of business about four years ago."

My feelings can be imagined. From the clouds of an exaltation of hope I was dashed to the solid grounds of despair.

"But it was taken over and all its assets, such as they were, and all its papers, were passed to The City Bank in Pitt

329

Street, It has the strong box. I have ascertained that and we should be able to view its contents tomorrow."

I started to say something and John held up a well manicured hand in warning, and told me that the land was probably worthless. It was in the Hunter Valley and had not been worked for a considerable period of time. He said that it lacked water so produces little and in addition there were squatters on it. My hopes sank again. Then rose as I thought of Beckridge and Blownding.   I became excited. Despite the lateness of the hour I wondered whether we should not be doing something. I rose and paced about. John eyed me with amusement.

" So we are friends again?" he asked enthusiastically.

"Partners."

"Oh come now Pip. We have been through a great deal together, been rivals in love and have established a solid merchant firm that is respected both here and in New Zealand."

He saw my frown as he said 'New Zealand' and hurried on:

"Do sit down. Tomorrow we shall go together to the bank and there establish either that Magwitch was successful in making you a gentleman of property or not. Think of that Pip. It's not a case of you having raised yourself by your own bootstraps in trade, with a little aid from me, to be a man of property. You could be landed gentry! You could be a real gentleman"

"But what if the land is valueless? What then?"

"My dear Pip, that's quite beside the point. How many 'gentlemen' were you acquainted with in England who had estates that were absolutely laden with debt? How many of those gilded gadflies of the upper class, who spent money like water and shared your life of ease, gave a fig for so being in debt that they were obliged to borrow from people like me? And how they despised people like me for not being gentlemen. You told me how you were nearly arrested for running up bills over jewellery for self-adornment and only Joe and Biddy saved you. So does it matter if your land is worthless? You could really be landed gentry! You could be a bone fide gentleman"

So we sat up late in the hot Australian night, opening several bottles, as we set aside our differences and speculated on the future. And the more glasses of wine that we took, the rosier that future seemed to be. I became philosophical. I felt my anger lessen. John fell asleep in his chair. I felt too full of I know not what to sleep. I thought about Abel and all his struggles to make me his gentleman. I thought about Amanda Jane and Joe and Biddy and Olivia. Ah! Olivia. What was I going to do about Olivia? I could not let her ruin young Pip's life.

Chapter 23

Magwitch's inheritance

The morning was considerable cooler as we rattled our way to the bank. The overnight rain had laid the dust but there was still a hint of some muggy weather to come. My head ached and the rebuilding that was going on everywhere with the consequent noise did little to help it. I ignored John's suggestion that we might have a little drink to settle ourselves. I was anxious to see what there was in the bank vaults.

The bank manager was new, didn't recognise us, and John and I were obviously an unnecessary interruption to his busy day. He rang a bell and, when a deferential clerk came in, handed us over, clearly glad to be rid of us. John muttered something about a jumped-up nothing riding on the coat tails of others efforts. I was too excited to say anything.

We were led downstairs, through several sets of iron gates that were unlocked and relocked as we went through them, reminding me of how I used to visit Abel before he died. As we went through the last one, I remembered how I told him about Estella being his daughter, and was brought back sharply from my reverie when we stopped before a row of drawers set in several aisles. With a complete lack of ceremony the clerk handed me a quite small key and pointed to one of the metal drawers. He then withdrew to sit upon a wooden bench nearby. I opened the drawer, and pulled it out to find a dusty packet of papers, brittle and somewhat faded. I handed them to John who opened them. The names Spens, Magwitch and O'Brian were written there on the first pages, so he simply put them into a little leather bag that I had brought for that purpose. I went to close the drawer, when at the back I saw there was another smaller packet; a linen pouch with a smooth hard something in it.

It was a watch. A handsome old fashioned one, slightly dented as if it had been dropped, although the glass was still intact. The scrap of paper that it was wrapped in had obviously been cut from a newspaper, as the edges were smooth and not torn. I put the watch into my bag, realising as I did so that the bottom of the linen bag contained something else. It was an envelope and it was addressed to:

P. Pirrip Esq

To be opened on my death.

Lady Amanda Jane Spens

We travelled back with our booty, in a state of some excitement, to our main office, where we gave instructions that we were not to be disturbed. There we found that the documents were copies of:

Abel Magwitch's will;
his employer's will;
letters from Amanda Jane Spens;
and letters from Mrs Jane O'Brian.

In other words, we had documents that showed that, through a correctly probated will, Abel had inherited money and property.　They also showed that Abel had willed all that property and money to me, before he had gone back to England.　It seemed to be correctly drawn up to leave all of Abel Magwitch's land, goods, chattels and property to a certain Pip Pirrip Gentleman C/O Jaggers, Barrister at Law etc etc

John looked at all this with some satisfaction.

"Now we have something for Beckridge and Blownding to get their legal teeth into."

I laid aside the papers and took up the watch.　I was about to throw away the scrap of paper that was wrapped around it when, having smoothed it out, I read:

MYSTERIOUS DEATH OF OFFICER

On Wednesday night the body of Captain Paffrey of the 53rd (Shropshire) Regiment of Foot was discovered near one of the large trees that remain in Hyde Park. His throat had been cut and nothing remained in his pockets thus giving credence to the theory that he had been the victim of a foul robbery.

Captain Paffrey had recently taken part in the largely abortive sweep in Tasmania where his conduct as an officer gave cause for concern. An undisclosed source of information indicated that he was not the most popular of officers, and having completed some time in Australia, where he was attached to the 63rd Regiment, was due to return to England.

We can reveal that he had made enquiries about travelling on the Sarah, but had not finalised his arrangements.

We have repeatedly warned the Governor General that the city is still a dangerous place. Since the Hyde Park Barracks were built more ruffians have been placed in them and we urge the authorities to maintain their vigilance in respect of containing them to the safety of the public.

It was a cutting from a Sydney daily and it had a date on it in faded handwriting. Also in the same hand was a note that I could just about make out.

Jane burned the other copy so I bought another paper and cut this out

I now took up the envelope

P. Pirrip Esq

To be opened on my death.

Lady Amanda Jane Spens

Opening it, I found the following letter.

Dearest Pip,

When you read this, if you ever do, I shall be dead, and you should be the heir to what Arthur and I are leaving behind in this world. I say *should* because life is never straightforward and the litigation and grasping that I have seen in my lifetime persuades me that once Arthur and I are gone his relatives may well have won out against our wishes.

You may wonder why Arthur and I did not make it over to you when we were alive. As I write this you are making your own way quite successfully which is as it should be. I know that you are not entirely satisfied with your present employment but I am confident that in time the name of Pip Pirrip will be recognised as the name of a successful respected gentleman.

I have protected one thing along with these papers that I should like you to have. You remember that when I told you how I helped Abel how I also was under threat from Freddy, and Jane was instrumental in getting back my father's watch.

Please keep it in memory of all those people who have struggled to help you become the Australian gentleman that you are.

Amanda Jane

Beckridge and Blownding were delighted with the papers, just as John had predicted. They immediately got to work, setting in train all sorts of legal processes that required my signature and much taking of oaths before witnesses, and all sorts of legal mumbo jumbo activities that were so arcane that great quantities of money were soon swallowed in all kinds of legal bills. Jaggers would have been delighted!

They were the very model of what one thought professional men should look like. I still have a picture of them both, done in water colours by Blownding's daughter, who went on to produce many more such likenesses. She had captured the solid respectable nature of both as they stood beside one another with their watch chains stretched across their ample stomachs, made ample by the fees that they charged us for their very successful work. I knew from my long experience of them that their chains ended in substantial watches that were frequently consulted in order to ensure that we were charged sufficiently for their time.

She had figured them against a background of their library of legal books, none of which I ever remembered them opening. But on this occasion one of them actually held one of the books open as if to demonstrate to the other some obscure point of law that he was going to use to support an assertion before a court of law. As I said, the very model of professional men.

With such luminaries working on my behalf I could not but suppose that I should eventually be seen as the legal heir of Abel Magwich, and therefore the owner of a substantial tract of land.

EPILOGUE

During this time I continued to work for the firm, despite the fact that I was nearly a real gentleman. John, now that Estella was with us no more, gave up any pretence at being other than he was and devoted himself assiduously to 'ladies', some of whom I felt were scarcely the sort of persons with whom I should be associated. I tried to remind him of the warning that the doctor had given him. His answer was merely to quote the bible about man's life being three score years and ten.

He explained that he was looking for a wife to produce an heir or heirs to inherit his empire. That empire became his alone, for I anticipated being a gentleman of property and leisure by selling him my share of "ADAM & PIRRIP". This duly occurred and

Adam and Pirrip
Purveyors of Excellent Supplies.

disappeared, and

Adams

appeared in its place.

My fears about Young Pip and Olivia proved groundless as their subsequent marriage proved.

When Beckridge and Blownding finally established that I owned land in the Hunter Valley, I took myself off there and had a house built, a Manor House that I called Satis Novis. It looked out over the valley, and was adjudged by all who saw it as an extremely suitable residence for an Australian gentleman.

The end

Those who are familiar with Australian history will recognise real people and real events in my stories. I have taken liberties with both for the sake of my narratives, for which I apologise.